"What happened to the woman?" he asked.

Walt regarded him expressionlessly. "Woman?"

"I thought I saw a woman in here," Lakesh said haltingly.

Clarence shook his head. "Just us, Dr. Singh. When a human being comes out of stasis, especially after such an unusually prolonged period, the senses are untrustworthy."

It took a few seconds for the implications of Clarence's comment to penetrate Lakesh's comprehension. "Unusually prolonged period?" he echoed. "Twenty years isn't unusual."

Walt said, "True, twenty years isn't unusual. But you've been in stasis much longer than that."

Lakesh stared at him. "How long?"

Clarence picked up a clipboard hanging from a hook at the end of the examination table. In a flat monotone he read aloud. "One hundred and forty-eight years, three months and thirteen days. Do you want the hours and minutes?"

Other titles in this series:

Exile to Hell
Destiny Run
Savage Sun
Omega Path
Parallax Red
Doomstar Relic
Iceblood
Hellbound Fury
Night Eternal
Outer Darkness

JAMES AXLER

OUTLANDERS®

ARMAGEDDON AXIS

A GOLD EAGLE BOOK FROM
WORLDWIDE®

TORONTO • NEW YORK • LONDON
AMSTERDAM • PARIS • SYDNEY • HAMBURG
STOCKHOLM • ATHENS • TOKYO • MILAN
MADRID • WARSAW • BUDAPEST • AUCKLAND

For Darryl Banks; may his lantern always shine.

First edition December 1999
ISBN 0-373-63824-8

ARMAGEDDON AXIS

Special thanks to Mark Ellis for his contribution to the Outlanders concept, developed for Gold Eagle Books.

Printed in U.S.A.

Earth used to spin on its axis,
now Armageddon spins around it.

—Entry found in the
private journal of
General H. E. Kettridge,
January 22, 2001

The Road to Outlands—
From Secret Government Files to the Future

Almost two hundred years after the global holocaust, Kane, a former Magistrate of Cobaltville, often thought the world had been lucky to survive at all after a nuclear device detonated in the Russian embassy in Washington, D.C. The aftermath—forever known as skydark—reshaped continents and turned civilization into ashes.

Nearly depopulated, America became the Deathlands—poisoned by radiation, home to chaos and mutated life forms. Feudal rule reappeared in the form of baronies, while remote outposts clung to a brutish existence.

What eventually helped shape this wasteland were the redoubts, the secret preholocaust military installations with stores of weapons, and the home of gateways, the locational matter-transfer facilities. Some of the redoubts hid clues that had once fed wild theories of government cover-ups and alien visitations.

Rearmed from redoubt stockpiles, the barons consolidated their power and reclaimed technology for the villes. Their power, supported by some invisible authority, extended beyond their fortified walls to what was now called the Outlands. It was here that the rootstock of humanity survived, living with hellzones and chemical storms, hounded by Magistrates.

In the villes, rigid laws were enforced—to atone for the sins of the past and prepare the way for a better future. That was the barons' public credo and their right-to-rule.

Kane, along with friend and fellow Magistrate Grant, had upheld that claim until a fateful Outlands expedition. A displaced piece of technology...a question to a keeper of the archives...a vague clue about alien masters—and their world shifted radically. Suddenly, Brigid Baptiste, the archivist, faced summary execution, and

Grant a quick termination. For Kane there was forgiveness if he pledged his unquestioning allegiance to Baron Cobalt and his unknown masters and abandoned his friends.

But that allegiance would make him support a mysterious and alien power and deny loyalty and friends. Then what else was there?

Kane had been brought up solely to serve the ville. Brigid's only link with her family was her mother's red-gold hair, green eyes and supple form. Grant's clues to his lineage were his ebony skin and powerful physique. But Domi, she of the white hair, was an Outlander pressed into sexual servitude in Cobaltville. She at least knew her roots and was a reminder to the exiles that the outcasts belonged in the human family.

Parents, friends, community—the very rootedness of humanity was denied. With no continuity, there was no forward momentum to the future. And that was the crux—when Kane began to wonder if there *was* a future.

For Kane, it wouldn't do. So the only way was out—way, way out.

After their escape, they found shelter at the forgotten Cerberus redoubt headed by Lakesh, a scientist, Cobaltville's head archivist, and secret opponent of the barons.

With their past turned into a lie, their future threatened, only one thing was left to give meaning to the outcasts. The hunger for freedom, the will to resist the hostile influences. And perhaps, by opposing, end them.

Prologue

Mount Rushmore, South Dakota
October 3, 2002

Mohandas Lakesh Singh began his fiftieth birthday by watching Lieutenant Hayden go mad.

Standing in the T junction of Level Six, Lakesh watched as the Air Force officer hammered his head repeatedly against a sealed security door. The man shrieked as he did so. Most of his words were unintelligible, but Lakesh caught Biblical quotes, garbled references to stars falling into rivers and transforming them to wormwood.

No one tried to stop Hayden. The people in the corridor stood and blandly observed the lieutenant batter himself against the vanadium alloy until his face and head were glistening blotches of pulped flesh and exposed bone. When he finally fell to the floor and lay there twitching, everyone turned away and went on about their business.

Public suicides had become fairly commonplace in the Anthill over the past six months, particularly among those suffering from radiation sickness. At first those so afflicted tended to kill themselves in the privacy of their quarters, but after General Kettridge had decreed only internal-security officers could carry weapons, more and more of the self-immolations were staged out in the open.

Lakesh couldn't be sure if the reason was insanity due to brain-cell deterioration or a terminal display of defiance. More than likely, he thought bitterly, six of one, half a dozen of the other. Certainly the number of suicides seemed to grow as the second anniversary of the nuclear holocaust approached. Still and all, repetition did not make the suicides any easier to witness.

His heart gave a painful jerk, and instinctively he put a hand over the left side of his chest, trying to regulate his breathing. The arrhythmia he had suffered over the past couple of years had become more frequent since his confinement in the Anthill. Although a physicist by training and trade, Lakesh knew the prescribed medications dealt only with the symptoms, not with the cause. Eventually, he would have to undergo open-heart surgery.

A voice murmured behind him. "Why don't we all just do ourselves in? I don't know how much longer I can take this."

Lakesh glanced over his shoulder and saw a white-faced Gregson staring at the oozing ruin of Hayden's head. Gregson was a civilian cyberneticist who had been permitted to bring his wife and nine-year-old daughter to the installation. Lakesh knew him only slightly, from his last couple of months in the Cerberus redoubt. He didn't respond to the younger man's comments, who was speaking for the vast majority of the people inside the Anthill complex.

Hayden had stopped twitching. Lakesh edged around him, careful not to step in the pool of blood spreading out from the man's head. As he did so, he saw two green-coveralled sanitation men approaching with a casual, almost bored gait. One of them carried a folded body bag under an arm. Lakesh didn't bother watching them insert Hayden's corpse into the bag, just as he didn't bother speculating on the disposition of the man's remains. All he could think about was his birthday, and how it was also his last day, insofar as the rest of the world was concerned. Not that there was much constituting a world any longer, he reminded himself bleakly.

For the past eighteen months, Lakesh's world had been the interior of Mount Rushmore, a vast labyrinth of passageways, tunnels and levels bounded on all sides by vanadium-shielded rock. Unlike many of his fellow inhabitants, he did not suffer from claustrophobia or feel oppressed by life inside of a mountain. He had spent the past thirty years in similar environments, from the installation beneath the Archuleta Mesa in New Mexico to Redoubt Bravo high on a plateau in Montana. At this point in his life, he would have felt far more uncomfortable in the wide-open spaces of the outdoors. Of course, he reminded himself, if he went outdoors now he would be more than uncomfortable—he'd be dead.

Lakesh didn't find that prospect particularly unsettling, at least at the moment. He dreaded telling Dian of how he planned to spend the next century far more than he did dying.

He strode along the corridor, resolutely ignoring the bustle of damage control and containment crews as they raced to attend one crisis after another. Radiation alarms seemed to warble constantly, always drowning out the bland Muzak filtering over the public-address system. The music was supposed to be comforting, but it could rarely be heard over the screaming of sirens.

As Lakesh entered the wide, sweeping curve of the main promenade, his attention was caught by a cluster of people near the decorative fountain. They were shouting and cheering. At the same instant he noted a pair of security officers in black uniforms and helmets jogging toward the disturbance, Shocksticks in their hands.

Lakesh quickened his pace and shouldered his way through the collection of shouting, laughing people. What he saw when he forced himself to the front line froze him in his tracks for a long moment.

A burly black man in military fatigues was endeavoring to push a young blond woman's head beneath the surface of the enclosed pool surrounding the fountain. The two combatants were grunting and snarling into each other's faces. While Lakesh watched, the woman raked the man's eyes with her fingernails.

"You Russkie whore!" the black man howled. He planted the heel of his broad hand beneath the woman's chin and shoved hard. The water closed over her head, and the man uttered a growl of triumph.

The security officers lunged forward, the crackling tips of the Shocksticks stroking the man along his back and midriff. He cried out shrilly as his limbs spasmed. He whirled away, falling in a heap as his legs tangled. Several onlookers muttered in disappointment.

One of the security men pulled the gasping, soaking-wet woman out of the pool while the other put himself between her and the crowd. He waved the Shockstick menacingly. "Get the fuck back."

"Let the bitch drown," a bearded man snapped. "She's a Russian—she doesn't need to be here with the rest of us. Her country started all this shit, blew away the world!"

Neither of the security officers responded to the man's declaration, even though half the crowd voiced fervent and profane agreement. The officers each took hold of one of the woman's arms and they hustled her away, ignoring the curses and catcalls hurled at them from the onlookers. They let the black man lie where he had fallen.

Lakesh turned and went on his way, his face registering no emotion. Over the past year, he had taught himself the technique of tuning out his surroundings. If he had not, he knew he would have gone mad as so many others had. Still, he couldn't help but wonder what had driven the woman to leave the guarded compound reserved for foreign personnel. In the lower levels lived a few Germans, Asians, Mideasterners and Russians. They were not naturalized American citizens like himself, but scientists, diplomats and their families. The Russians were kept segregated from the general population for a very good reason: officially their nation had touched off the nuclear holocaust with the detonation of a nuclear warhead hidden within the Soviet embassy in Washington, D.C.

Lakesh had very good reason to suspect the official version of events, but he kept his doubts to himself. More than likely, in a hundred years or less, all history prior to January 20, 2001, would be revised, disguised and rewritten out of all recognition.

As he passed the main operations room, he glanced in through the open doors. Men in neat dark business suits sat shoulder to shoulder with men in military fatigues at the various consoles. As the brain of the Anthill, the huge chamber was crammed with chassis upon chassis of complex electronic equipment. A bank of closed-circuit monitor screens ran the length of one wall, transmitting images from the various redoubts scattered across—and even beneath—the country. Most of the screens displayed nothing but dark and empty rooms. Others were filled with faces, their expressions ranging from outright terror to fury. He heard a babble of demands and pleas for permission to leave the redoubts and return to the Anthill.

The people on the monitor screens were cursed with security clearances below the ubiquitous B-12 and had been left behind when the mushroom clouds bloomed and the surface of the planet was covered by a blanket of scorching atomic fire. They begged for sanctuary, and Lakesh couldn't help but notice how almost no one in the operations center looked at the faces on the monitors or responded to their words.

He moved on, stamping hard on his pity for the hapless personnel trapped in the redoubts. With the gateway jump lines to the Anthill complex closed, there could be no escape. Jumping to another redoubt was certainly no solution, since they would encounter the same problems as those in their own installations. And since the Anthill was plagued by those same difficulties but magnified due to its size and the number of people it had to support, it could not serve as a sanctuary. Those who pleaded for entrance did not know the Anthill installation was less than a dream that had failed; it was a vision that had never taken full shape.

Certainly there had been sufficient time for the Anthill and similar installations to achieve optimum operational status. As many as fifty years before, in the paranoid period following World War II and the detonation of the first nuclear device in Hiroshima, the Continuity of Government program was conceived and implemented.

COG was viewed as the ultimate insurance policy against an atomic attack, and to this end many subterranean command posts were constructed all over the country. The Anthill was by far the most ambitious, and all of Mount Rushmore was honeycombed with interconnected levels, passageways, stores, theaters and even a small sports arena. The interior vanadium-alloy walls were reinforced with a mixture of silicon foam and molten lead to provide radiation shielding.

But all of the precautions were insufficient when the first mushroom cloud billowed up over Washington, D.C. on January 20. The devastation wrought by the atomic conflagration had been far more extensive than even the most pessimistic strategists had warned.

The full horrors of the nuclear winter hadn't been foreseen at all. For more than a year, a perpetual twilight lay over the world as megatons of pulverized dust and fallout clogged the sky.

Not even the heads of the presidents had come through the destruction unscathed. Three of the four stone images outside the Anthill had collapsed due to the ferocious, days-long quakes birthed by Soviet earthshaker bombs detonated off the Pacific Coast. Only Lincoln's head remained intact, but just barely. His high forehead had crumbled, and one of his huge eyes was deeply riven by ugly cracks.

The original timetable for outlasting the effects of the nuclear winter had stipulated five years or so. Now it appeared close to twenty years would pass before the people in Mount Rushmore could safely emerge into the new world their machinations had brought into existence.

After much thought and soul-searching, Lakesh decided he would rather wake up into that new world than die of heart disease within the walls of the Anthill. He certainly wasn't the only one of the facility's inhabitants to make that decision. He imagined that sooner than later, it would no longer be a matter of choice.

As he turned a corner, he saw a security drone hovering in front of him. The mechanical device was barely two feet long, its body made of interlocking metal segments, like the carapace of an insect. Extensors and hooks studded its dully gleaming silver skin. The red photoreceptor shone down on him, fixing on the light-sensitive lozenge on his ID badge. The beam interacted with the electrochemical components of the cell, which confirmed Lakesh's identity and security clearance.

The drone moved on, humming purposefully. The machines had only recently been pressed into service, used more for monitoring than interference. They were referred to as "beetles," and the rumor mill whispered the buglike devices would soon be equipped with stings—tasers and voltage projectors.

The lozenge on Lakesh's badge allowed him to pass through the various security checkpoints without triggering so much as a beep from the sensors. Pausing before the double doors leading to the medical section, Lakesh automatically checked his reflection in the metal sheathing. He was neat and trim as always in his crisp white coveralls. His thick, jet-black hair showed not a thread of gray nor did his glossy mustache. His faintly olive complexion was still unlined, holding few creases from either age or stress, although he certainly had a stockpile of both. He used to enjoy a certain vanity in the fact he looked a decade or more younger than his actual age, but now he couldn't care less.

Still, because of that vanity he refused to wear his eyeglasses with their thick prescription lenses. Some months before, he had been diagnosed with incipient glaucoma, but he continued to postpone the recommended surgery. There seemed little point in it now. Besides, if matters in the Anthill continued on the present downslide, he would welcome blindness.

As he stepped close to the doors, his ID badge interacted with the sensors and the lock clicked open.

He pushed aside a door and entered the medical section. He strode down the corridor, not glancing into the examination rooms and laboratories lining both sides of the hall.

Lakesh had a broad idea of some of the biological research and experiments that had been transferred from the Dulce facility, but he didn't like to think of them or some of the whispered stories he'd been told by scientists attached to the subdivisions of Overproject Excalibur. Partly due to those hints, Lakesh had checked out the sublevel of the installation, referred to in whispers as Nightmare Alley. The memories of the monstrosities he glimpsed there still gave him anxiety attacks. The appellation had been borrowed from a 1940s film noir classic dealing with the gallery of human deformities and freaks found on a carnival midway.

Lakesh had never seen the movie, and after his covert visit to that sublevel he had no inclination whatever to do so.

He turned left into a laboratory, wending his way through a maze of heavy tables laden with networks of glass tubes, microscopes, centrifuges, stainless-steel fermentation tanks and a fluoroscope.

The few people concentrating on their work paid him no attention as he passed. Not even Dian realized he was there until he stood right at her elbow and softly cleared his throat.

She lifted her head from the eyepieces of the microscope and smiled at him. As always, the smile transformed her face, turning it from merely attractive to radiantly beautiful. The white lab smock she wore did little to conceal the bountiful curves and willowy slenderness of her figure. Her long wavy hair, swept back from a high forehead and pronounced widow's peak, held the color of sunset. Her eyes were such a deep blue as to be almost black. The complexion of her high-planed face was the hue of fine honey.

"Happy birthday," she said, reaching for his hand.

Lakesh tried to return her smile. "My happy returns won't be for some years yet."

Her smile faltered. She gazed at him steadily for a long, tense moment, then turned back to the microscope, but not before Lakesh glimpsed tears glimmering in her eyes. She understood his enigmatic reply, so he saw no reason to expand upon it. Instead he asked, "How goes the gene therapy?"

In a voice pitched so low it was barely a murmur, Dian answered, "Not well. If we'd been able to coordinate all of the Overproject Excalibur subdivisions from here like the original plan, the process would be further along. Right now, it's a classic case of the right hand not knowing what the left foot is doing."

Lakesh did not feel dismay or surprise by her response. It was standard by now. The various researches under the umbrella of Excalibur devoted to pantropic sciences and genetic engineering were too scattered, too separated to be efficiently coordinated. Project Genesis was down south in Louisiana, Project Invictus was stuck literally in the middle of nowhere out in the Guadalupe desert and Wild Wil Longley had allegedly absconded with its most crucial data shortly before the nukecaust.

Other experiments and researches into developing

life-forms capable of adapting to the postholocaust environment were ongoing in the Anthill, but so far only horrors had been spawned. At least, that was how Lakesh thought of them, basing his assessment on the creatures he'd seen in Nightmare Alley.

Repressing a shudder, he laid a hand on Dian's shoulder and said quietly, "We discussed this, you know. At great length. It's not an arbitrary decision."

Her "yes" was a deliberately distracted whisper. She kept her face fastened to the microscope's eyepieces.

"Join me," Lakesh said.

Dian straightened up, face set in a tight, unreadable mask. "We discussed that, too. I'm needed here. I'm essential, at least for the immediate future."

A hard lump formed in Lakesh's throat and he swallowed it down, tasting bitter anger and disappointment. As a physicist, his presence in the Anthill was not particularly important, so when the option of entering cryostasis was offered to him, his initial reaction had been one of feeling useless.

But, after considering it for a couple of weeks, he had seen the logic of the offer. The Anthill's resources were already strained, and every day brought a new crisis. The prospect of going to sleep for twenty years and awakening into a world on its way to recovery became more enticing the longer he thought about it. And even if Dian elected to remain unfrozen, at least they would be the same age when he revived. She would no longer be twenty years his junior.

Other than that, the form of cryogenesis employed at the installation wasn't a standard freezing process.

It utilized technology that did not rely on liquid nitrogen or the removal of the subject's blood and organs. Lakesh never wondered aloud where the technology came from. Three words, which he had learned years ago in Dulce and been ordered never to repeat under pain of death explained it all: the Archon Directive.

Forcing a smile to his face, Lakesh asked, "Can your work spare you for a little while so you can spend some time with me?"

"As a birthday gift?" Dian's voice held a hard edge. "Or a bon voyage present?"

Lakesh's smile remained stitched to his face even as he turned away.

Swiftly, Dian rose from her stool and took him by the arm. Then she caught him in a tight embrace. "I'm sorry," she said in a voice tight with grief and sadness. "You're the only person in this hellhole who reminds me there was sanity in the world once. Without you here as my anchor, I'm afraid I'll go as mad as everybody else."

Lakesh clumsily caressed her hair. "Join me in stasis, then. When we're revived, things will be different. Things will be better. The world will be secure."

She laid her head against his shoulder. "I can't, not immediately. Maybe in a few months."

Stepping back from him, she gazed deeply into his eyes. "But for right now, my work can wait."

IN THE DARKNESS of his quarters, Lakesh lay with Dian in his arms and tried to slow his almost painfully speeding heartbeat. Even if he suffered an infarction—or a coronary—the past half hour would have been worth it. With Dian's long sleek body pressed against his, Lakesh could feel her own heart beating fast.

Although his experience with women was embarrassingly limited, he knew he had performed more than adequately. And Dian had been more than enthusiastic; she had been pagan. He laughed to himself when he recalled how one of his colleagues had described her as frigid, with ice water instead of hot blood in her veins.

Dian snuggled close to him, breathing into his ear, and said in a drowsy voice, "Many happy returns, Mohandas. We'll make this a birthday tradition."

Lakesh stroked her silken tresses. "By the time we see each other again, I'll have quite the stockpile."

She laughed softly, running her hands over his chest. "It's something to look forward to." She sighed, resting her head on his shoulder. "I think I'll take a nap. Please stay with me until I wake up."

Lakesh smiled in the darkness and kissed her cheek. "I will if you promise me the same thing. Please be there for me when I wake up...twenty years from now."

Dian didn't answer for such a long time he thought she had drifted off to sleep. Then, in a husky whisper, she said, "No matter how many birthdays pass, I'll be there."

Lakesh kissed her again. He believed her, and for one of the few times in his life he was happy. It was an emotion that could never be frozen out of him.

LAKESH FLOATED in the eternal night, aware of metal inside and out, but seeing and feeling nothing but the vast darkness.

A field of changing colors sifted into his perceptions, then there was total black again. The colored dots returned, bobbing before him, shifting shape and tint. Lakesh tried to become interested in the phenomena, but it was like trying to make sense of the constantly changing view through a kaleidoscope.

Sluggishly, Lakesh finally understood he was actually seeing the wavering colors. The light drove back the eternal dark and seeped behind his eyes.

He knew his mind was stumbling through the last moments of stasis. He blinked at the shadows wavering above him. He felt a cold so fierce and deep that he suspected his blood had congealed in his veins and frost rimed the valves of his heart.

Suddenly warmth began to spread through him, pushing away the marrow-freezing chill. As the cold receded, his eyes became less cloudy and he tried to see more than shadows. He blinked hard and the woman-thing slid into his field of vision. He wasn't sure if he was actually seeing her or thinking he did.

The woman's body was sleek and trim, perfectly proportioned and beautiful. But when he glimpsed the head, all resemblance to a woman ended. The face was distorted, discolored, with moist dark eyes peering from sockets sunk deep in the skull. The nose was almost nonexistent, the mouth a damp gaping triangle that glistened beneath the pocked yellow flesh of the cheekbones. He thought he saw the dull glint of silver there.

The hair was a wild, Gorgon-like tangle of no particular color or texture. Lakesh shut his eyes and opened them again. The woman-thing's form became indistinct, as if she had wrapped a cloak of shadow around her. Then she and the shadow disappeared altogether. It was as if she had existed only between one eye blink and another.

"Easy," a man's voice whispered from far, far away. "Don't force it, Dr. Singh."

Lakesh tried to lifted his head, straining to see who had spoken to him. Then he realized he was sitting up, an arm at his back and a hand on the rear of his head.

"Shallow, regular breaths, please. Remember the orientation."

Lakesh tried to do as the voice said, but his respiration was painful, labored, sounding like the wheeze of punctured fireplace bellows.

"Not too deep at first. Let your lungs become accustomed to expanding and contracting again. It will hurt at first, like a muscle that hasn't been exercised in a long time."

As Lakesh followed the instructions, he realized he was sitting inside an eight-foot-long crystalline ovoid that rested on four small pyramids crafted from a pale golden alloy, placed at equidistant points around it. He could barely make out the bulky outlines of two other stasis units in a corner.

Two men in dark suits and neckties stood on either side of the cylinder. He didn't recognize either of them. Their pallid faces were completely expressionless. They wore rectangular ID badges with the photocell lozenges attached. By squinting, Lakesh saw the names on the badges—Walt and Clarence.

Walt lifted a hand, shot his shirt cuff, checked his wristwatch and stated flatly, "You should be properly acclimatized by now."

Lakesh noticed how his breath puffed out with every word, as if they were standing inside a meat locker. He allowed himself to be led one doddering step at a time from the unit to an examination table. Clarence helped him sit down on it, and he grunted as the icy metal surface touched his bare flank.

"What happened to the woman?" he asked.

Walt regarded him expressionlessly. "Woman?"

"I thought I saw a woman in here," Lakesh said haltingly.

Clarence shook his head. "Just us, Dr. Lakesh. When a human being comes out of stasis, especially after such an unusually prolonged period, the senses are untrustworthy."

It took a few seconds for the implications of Clarence's comment to penetrate Lakesh's comprehension. "Unusually prolonged period?" he echoed. "Twenty years isn't unusual."

"True, twenty years isn't unusual," Walt said. "But you've been in stasis for much longer than that."

Lakesh stared at him. "How long?"

Clarence picked up a clipboard hanging from a hook at the end of the examination table. In a flat monotone, he read aloud, "One hundred and forty-eight years, three months and thirteen days. Do you want the hours and minutes?"

Lakesh gaped at him, utterly confused, bewildered and even frightened. Suspicion and desperate denial fought within the walls of his skull. Finally he found his voice again and demanded stridently, "A century and a half? The stasis factor was set for only twenty years!"

"Adjustments had to be made," Walt explained. "Circumstances arose from within and without that made extending the factor a necessity."

Walt spoke matter-of-factly, as if he were reciting a speech by rote. "Within weeks of your containment, a rebellion arose among some of the personnel here. It lasted for nearly twenty years. It was thought best to extend the time of those already in stasis—in order to best protect them."

"That only accounts for the first twenty years," snapped Lakesh. "What about the other 128?"

Clarence responded blandly. "Fifty-three years ago the installation suffered near-catastrophic damage. General Kettridge was killed, and a number of stasis units malfunctioned. Others were intentionally shut down to conserve power in order to preserve our more essential personnel. You and a handful of others should consider yourself fortunate you are being revived at all."

Lakesh ran a shaking hand over his face. His fingers recoiled when they touched smooth flesh between his nose and upper lip. Tentatively, he felt the top of his head, fingertips encountering a hairless scalp.

"A form of *alopecia areata,*" said Clarence genially. "A temporary side effect of such a long stasis period. Your hair will grow back in time."

Lakesh didn't want to ask the next question, but it burst from his lips, almost against his will. "Dian—"

He shut his mouth, refusing to vocalize his anguish.

Smoothly, as if he had rehearsed his reply, Walt said, "There is no one here by that name. If you had an emotional attachment to her, then you must come to terms with your loss. You must put your grief behind you and look to the future."

Lakesh hung his head. "Is there one?"

"There is indeed," Clarence declared. "The seeds planted long ago have at last taken root. You are needed to aid the growth and tend the crop."

A groan worked its way up his throat, but he managed to turn it into a sigh of resignation. He reminded himself of all the inevitabilities he had accepted over the course of his life; this was just one more in a very long list.

He knew he would never feel happiness or see Dian Baptiste again.

Chapter 1

Dulce, New Mexico
Fifty-One Years Later

The sentry came as a surprise.

The terrain around the Archuleta Mesa was as dead as the most rad-scoured hellzone. The harsh, dry sands had been baked for centuries in the pitiless blaze of the sun. The few thorny shrubs crowning the low, gravel-strewed hills were the only signs of life. Great boulders of limestone thrust up from the desert floor like the headstones of long-dead giants.

The mesa itself rose sheer from the surrounding sands, a gigantic monolith of stone that blotted out the first stars of twilight. Four to five hundred feet high, its vertical sides seemed unscalable. Ages of erosion had cut deep fissures and furrows across its surface. A series of crumbling crags girded its base.

For a half day, Kane, Grant, Brigid Baptiste and Domi had toiled across the desert with never a sign of another living thing, not even vultures wheeling in the sky. Now, as a quarter moon slowly rose in the sky, gleaming like a curve of polished metal, a scuff of feet reached them, the unmistakable sound of boots crunching on gravel.

Kane, on point as always, scarcely had time to conceal himself behind a broken outcrop of rock when the sentry strode toward him. He walked in a leisurely manner, a Copperhead dangling from a lanyard over his right shoulder. A chopped-down autoblaster, the Copperhead was barely two feet in length. The magazine held fifteen 4.85 mm steel-jacketed rounds, which could be fired at a rate of 700 per minute. Even with its optical image intensifier and laser autotarget scope, the Copperhead weighed less than eight pounds.

The sentry was a long-legged man with a dark blond brush cut. He wore a black, calf-length Magistrate-issue coat of Kevlar weave. A pair of night-vision glasses masked his eyes, and a transceiver headset was plugged into his right ear, with the stem of a microphone angling around in front of his mouth.

Kane gritted his teeth in angry frustration when he saw that the overcoat was buttoned, not hanging open. The fabric could turn anything from a knife to a .38-caliber round. Kane had no intention of shooting the man because the sound of the shot would carry for miles, but now even using his combat knife wasn't an option.

He crouched lower in the shadows as the sentry approached his position. Like his companions, Kane wore a Stealth cloak, which was a black material that, according to Lakesh, concealed their heat signatures from thermal-imaging proximity sensors. Zippered hoods concealed their heads, leaving only a small area around the eyes exposed.

Kane found the term "Stealth cloak" a misnomer. The fabric, though lightweight, was stiff and tended to crackle when they moved. An infrared scanner might be deceived, but not a buried seismic detector or even a pair of human ears. He tried not to move at all, or even breathe. He even slitted his eyes in order to keep ambient moonlight from reflecting off them.

The sentry paused and made a slow visual scan of the area, turning his head in a maddeningly methodical way. Kane held his breath during the entire survey, praying his companions did the same. Finally, when Kane's lungs were aching and temples throbbing, the sentry started walking again. Kane inhaled short, shallow sips of air, timing them to coincide with the man's footfalls on the gravelly ground.

The sentry had to be taken out. This was obviously his assigned patrol zone, and his shift probably lasted from sunset to sunrise. The mission objective could not afford a protracted game of hide-and-seek with guards. Although Kane and his companions were armed, none of their blasters was equipped with a noise suppressor. And because he had moved out ahead, Kane wasn't even sure of the locations of the rest of the team.

The sentry marched past him, his gait confident. Kane turned his head slowly, following the guard with his eyes. The man went only a few yards when a sound floated through the air, a delicate, almost apologetic cough. An icy hand clenched around the base of Kane's spine as he watched the sentry wheel around, teeth bared in a startled snarl, leading with his subgun. The cough, though faint, came from an undeniably female throat.

Even if Kane hadn't been afraid to move, the sound still shocked him into immobility. He was almost as surprised as the black-garbed guard. He didn't know if Domi or Brigid was responsible for the cough, but he was overwhelmed by her sheer stupidity.

Then a small, almost shapeless mass rose from the ground behind the sentry, as if a section of the desert floor had detached itself. Fabric rustled, sand sifted down with a hiss and the guard pivoted around on his heel.

Kane couldn't really see what happened. He glimpsed only a blur of movement, then the sentry went into wild convulsions. Reeling backward, he clawed at his face, a gargling cry bursting from his lips. His limbs spasmed and his arms flew wide, the Copperhead falling from his shoulder. Collapsing onto his back, the man lay there, legs flopping like landed fish. A film of moisture gleamed on his face. Another cloaked form flowed from the shadows and planted a foot firmly on the sentry's chest, pinning his twitching body to the ground.

Kane came to his feet in a rush and reached the guard in three long-legged bounds. Domi bent over the man, stripping off his headset and handing it up to Kane. Looming out of the murk, Grant pointed his Sin Eater at the sentry squirming and gasping on the sands.

"He's neutralized," Kane said softly.

Grant made a rumbling sound deep in his broad chest and muttered wryly, "I'm glad we could be of help."

Domi chuckled, voice muffled beneath the hood.

She brandished a small metal cylinder topped with an aerosol-spray push button. "Figured this was the cleanest and quietest way to take him out."

Both Grant and Kane recognized the nerve toxin. It dispensed a chemical fluid that was absorbed through the pores of the skin and disrupted the nervous system for a short time. They had used it before, but neither man had thought to bring the spray with them on the mission.

"At least now we have a source of information," Brigid declared, her booted foot still on the guard's chest.

"Mebbe." Kane's tone was doubtful. A man assigned to the Dulce installation wasn't a raw recruit, randomly selected from the rank and file of a ville's Magistrate Division. Such a man would be chosen because he had the conscience of a stickie and the imagination of a tree stump.

Unzipping and peeling down his hood, Kane put on the sentry's headset, firmly seating the earpiece. A bland male voice said, "Zone six, report."

Kane gnawed nervously on his underlip. He had no idea what zone they had penetrated, and the sentry was in no shape to tell them, even if they could count on a straight answer.

"Zone six, all clear," said another man's voice.

"Acknowledged, zone six."

Kane stopped himself from sighing with relief. The security communications network was coordinated by a central dispatcher.

"Zone seven," came the first man's voice again. "Report."

Kane waited to hear a response. After a handful of seconds, the voice repeated the request, this time with a slight edge. "Zone seven, report. Rhine, report."

Trying to strike a balance between a mumble and a loud whisper, Kane replied, "Zone seven, all clear."

If the dispatcher thought his voice sounded strange, he gave no indication of it. "Acknowledged," said the dispatcher's crisp voice.

Kane covered the mouthpiece with a thumb and said, "We got away with it."

"This time," Grant pointed out dourly. Following Kane's example, he opened his hood so he could breathe unencumbered. Despite the arrival of twilight, the air was stuffy and still.

A tall, very broad-shouldered man, Grant had heavy eyebrows, which were drawn, shadowing his dark eyes. A down-sweeping mustache showed jet-black against the coffee brown of his skin. His heavy-jawed face was set in a perpetual scowl. A sprinkling of gray showed at the temples of his short hair.

Brigid tapped the sentry's chest with her foot. "You want him to see your face and be able to identify you?"

Grant snorted. "What difference does it make? We'd get blamed for this even if we weren't here."

Brigid considered Grant's comment for a thoughtful moment and stepped away from the sentry. She unzipped her own hood and inhaled gratefully. The unflattering Stealth cloak concealed her willowy, athletic figure, but her unruly mane of long red-gold hair spilling out made for a sharp contrast to the dark fabric. Her hair framed a smoothly sculpted face with a rosy complexion dusted lightly with freckles across her nose and cheeks. There was a softness in her features that bespoke a deep wellspring of compassion, yet a hint of steely resolve was there, too. The color of emeralds glittered in her big, feline-slanted eyes.

When Domi pulled down her hood, the effect was startling, almost eerie. She was an albino, her skin beautifully white, her bone-colored hair cut close to her head. Her eyes were crimson, the color of fresh-spilled blood. Because of the black cloak draping her slight body, it was as if her disembodied head floated less than five feet above the ground. She seemed unaware of how unearthly she appeared, her delicate, piquant features tight and composed.

Kane couldn't help but grin. At an inch over six feet, he was not as tall or as broad as Grant. Every line of his supple, compact body was hard and stripped of excess flesh, from his corded neck to the square shoulders and the lean hips and long legs. Though his high-planed face showed a grin, his gray-blue eyes were alert and watchful. Brushing a lock of dark hair back from his forehead, he went to one knee beside the sentry. He stiffened his wrist tendons, and his Sin Eater popped from his forearm holster into his right hand.

The man's eyes gazed up at him, glassy and unfocused, wet lips writhing over his teeth in a silent question.

"You'll be all right," Kane told him quietly. "The paralysis isn't permanent."

"Your name is Rhine?" Brigid asked.

The man jerked his head once, in a spasmodic imitation of a nod. He inhaled a shuddery breath and exhaled one husky word. "Who?"

"It doesn't matter who we are," Kane replied flatly. "All you should worry about is cooperating so you can be alive this time tomorrow."

Legs and arms moving in fitful twitches, Rhine managed to hike himself up into a sitting position. His eyes darted from Kane to Domi to Grant and then to Brigid. In a guttural whisper, he said, "I know who you are now. Three of you have been here before. I saw the sec record tapes."

Pausing, Rhine pursed his lips and spit contemptuously. Because his lips were still partially numbed, the saliva only drooled down onto the front of his coat.

Still, Domi bristled at the disrespectful display and kicked him hard in the chest, knocking him back onto the sand. "Do that again," she grated between clenched teeth, "and lots more than spit will come out of your mouth."

Rhine didn't respond to the threat. He slowly pushed himself back to a sitting position. "What are you doing here again?"

The question was valid enough, and if Kane had been in Rhine's place he might have asked it himself. What he knew of the Archuleta Mesa derived both from what Lakesh had told them long months ago and from personal experience.

The tiny ville of Dulce, on the border of New Mexico and Colorado, had served as the headquarters for two overprojects relating to the Totality Concept, which was the umbrella designation of various arcane and esoteric scientific areas. The research dated back to World War II, when German scientists were laboring to build what turned out to be purely theoretical secret weapons for the Third Reich. The Allied powers adopted the research, as well as many of the scientists, and constructed underground bases, primarily in the western United States, to further the experiments.

The Totality Concept was classified Above Top Secret. It was known only to a few very high-ranking military officers and politicians. Few of the Presidents who held office during its existence were ever aware of the full ramifications.

Buried beneath the Archuleta Mesa was a six-level research complex, built solely to house two major divisions of the Totality Concept. One of them, Overproject Whisper, was subdivided into Operation Chronos and Project Cerberus.

The other major division was Overproject Excalibur, which dealt primarily with bioengineering. Kane knew of at least three subdivisions—the Genesis Project, Project Invictus and Scenario Joshua.

Although Kane, Brigid and Grant had penetrated the complex, they'd done so by mat-trans unit. They hadn't seen the exterior of the mesa until now. The brooding, dark monolith rising from the wasteland evoked a sense of dread in Kane. To him it was not just an ancient rock formation sculpted by aeons of erosion and geological changes but a signpost marking the entrance to hell.

Kane would never forget the secret sublevel far beneath the rest of the installation. Lakesh referred to it as Nightmare Alley.

The worst part of Kane's visit to the secret sublevel was learning the fate of his father, suspended in cryonic stasis, his body now supplying its superior genetic material to create nonhuman and human hybrids.

Although Brigid, Kane and Grant barely escaped the installation, they had left it aflame, littered with the corpses of the unholy hybrids. Obviously, the memory of that assault ran deep, and humans had been recruited to supplement the number of hybrids in the installation.

"You want to know why we're back?" Kane asked Rhine, pitching his voice to a low, deadly monotone.

Rhine nodded.

"We know that some kind of aircraft is launched from here. It flies to some preselected Outland area where the local residents are killed, their organs and tissues harvested and returned here for processing. By our estimation, the last harvest was six months ago in Idaho. We figure you're due for another one."

Kane didn't tell the sentry they had arrived at that conclusion after encountering the aftermath of the Idaho harvest. Domi had been born and raised in the squalid little collection of huts on the banks of the Snake River. The sole survivor of the massacre, an old half-blind man, had reported seeing a strange silent aircraft with black helicopters flying escort.

Rhine listened, his face blank, his eyes fixed on the hollow bore of the Sin Eater. "Nothing to say?" Kane inquired.

In a husky whisper, the sentry replied, "Not yet."

Kane gave him a bleak half grin, showing only the edges of his teeth. "On your feet."

Carefully, Rhine pushed himself erect, bracketed by Grant and Domi.

"Take off your coat," Kane ordered.

Rhine obediently unbuttoned the coat and let it fall at his feet. Without much surprise, Kane saw the man wore the pearl-gray, high-collared bodysuit of a Magistrate duty uniform.

"What ville division are you from?" Kane asked.

"Mandeville. I was assigned here just two months ago."

"That's long enough to know your way around," Grant stated matter-of-factly. "There's an entrance to the complex somewhere around here. Show us."

Rhine's lips compressed tightly, and silver flashed in the moonlight. Domi placed the serrated edge of a long knife at the base of the man's throat. In a fierce hiss, she said, "Don't even think about clamming up. If you do, I'll clam you up permanently. I'll cut out your tongue and wipe my ass with it."

Rhine regarded the diminutive white wraith expressionlessly.

"Show us," Grant repeated, biting out both words.

Rhine nodded in a southwesterly direction. "That way."

As he began walking, Grant stepped back a few feet into the shadows and returned a moment later carrying a long, zippered canvas bag in one hand. Kane picked up the man's Kevlar-weave coat and slung it over a shoulder as they followed Rhine along a circuitous route around upthrusts of rock.

"He's stalling," Brigid sidemouthed to Kane.

Kane responded to her observation with a quick nod. His pointman's sense rang an insistent alarm. He suspected Rhine of misdirecting them. He scanned the sloping, deeply furrowed base of the mesa for openings of any kind, but they were still too far away.

Rhine suddenly came to a halt. "Here," he said simply.

They saw nothing but a few loose rocks and sand.

"Here what?" Grant demanded.

Rhine gestured to the ground and repeated, "Here."

Brigid was the first to see the square concrete slab rising from the desert floor. It was the same color as the sand and almost invisible in the stark pattern of light and shadow.

Kane stepped forward, stooping over the slab and touching the metal ring handle recessed into its pitted surface. He cast a questioning glance at Rhine.

The sentry said, "That's what I use when I come and go. Turn the handle clockwise and pull straight up."

Kane grasped the metal circlet, then removed his hand. He beckoned to Rhine with a forefinger. "You're a fine, strapping young Magistrate. Demonstrate it for me."

The sentry moved to the slab and, seeming oblivious to the blaster barrel inches away from his head, twisted and pulled the handle. The slab swung up silently, as if counterbalanced. Glinting dully against the darkness of the square cavity, Kane saw the rungs of a steel ladder. A faint hum wafted out of the shaft.

"What's down there?" Grant asked.

"It's only twenty feet deep. Then you'll be in a tunnel." Rhine spoke quietly, with no emotion.

Kane looked from the opening to the bulk of the mesa and to the sentry's face. "You'll stay here. Domi, you can nursemaid him until we get back."

Domi frowned, full lips parting as if to voice an objection. She cast a glance toward Grant, who scowled at her. The albino girl shrugged in resignation and drew her Detonics Combat Master handblaster from a shoulder rig. She cycled a round into the breech with a deliberate show of menace.

Gesturing with the barrel, she said to Rhine, "Sit down over there. On hands. Don't move, don't talk."

Under stress, her abbreviated mode of Outlander speech became more pronounced. Rhine did as she ordered, putting his hands, palms up, beneath his buttocks.

Shouldering the canvas bag, Grant planted his feet on the first rungs of the ladder. "I'll go first, make a recce. I'll signal you if it's all clear."

He brandished the Nighthawk microlight strapped around his left wrist, clicking the beam on and off. Then he descended the ladder.

Chapter 2

The air at the bottom of the shaft smelled surprisingly fresh. The diffused glow of Grant's microlight illuminated walls and floors of natural stone, smoothed in the long-ago excavation process. The tunnel stretched away into deep gloom.

Stenciled on the right-hand wall in red paint faded to near illegibility were the words Exit To Zone 7. An arrow pointed upward. Grant, Kane and Brigid knew the directions dated back to the twentieth century.

The three people moved carefully down the tunnel. By unspoken agreement, Kane assumed the pointman's position. It was something he always did, had always done even when he and Grant were Mags. When he acted as pointman, he felt electrically alive, sharply tuned to every nuance of his surroundings.

The arched stone ceiling close above their heads made the whisper of their footfalls a reverberating scrape. Air blew softly in their faces. A circulation vent was somewhere up ahead, judging from the high-pitched whine that grew in volume with every step. Kane made periodic sweeps with the compact motion detector strapped around his left wrist. Made of molded plastic and stamped metal with an expandable band, the motion detector featured a liquid-crystal digital display window that showed his position as a centered, pulsing green disk.

Tiny, regularly shaped slits of white light showed in the darkness before them. When they drew closer, they peered through the metal shutters of a framed portal on the right wall.

They took up positions on either side of the opening, Grant silently pointing out a pull cable. The electronic hum was much louder now, almost painful in its piercing intensity. Kane nodded to Grant and very slowly he began to tug on the cable. As the shutters slowly opened, the threads of light became slits, then narrow rectangles of dazzling white. Kane, Grant and Brigid narrowed their eyes until their vision became accustomed to the brightness.

The three people looked down into a vast, barnlike hangar, lit from above by a hundred halogen lamps. The walls were lined by worktables, tool cabinets and comp stations. Men in dark coveralls bustled about, some holding odds and ends of machinery and electronic components.

In the center of the floor, resting on an individually lit raised platform, squatted a giant wedge of dark metal. Its obsidian surface did not reflect so much as a pinpoint of light from the array of lamps above it.

Kane estimated the craft to be around fifty feet in length, from the beveled tip of the triangular prow to its squared-off rearward section. The hull was smooth, with barely perceptible seams where the metal plates joined. The craft had no external apparatus at all, no ailerons, no fins, no wings, no exhaust ports.

Three steel legs supported the black wedge above the platform. A metal ladder extended from a lighted hatch on its undercarriage. Kane's eyes followed thick power cables snaking from the base of the craft to a two-tiered generator. Twelve feet tall, the generator appeared to consist of two solid black cubes, the slightly smaller one balanced atop the larger. The top cube rotated slowly, producing the rhythmic drone. He didn't bother exchanging knowing glances with Brigid and Grant. The sight of the strangely shaped generator was no surprise considering their location. They had seen identical devices in several places across the world over the past months. They still didn't know on what principles it operated or what kind of energy it produced.

As they watched, four figures emerged from a door at the far side of the hangar. Despite the black, multi-pocketed coveralls they wore and the helmets that concealed most of their heads, there was no mistaking the slight, graceful build of hybrids. Their presence was no more of a surprise than the generator.

As the hybrids marched purposefully toward the craft, Kane noted that two of them carried wide, flat aluminum cases slung over their shoulders. He suspected the cases contained medical equipment. He backed away from the shutter, gesturing for Brigid and Grant to follow.

"They're prepping that ship," Grant declared.

"The question is whether we knock it out of the sky or hit it now."

He glanced expectantly at Brigid and Kane, waiting for an opinion.

"We don't know a hell of a lot about that aircraft," Kane mused. "If we start something while it's grounded, while it's still hooked up to the generator, we might trigger a chain reaction that will flash-fry us. Remember what happened when we blew the same kind of generator in Mongolia."

Brigid nodded grimly. "I'm not likely to forget."

Her tone held no note of irony, even though her statement was rife with it. Possessed of an eidetic memory, Brigid Baptiste was not likely to forget anything, regardless of its triviality, and the incident Kane referred to in Mongolia was certainly not trivial.

When one of the two-tiered generators had been destroyed, it triggered an explosion of near apocalyptic proportions. The ancient city of Kharo-Khoto, which had withstood not only the ravages of time but also the nukecaust, was obliterated in a matter of seconds.

"On the other hand," Grant interjected, "we might succeed in blowing the shit out of this entire pest-hole."

Brigid gave him a hard-eyed stare. "And us, too. This isn't a suicide mission."

Kane smiled wryly. "Since we don't know what will happen, it's not worth sacrificing ourselves on a 'might,' no matter how attractive it is." He hooked a thumb over his shoulder back toward the shuttered portal. "Once the thing is airborne, we can try to knock it down before it's out of range."

"Or engages its cloaking field," Brigid argued.

"If it has such a thing," Kane retorted, trying to suppress a note of irritation in his voice. The irritation was directed toward Lakesh, even though the lack of detailed data about the aircraft wasn't really his fault.

One of the most closely guarded military secrets in the two decades preceding the nukecaust, the silent flying triangles employed a pyroceramic hull finish to baffle radar signals and a ninety percent inertialess acceleration quotient. Code-named Aurora, the aircraft were capable of unbelievably swift ascent and descent, could take off vertically and hover absolutely motionless. Allegedly they were able to produce a parabolic energy screen that rendered them for all intents and purposes invisible.

Supremely maneuverable, the Auroras' top speed was unknown, although the craft were certainly capable of achieving Mach 5 or 6 during an upper atmospheric flight. Their flight ceilings were also unknown, though Lakesh was positive they could easily rise into the stratosphere, a distance of about twelve miles. However, he wasn't sure of the ships' method of propulsion, although he speculated they utilized pulse-detonation-wave engines and a form of gravity nullification.

As another aspect of the Totality Concept, the technology for the Aurora program had derived from the so-called Archon Directive. As part of Mission Snowbird, militarists had envisioned fleets of the ultra-advanced ships skimming over Earth and beyond, invisible to detection, visiting death from above on America's enemies. They were designed to make all other aircraft seem like children's gliders in comparison.

Kakesh couldn't say whether more than a few prototypes of the Aurora were ever built. It was a stupendously moot point; when the atomic firestorms raged over the planet in the global megacull of 2001, any kind of air vehicle was rendered superfluous. But at least one Aurora had survived and been put to uses never imagined by its long-dead builders.

All of this flitted through Kane's mind within a second. "All right," he said. "Let's try to take it out when it gets airborne, presuming it's going to be."

Grant and Brigid nodded in agreement. They retraced their steps through the tunnel to the ladder. Kane only glanced back once, wondering where the passageway terminated, then he led the way up the ladder.

Domi still held her blaster on Rhine and spared them only a single over-the-shoulder glance as they emerged from the opening in the desert floor.

"He give you any trouble?" Grant inquired.

Domi shook her white-haired head. "Not a move, not a peep. Just staring at me."

Kane felt a flash of grudging admiration for the man's rigid self-possession. Most Magistrates, if they found themselves in the same position, would have kept up a steady stream of sneers, insults and threats to cover their humiliation. Of course, if Rhine had tried that, Domi would have chilled him without blinking.

Kane walked over to the sentry. "Is there any point in asking you if a launch is scheduled in the immediate future?"

"No." The word passed Rhine's lips in an unemotional whisper.

Grant gave the surrounding terrain an appraising visual inspection. He thrust out his right arm toward an open expanse of sand and sere brush about fifty yards to the east. "That's the most likely spot for the launch zone. Matches up with the layout below," he announced.

Brigid consulted her wrist chron and then the sky. "If they don't launch tonight, we can't hang around much past dawn. If the heat of the day doesn't kill us, they're sure to miss Rhine and send out a search party."

"I think we managed to arrive on the right night," Kane said. "For some reason, I doubt foot patrols are assigned every evening." He angled an eyebrow toward Rhine. "Am I cold or am I warm?"

As if on cue, static suddenly hissed from the receiver plug in Kane's ear. The bland voice he had heard earlier said, "Zone seven, take up safety position. Launch in T minus three."

"Zone seven acknowledging," Kane said. "Will comply."

When he spoke, Grant and Brigid and Domi swung their heads toward him, eyes questioning.

"Three minutes," he declared. "Let's get it done."

CROUCHING in a smear of shadow provided by a boulder, Grant unzipped the long canvas bag and lifted out a four-foot-long hollow tube, six inches in diameter. One end of it flared out like the mouth of a trumpet. A smaller cylinder was attached to one side of the tube.

Kneeling beside him, Kane checked his wrist chron. "One minute, fifty-five seconds."

Grant acted as if he hadn't heard. Dipping into the bag again, he brought out a cuplike object shaped like a flowerpot with a thick rim. Hands moving with expert ease, he plucked a two-foot-long blunt-nosed missile from the carrying case and fitted its tapered end into a socket in the cup. It clicked into place.

Kane stuffed Rhine's Kevlar-weave coat into the bag. "I've been wondering when I could replace the one I lost."

Grant made no comment to the reference. He remembered how Kane had been forced to abandon his own Mag-issue coat during the mission that took them to Ireland.

"Time," said Grant tensely.

Kane checked his chron again. "One minute, fifteen seconds."

Grant slapped the flowerpot object over the flared opening of the tube. He gave it a twist, and ratchets locked into place. Shifting position, Grant sat down on the ground, resting his elbows on his upraised knees. He placed the M-47 Dragon rocket launcher on his left shoulder, squinting through the cylindrical eyepiece of the top-mounted tracker unit. He adjusted the focus.

Kane removed the telescoping support stanchion from the bag and hooked it to the eyebolt below the launcher's muzzle.

The Dragon was a one-man, optically tracked missile launcher. The projectile carrier attached to the tube launched a Cobra 2000 one-stage rocket with a 2000-meter maximum range. The warhead contained a HEAT hollow charge. The targeting system used command-to-line-of-sight guidance with infrared tracking.

The Dragon came from the same source as most of their other ordnance—the armory in the Cerberus redoubt. Fantastically well equipped, the armory also contained numerous subguns, semiautomatic pistols and revolvers. The arsenal was a treasure trove of death-dealing armament.

Grant flicked a switch to activate the system. The tracker and ignition units emitted faint electronic whines.

"Thirty-six seconds," Kane intoned.

"Set," Grant announced.

Glancing back over his shoulder, Kane looked for but couldn't see Brigid, Domi or Rhine. They were hunkered down yards away in the murk with their cache of equipment.

Half a minute later, with the muffled groaning of buried gears, pulleys and hydraulics, the ground beneath them began to tremble. Heaps of sand shifted and vibrated.

A dozen yards beyond Kane and Grant, the desert floor suddenly seemed to split in two, as if a fault line had suddenly been exposed. A prolonged hiss penetrated the night as two huge sections of the ground lifted up. Sand sifted down in miniature avalanches from the pair of multiton slabs of rockcrete. On the underside of them, Kane saw pistons and steel pylons, twice the length and breadth of his body. The twin slabs were themselves at least seventy feet long by fifty wide. As they rose ponderously Kane's tension increased.

The hissing ceased, as if a lever had been thrown. A buzzing sound built softly, slowly, increasing to a steady murmur. From below and between the open squares of rockcrete floated a dark, massive shape like a gargantuan killer whale rising to the surface.

The Aurora ascended very slowly, as if it were being drawn up to the sky by an invisible winch-and-pulley system. There was no sound of engines or thrusters, only a faint murmur. Three disks of light, at equidistant points on the bottom of the giant triangle, exuded misty halos.

Grant carefully tracked the craft with the Dragon as it rose from the subterranean hangar. Kane resisted the urge to offer Grant instruction. The man was a superb marksman, gifted with the ability to handle all sorts of weapons. Although Kane had been around and used firearms most of his adult life, he felt like a novice compared to Grant.

The wedge-shaped aircraft lifted to twenty feet above the outer rims of the upraised slabs and halted, hovering. From his angle, Kane could easily understand why so many predarkers who had glimpsed the Auroras' test flights had assumed the ships were of extraterrestrial origin. Of course, according to Lakesh, those assumptions weren't completely incorrect.

Peering through the Dragon's eyepiece, Grant whispered calmly, "Harvest *this.*" Then he squeezed the trigger.

Chapter 3

Flame and smoke gouted from the hollow bore of the missile launcher. Trailing a ribbon of vapor and sparks, the Cobra rocket leaped from the muzzle, accompanied by a ripping roar. Small fins popped open at the tail of the projectile as it rotated, snaking up in an arc.

The rocket impacted on the Aurora's underbelly exactly between the three glimmering light disks. The missile vanished in an eruption of billowing orange-white flame and a thunderous concussion. The echoes of the detonation rolled over the desert, bouncing off the wall of the Archuleta Mesa.

The Aurora's leeward side lurched violently upward as if it had received a kick from below. One of the light disks flashed erratically and went out with the suddenness of a candle flame being extinguished.

Lowering the Dragon missile launcher, Grant climbed to his feet and stood shoulder to shoulder with Kane. They watched as the wedge-shaped craft seemed to hang suspended at a crooked angle in the sky. A thick corkscrew of smoke boiled out of the fireball searing through the Aurora's undercarriage. They saw another of the light disks flicker and go dark.

The Aurora shuddered and its prow slowly lifted as the ship struggled to gain altitude. It hung there for what seemed like a very long time, straining and smoking. Then its nose began to dip, like a broad arrowhead that had lost its velocity and now dropped back to Earth.

The aircraft did not so much fall as gracefully slide down between the open rockcrete slabs. It disappeared beneath the desert, its electronic murmur also fading. They waited for the sound of a crash. Instead, they felt a fierce, throbbing vibration like a silent surf rising from below.

Kane took a swift step back, snarling, "Oh, *shit!*"

Both men heeled around and started running. A deafening blast cannonaded up from the depths beneath them. A roaring sheet of yellow flame mushroomed up and out of the opening, turning the desert as bright as high noon on a cloudless summer's day.

A consecutive series of brutal shock waves crashed into Grant and Kane like invisible breakers, picking them up, knocking them flat and then rolling them headlong over the sand.

The ground heaved violently, riven by fissures of superheated air that spewed dust and rock fragments. Kane's main fear was that the roof of the subterranean hangar would be driven upward by the enormous pressure of the explosions and then collapse, but the desert floor did not yield. Debris began to fall, pieces of slagged and smoldering metal mixed in with blackened chunks of rockcrete.

They picked themselves up, spitting out grit and

knuckling sand particles from their eyes. The two men blinked in stunned surprise as the pillar of hell-fire climbed higher and higher, as if it intended to punch a hole in the canopy of the sky. Flaring fingers of energy crackled up and down its coruscating length.

"Goddamn," Grant said inanely.

"Yeah," Kane muttered in the same subdued tone.

The column of raging flame slowly receded, and so did the ground quakes. They turned away, Grant cradling the Dragon missile launcher in his arms, Kane seizing its canvas carrying case.

They sprinted toward the area where Brigid and Domi waited, once taking a detour around a crack in the ground from which a tongue of flame erupted.

Both knew what had happened—what they hadn't wanted to happen. When the Aurora crashed, whatever powered it had interacted with the two-tiered generator in the hangar and triggered an apocalyptic chain reaction.

Despite the disaster, Kane fervently hoped the destruction wrought in the hangar had spread farther into the installation, particularly to the loathsome Nightmare Alley.

"Kind of a shame. I wish I could have had the chance to jockey that bird," Grant said wistfully.

Kane smiled sourly but said nothing. Grant had been one of the most experienced pilots in Cobaltville's Magistrate Division. He missed flying the only type of aircraft available in the villes, the modified Apache AH-64 gunships known as Deathbirds. He'd heard rumors about air travel making a limited comeback in some areas, with old prop planes and the like being restored and used for short flights.

Brigid moved out of the shadows to meet them, the wavering glow of the flames casting unnatural highlights on her face. "You blew the damn generator anyway!" she said angrily.

"Not on purpose," Kane retorted a little defensively. He peered behind her. "Where's Domi and Rhine?"

Brigid gestured. "They're back there. What are we going to do with him?"

A searchlight beam suddenly stabbed through the indigo sky and swept toward them. The rod of white incandescence bisected the blue-black tapestry of the sky, stretching back to the indistinct mass near the top rim of the mesa. A small speck seemed to crawl along the beam.

Kane was not surprised by the appearance of the Deathbird, but he was dismayed by it. Now he understood why the Aurora had hovered above the hangar doors—the crew had been waiting for their chopper escort to arrive.

The three of them ran deeper into the gloom. When they reached Domi and the sentry, Grant snapped to her, "Let the bastard go, grab our stuff and let's move!"

Domi hesitated only a fraction of a second before removing her blaster from Rhine. She obviously wanted to chill the man, but she didn't question Grant's command. Turning, she grabbed a leather rifle case from the ground, slung it over her shoulder by the strap and sprinted quickly away from the blazing wall of flame, desperate to get out of the glow it shed. Brigid picked up the case of survival stores and Kane snatched the bag containing grens and extra ammo.

Rhine scrambled away in the opposite direction, waving his arms to attract the attention of the Deathbird. The searchlight beam dropped straight down from the sky and transfixed him in a circle of blinding white. He covered his eyes with one hand, gesturing wildly with the other.

Pinpoints of fire rippled in a rotating sequence from the Deathbird. The roar of the M-230A1 chain gun in the chin turret sounded like stuttering thunderclaps.

As fountains of dust exploded all around him, Rhine expressed emotion for the first time. He voiced a wordless scream of terror and anger. The scream clogged in his throat as he hurtled backward, pounded by a storm of 30 mm slugs. His coverall flew apart in tatters. Coils of intestines spilled out at his feet.

Grant, Domi, Kane and Brigid ducked into the sheltering shadows of a small outcrop. Swiftly they raised their Stealth hoods over their heads to baffle the Deathbird's forward-looking infrared tracker.

The helicopter skimmed into view, dropping altitude, its searchlight fixed on Rhine's mutilated body. Kane imagined the outrage of the two-man crew when they got a good look at their victim. His lips creased in a thin smile as the Deathbird hung over the corpse like a hovering vulture.

Painted a matte, nonreflective black, the chopper's

sleek contours were interrupted only by the two ventral stub wings. Each wing carried a pod of sixteen 57 mm missiles. Both T700-701 turboshaft engines were equipped with noise baffles so only the sound of the steel vanes slicing through the air was audible.

The maximum speed of a Deathbird was 186 miles per hour and its internal fuel range was 300 miles, so there was no chance of either outrunning or outdistancing the chopper, even if they made it back to the Land Rover in one piece. The foreport of the black chopper was tinted a smoky hue, so neither Kane nor Grant could tell if the pilot was someone they might recognize from their years as Mags.

The searchlight slid away from Rhine's corpse, inching across the desert floor. With no body-heat signatures registering on their FLIR instruments, the crew had to look for intruders the old-fashioned way—visually, by tracks on the ground.

Kane was fairly certain they could evade one Deathbird, perhaps even two of them. But that would require a protracted game of cat and mouse, and the longer they waited, the greater the likelihood of ground troops being put into the field, too.

When they had invaded the installation nearly a year earlier, normal humans had been conspicuously absent, except for three members of the Cobaltville Trust, and they were there on business. All of the opposition had been composed of the hybrids, the so-called new humans.

After the death and destruction the three of them had wreaked in the place, it seemed reasonable to presume that a garrison of Mag-trained humans had been permanently stationed there. They had eight miles of open desert to cover, and though dawn was at least twelve hours away, they couldn't afford to expend the time they needed to cover that distance in eluding capture. If they hadn't escaped the area by sunrise, Kane knew they never would.

With a strong thrumming of blades, the Deathbird gained altitude and swung off, cutting over to the east. When the shape of the chopper was little more than a smudge against the dark sky, the four people moved out again. Domi continually watched their backtrack. Full night swallowed the twilight and the stars winked on, cold, white and impersonal. No sound but their careful footfalls disturbed the brooding quiet.

They didn't retrace their route, but chose one roughly parallel to it so if their tracks were discovered, they wouldn't lead back to them. Several times they were forced to take cover as the Deathbird soared close, its searchlight crawling over the desert.

"It seems strange only one chopper has been deployed," Brigid murmured.

"Not so strange," Grant said grimly. "Whoever gives the Bird crew their orders knows damn well what happened to the Aurora wasn't an accident."

Brigid looked at him in puzzlement, then understanding shone in her jade eyes. "The Deathbird is a diversion—is that what you mean?"

"Yeah," Kane muttered, eyes still on the hovering helicopter. "It's supposed to keep us pinned down and our attention focused only on it. Simple way to buy enough time to put more opposition into play.''

Grant hefted the missile launcher. ''Shooting down the Bird would free us up to some extent, but we'd pinpoint our position.''

As the chopper wheeled away from them, they rose and began a skulking sprint, alternating running with creeping.

Kane estimated they had traveled less than a mile before a peculiar swishing sound reached his ears, like the wind rustling through dry weeds. He felt not the faintest breath of a breeze. Signaling a halt, he crouched, eyes searching the terrain that lay before them.

Domi tilted her head, listening intently. ''What's that?'' she whispered curtly.

Within a second, her question received an answer. From a declivity in the flatlands, an open-topped vehicle hove into view some thirty yards away. At first glance it resembled a slightly flattened box. A pair of MG-73 swivel-mounted machine guns sprouted from the open deck. From a shielded assembly protruded the ten-foot-long snout of a 75 mm smoothbore cannon.

Skirts of alloy fell almost to the ground, and they rose and fell gently as the vehicle moved. Dust and grit puffed up all around it in a cloud. It looked like a cross between a tank and an infantry combat vehicle, but it did not produce the clatter of treads or the squeak of return rollers. All they heard was a faint throb.

Sounding nonplussed, Grant said softly, "I'll be triple damned. A hovertank."

Kane kept his eyes on the machine, counting three black-uniformed figures within the raised superstructure, one manning the cannon, the others at the MG-73 emplacements. "A hover*what?*"

"Something the predark military was developing as part of the Super Infantry Program. It operates on the air-cushion principle with big-ass fans providing the lift. It rides above the ground."

"How do you know that?" Brigid asked skeptically.

Grant cast her a glance, irritation glittering briefly in his eyes. "You're not the only one who skims through the historical database, you know."

Kane stared at the tank, admiring the effortless way it appeared to glide over the sand. The metal skin seemed smooth at first glance, but he discerned a number of irregularities inset into the armor. He guessed they were proximity sensors and maybe even close-range-defense devices. "Only see three crew."

"There's a pilot's compartment below the combat deck," Grant declared. "At least one man is down there, mebbe two."

"What kind of armor does that thing pack?"

Grant did not reply.

After a moment, Kane said impatiently, "I asked—"

"I heard you," Grant broke in. "I'm trying to remember. I read about it months ago."

Kane said wryly to Brigid, "Too bad you weren't the one who'd read about the damn thing."

Grant uttered a noise of disgust. "Some kind of steel-ceramic bond, like on the Sandcats. Nothing a Cobra can't disable if we hit it in the right place."

Kane shook his head. "I'm not interested in disabling it. I want to hijack it."

"Nice concept, but how do you figure to do it?" Brigid asked.

Grant reached for the rifle case slung from Domi's shoulder. "Take out the gunners, first thing."

He unzipped the leather scabbard and removed the big Barrett sniper rifle from its cushioned interior. He checked over the telescopic sights, tested the built-in bipod and chambered a .50-caliber round from the box magazine into the breech. His left hand cradled the thirty-three-inch barrel, while his right hand curled around the pistol grip backing the trigger guard.

"They looking for us," Domi pointed out. "No cover, no way to sneak up on 'em."

Kane hiked around and spotted the Deathbird. He estimated it was about three-quarters of a mile away, about 150 feet in altitude. "We might be able to do it," he said slowly, "if we do to them what they've been doing to us."

Chapter 4

Maddock fixed his attention on the small screen above the hatch leading to the pilot's compartment. It had been black and blank for the past thirty minutes, but now concentric red lines radiated from the center around a pulsing, inch-wide circle, accompanied by a series of soft electronic pings.

"We've got an infratrace hit!" he crowed jubilantly. "Body heat and motion signature!"

Howse, the pilot, shouted up through the hatch, "Coordinates!"

Staring at the numerals flickering on the upper right corner of the screen, Maddock called out, "Six-niner-six, fifty-four meters. Target is moving fast."

Howse wrenched on the wheel, and the tank shifted direction smoothly, the lift fans whirring and sighing. Beck, at the port-side machine-gun emplacement, tightened his hands on the firing studs. Across from him, Duncan did the same. Neither one said anything.

Maddock envied the studied ease of the two men, but he suspected they were just as strung-out and nervous as he was. He was the newest member of the security force, recruited from the ranks of freshly badged Magistrates in Cobaltville. He still wasn't certain if this assignment was superior to walking patrol in the Tartarus Pits.

At least there he knew what to expect, understood the kind of people he would be dealing with. Slaggers mainly, since that sector of Cobaltville was a melting pot of cheap labor, petty criminals and outlanders. The Archuleta Mesa duty was like nothing he expected or even imagined pulling when he entered the Mag academy.

The high level of technology in use in the installation came as more than a surprise; it was profoundly shocking. Machines, wags and devices of all types far outstripped anything in Cobaltville. And if he thought some of the residents of the Tatarus were strange, the permanent personnel in the subterranean complex made the Pitters seem mundane in comparison.

None of the security force dealt with the slightly built, delicate-featured people directly. They were kept segregated, although each of the four sec squads had a designated intermediary who conveyed their orders. As far as Maddock had been able to determine, all of the squads comprised only five men.

The people, if that's what they were, spooked Maddock, made his skin crawl and his short hair tingle on his scalp. He had only caught glimpses of them from time to time, and they struck him as more than human but at the same time somehow other than human, too. All shared similar characteristics—besides slender, almost childish builds, they had large domed heads, huge slanting eyes and faces that seemed all brow ridges and cheekbones. He had seen a couple of them walking around with plastic tube-shaped holsters strapped to their thighs.

Shortly after arriving at the mesa, he'd asked Howse if the people were a breed of mutie. Since the man also hailed from Cobaltville, he figured he'd share his curiosity, especially since the small, big-headed people didn't fit any of the descriptions of stickies, scalies, swampies or scabbies he had ever heard of.

"The desert is full of the bones of stupes like you who started asking questions about this place," Maddock was told.

Maddock immediately ceased further inquiries, but try as he might, he couldn't smother his curiosity. Right at the moment, his curiosity burned at a fever pitch, threatening to consume his training. He struggled to keep from yelling a series of questions at everyone around him.

Every night, from dusk till dawn for the past month, he and the tank crew had patrolled the perimeter, to the edge of the shock field and back. This night they had been ordered to stand down and confine themselves to barracks. His companions did not seem surprised, and Maddock received the distinct and uneasy impression something was going on they weren't meant to see. The rest of the sec crew accepted the change in procedure with resigned equanimity. Maddock pretended to do so, as well.

Then, barely half an hour ago he had felt the concussion of an explosion, the power failed for a few minutes and then came the screaming of the high-alert siren. Within moments of the siren, the hovertank rolled from a camouflaged entrance and out into the desert night. The orders were simple—locate and apprehend intruders, terminate if necessary.

Maddock saw the flames staining the sky but he knew better than to ask his comrades about their source. The notion of intruders agitated him far more than a mysterious fire.

"I see something!" Duncan swung the machine gun around on its oiled swivel mount.

Maddock looked up from the screen, eyes scanning the desert. He saw nothing but shadow-splotched sand and ocotillo scrub. Then he caught a fleeting glimpse of a shape, little more than a flitting blur, white against the murk only twenty yards away.

Duncan squeezed the double triggers of the MG-73. The heavy weapon roared with a sound like a hailstorm confined inside of a steel drum. Orange flashes stabbed the gloom, and cartridge cases spewed from the ejector port in a smoking rain.

Duncan hadn't established either proper range or target acquisition. The wild volley chewed into the desert floor, kicking up sand in high fountains. Maddock returned his gaze to the red pulsing dot that represented Duncan's target. The range decreased with every passing microsecond, but it still moved.

Thick liquid a deeper shade of red than the dot sprayed across the screen. The steady drumming of the MG-73 ceased almost at the same time. Maddock whirled, a profanity-seasoned demand on his lips. It died there.

The first thing he saw was Duncan's lower leg lying on the combat deck, severed at the knee, still clothed in coverall and the foot still booted. The second thing he saw was Duncan himself, sagging down behind the gun emplacement, clutching at the stump of his left leg, squeezing it to keep the femoral artery from squirting any more blood. His eyes bugged out, his mouth worked, but he was too overwhelmed by shock and pain even to scream.

On the raised housing encircling the deck, Maddock noticed a gaping hole punched through the metal, surrounded by a shiny ring of alloy. Beck, squatting behind his own MG-73 on the opposite side of the vehicle, hadn't seen a thing.

Maddock finally found his voice. He meant to yell Beck's name, to attract his attention to their downed comrade. Instead he shrieked, "*Fuck!*"

That drew Beck's attention. He took a step toward Duncan just as the hovertank shuddered brutally. Pulverized grit blew out between and beneath its skirts in a cloud. The lift fans keened and the tank lurched. It tipped to one side for an instant as a cursing Howse frantically fed more power to the stabilizers, trying to coax the other blades to compensate. Maddock gripped the frame of the sensor screen to keep from plummeting headfirst into the pilot's module.

Beck blurted in wordless surprise as he toppled backward, the backs of his thighs striking the lip of the housing. Maddock thrust out a hand toward him, but with arms windmilling, the gunner pitched off the combat deck.

The tank righted itself with a violent, spine-compressing jolt, hurling Duncan across the deck, leaving a scarlet stream in his rolling wake. He fell into Maddock, piling him up against the bulkhead. The rear of his skull hit the superstructure holding the cannon very hard. Howse shouted a steady stream of expletives.

Maddock wasn't thinking; he only reacted. When he managed to disentangle himself from Duncan and achieve a half-standing position, he saw a black-gloved hand gripping the rim of the deck housing.

Scrambling forward, he slapped his hand around Beck's wrist, heaving and pulling the gunner back aboard. It wasn't until the ebony-clad, masked figure stood on the deck that Maddock realized it wasn't Beck.

"Much obliged," Kane said a shaved sliver of a second before he sprayed a fluid directly into Maddock's face.

AS THE TROOPER WENT into convulsions, Kane slammed a shoulder into him. He fell down amid a wild spasm of arms and legs, smearing blood all over the deck. The other gunner was obviously dead, bled almost white. The .50-caliber AP round from the Barrett had easily penetrated the housing and ripped off the trooper's leg like a man tearing a drumstick from a baked chicken.

Toeing aside the bullet-amputated leg, Kane moved to the hatch leading to the pilot's compartment. The man seated before the control panel still struggled with the wheel, trying to stabilize the hovertank. The pilot wore a headset, and Kane assumed he was in radio contact with the Deathbird crew. He cast a swift glance behind him. The flight lights of the chopper shone like pinpoints in the sky, its search beam still probing the ground like a questing finger. As yet, the aircraft wasn't coming to investigate the problems of the ground vehicle.

The stuttering whine of the fans smoothed and the tank came to a halt, rising and falling gently, the deck swaying underfoot.

"Papa Bird, we've got a malfunction here," the driver declared.

Kane shoved his upper body into the module, jamming the bore of his Sin Eater against the side of the driver's neck. Quietly he said, "Advise them to stand by."

The pilot wasn't as rigidly self-controlled as Rhine the sentry, but he came close. After a handful of seconds spent gaping at the masked apparition, the man said into the microphone. "Papa Bird, stand by."

He looked at Kane intently and asked, "What did you use, a gren?"

"Concussion type. Damage is minimal. Don't bother thanking me for my restraint."

As he spoke, he scanned the interior of the module and spotted the Intratec 9 autoblaster clipped below the instrument panel, within easy reach of the pilot. Still holding the barrel of his Sin Eater against the man's neck, Kane stretched out a hand and removed the gun.

"What's your name?" Kane asked.

"Howse."

"Howse, keep this thing grounded until I say otherwise."

Hearing the scuff of feet behind him, Kane backed out of the module carefully, still aiming his blaster down into the hatch. Grant pulled himself up onto the deck and took the Barrett rifle Domi handed up to him, then helped her and Brigid aboard.

Grant nudged the body of the one-legged gunner with a boot. The man didn't move. "I meant to hit him in the hip. Hydrostatic shock would've stopped his heart and dropped him dead. He wouldn't have bled to death."

"He still just as dead," Domi said bluntly, her Stealth cloak folded over one arm.

Kane saw a crimson scratch marring the pearly hue of her rounded chin. "Are you all right?"

"Yeah. A couple of rounds came close, though."

Kane nodded, not outwardly expressing his relief. The plan to divert the hovertank's crew had been primarily Domi's. Stripping off the Stealth cloak in order to be detected by the vehicle's infrared imagers while Grant used the Barrett to take out the gunners and Kane crept up with the gren had been a big risk—so big Brigid had strenuously objected to it.

Kane returned his attention to Howse. The illuminated instrument panel cast a greenish glow over his features, giving him the appearance of a drowned corpse. "Start rolling or floating or whatever. Call the

Bird and report a minor problem that won't affect the patrol."

Howse complied with both commands, and though alert for hidden messages in the man's words to the chopper, Kane detected no hint of deception.

As the hovertank began gliding forward again, Kane said, "Only one of your crew is halfway functional. Young guy."

Howse sighed. "That's Maddock. He has the luck of the cherry. Guess it's no mystery who you are."

"It isn't?" Kane's voice held a slight mocking edge.

"No. I'm from Cobaltville." Howse said nothing more, as if his statement explained everything.

Wryly, Kane reflected that it probably did. He, Grant and most likely Brigid had achieved near legendary status in the ville network—half traitors, half insurrectionist monsters, a blend of ghost and outlaw.

"Thing is," Howse continued conversationally, "officially you're dead."

"Is that so?" Kane's tone was deliberately uninterested.

Grant's voice drew his attention away from Howse. "What about these bastards?"

Glancing over his shoulder, he saw Domi and Brigid standing over the trooper he had dosed with the nerve disrupter. He showed signs of reviving. Grant stood next to the dead man.

Kane crossed the deck and helped Grant pick up the gunner's body and heave it overboard. The man's leg followed.

The young trooper Howse had identified as Maddock lifted his head and stared around. His eyes showed his terror, and he tried to thrash into a sitting position.

"We have no intention of killing you," Brigid said.

Maddock reacted to her soothing voice even though it was muffled by her hood. He swallowed several times before asking, "What happened to Beck?"

"Worry about yourself," Grant growled in his best menacing tone, holding the sniper rifle in a suggestive way.

Kane returned to the hatch and gave Howse directions. "Keep your speed steady and don't do anything out of the ordinary."

The driver nodded and inquired, "If you don't mind me asking, what are you doing here?"

"It's done already. Now we're leaving."

"You won't get away with it."

"If you know who I am, you know that's not true." Kane prodded the man's back with his Sin Eater. "Shut up and drive."

Howse did both, but far from being comforted by the man's show of compliance, Kane's pointman's instincts began raising an alarm. After the devastation they had visited on the installation, the manpower in the field seemed inadequate to execute a thorough search for the saboteurs. The rational, tactical part of his mind coolly informed him that the destruction of the Aurora had been so extensive that substantial losses of personnel and matériel had been achieved.

The Deathbird was already airborne and the hovertank was the best that could be mustered.

His feral wolf's mind snarled in suspicion. The wolf sensed something gravely amiss. Kane tried to combine the two aspects of his mind, attempting to imagine the nature of a possible trap, but he drew a blank. He put a muzzle on the wolf and turned to Brigid and Grant.

"Has it occurred to you," he ventured, "how light the security seems?"

Grant nodded. "Yeah. One foot sentry, one Bird, one tank with a crew of four. Pretty low-rent for such a high-maintenance compound."

Brigid tugged impatiently at her face-concealing hood. "There are probably a lot of reasons. Too many secrets to keep, for one thing, and the more people you have here the greater the danger of having them exposed. More than likely there's only a skeleton force garrisoned here."

"Makes sense," Kane admitted. "But what about the hybrids? The place was crawling with them, remember?"

"Very clearly. I also remember we killed an awful lot of them, too. That, combined with the damage we caused to their breeding facility and incubation system, means not many replacements could have been born over the past ten months. And since we don't know the gestation periods, it's possible there are only a handful of them left."

"And," put in Grant, "the hybrids aren't fighters. They're fragile. Without those infrasound weapons of theirs, they weren't any kind of match for us even though they had us outnumbered four to one."

"Keep in mind," Brigid said, "the last thing the warders of this place expected was that we'd ever return, especially overland."

"I figured they wouldn't expect it," replied Kane.

"Exactly," she agreed.

Kane nodded. "Yeah, but I still don't feel what we've seen so far is all we're going to get."

After a moment, Grant said heavily, "Me either."

The opinions of the two people quieted Kane's wolf. It stopped snarling, although it growled from time to time.

The hovertank bore them farther and farther away from the great black block of the Archuleta Mesa and the Deathbird, but he still didn't relax. He crouched near the pilot's hatch so he could keep his eye on Howse. The man guided the vehicle smoothly over the desert hardpan, swerving around boulders but always returning to the course Kane had laid out.

Maddock fully recovered from the nerve toxin, and Brigid gave him permission to sit up. He stared in horror at his comrade's blood congealing on the deck and drying on his clothes and hands. Kane guessed he had just received his first taste of true violence, not the structured, almost clinical violence he'd experienced during his Mag training.

Addressing Kane, Brigid said, "I don't see any reason for his presence any longer. We don't need another liability."

Shifting the barrel of his Sin Eater toward Maddock, Kane said sharply, "Stand up."

Stiffly, as if he were ninety years old, Maddock climbed to his feet.

"Pat him down," Kane directed.

Brigid frisked him quickly, running her hands over the multipocketed coverall. Maddock did not react. If he took any pleasure in the masked woman's touch, it did not register on his face.

Stepping away from him, Brigid announced, "He's clean. No comm, no weapons. Not even a jackknife."

Gesturing with his blaster, Kane ordered, "Move to the side."

Maddock obeyed, stepping in the direction the gun barrel indicated. He waited.

"Do you have a superior officer," Kane asked, "somebody you report to other than Howse here?"

Maddock nodded uncertainly. "I guess I can find one."

"Give him a message. Tell him the revolution has officially started."

"I don't understand."

"Neither will he. But the message will eventually reach somebody who does understand." He pointed to the desert with his Sin Eater. "Take a flier."

Relief flooded the young man's eyes, but he didn't hesitate. Balancing one foot atop the raised wall around the deck, he kicked himself up and off the tank. Kane stood up and watched the young man fall hard and roll across the ground, raising a cloud of sand in his wake. Once he stopped rolling, Kane waited to see if he stood up, but the tank was traveling at such a rapid clip, Maddock's black-garbed body was quickly lost in the darkness.

Kane turned back to the hatch. "Slow down," he called.

Howse didn't look at him. "The faster we go, the sooner you can get out of here and the sooner I'm rid of you."

"Do as I say. Slow it down."

Sighing in exasperation, Howse shifted his foot over the accelerator, easing the pressure. Then he stamped down on the pedal as hard as he could. The steady drone of the lift fans hit a shrieking high note.

The abrupt surge threw Kane off balance, nearly back-somersaulting him across the combat deck. He heard Grant curse and Domi cry out as they staggered under the sudden increase in velocity.

The increase ended as unexpectedly as it began. The hovertank did not gradually lose its momentum or speed; it just stopped as violently as if it had collided with a brick wall.

Chapter 5

Kane heard no sound of a crash, but electricity crackled in dazzling blue skeins all over the metal hull of the vehicle, weaving a web of voltage. For an instant, he felt the current swarming all over him, like a million ants biting him simultaneously.

The rear end of the hovertank tilted sharply upward, then it dropped. The entire vehicle settled down on the ground, as if it were an animal that had suddenly decided to take a nap. The drone of the lift fans ceased. The only sound was the faint creak of the metal skirts as they came to rest on the sand.

Pushing himself to a crouch, Kane noticed the deck beneath him no longer vibrated with power. The hovertank was dead. He turned toward the control compartment and saw the instrument consoles were black.

Howse hitched around in his seat. Blood flowed from both nostrils, the result of slamming into the steering yoke. Baring red-filmed teeth in a grin, he said, "We're in a shock field, Kane. It automatically activated when the intruder alert went out. It kills all the power of anything with an electrical system that crosses it."

Howse chuckled, blowing little droplets of crimson

from his lips. "You may have gotten in here alive, but you sure as shit ain't gonna leave the same way."

Kane repressed the wrathful urge to put a 9 mm bullet into the middle of the man's smirk. "Get out of there," he commanded.

As Howse unbuckled his seat harness, Kane repeated to his companions what the man had said about the shock field. Grant experimentally worked the triggers of an MG emplacement. When they clicked impotently, he slapped the barrel in frustration, swinging it around on its swivel mount. "Batteries are dead."

"There must be some kind of voltage carrier beneath the sand," Brigid declared. "Probably like a carpet or a net."

Kane scanned the dark terrain ahead of them. He estimated their Land Rover lay hidden only a mile or so away. "If we parked our wag on the field..."

It wasn't necessary to complete the sentence.

As Howse emerged onto the deck, Brigid demanded, "How far does the field extend?"

The man shook his head. "I don't know."

"What will it do to a person if we walk on it?" asked Grant.

Again, Howse shook his head. "I don't know that, either."

"Let's find out," Domi snapped.

She rushed forward, head tucked against her shoulder. When she hurled her entire body weight against Howse's midriff, the air left his lungs in a surprised grunt. He stumbled backward against the raised rim of the deck and tumbled headlong over it. He hit the sand hard with a crunching thud.

They watched curiously as Howse climbed unsteadily to his feet. He looked up at them and spit, "Fuck you." Then he began a shambling sprint in the direction they had come.

Domi drew a bead on him with her Combat Master, holding it in a two-fisted grip, finger lightly touching the trigger.

"What are you waiting for?" Grant rasped angrily.

"Wait till the bastard thinks he safe," she replied, ruby eyes glinting with malice. "He'll get a big-time surprise."

Brigid uttered a wordless murmur of disapproval, but she knew better than to intervene when Domi's uncompromising Outland code demanded a bloodletting. She watched the girl's finger curl around the trigger.

A sheet of blue energy burst up from the ground, completely engulfing the running man. His figure became an indistinct shadow, frozen in midstride. A sound like the cracking of a monster whip rolled across the desert. A mass of fire swallowed Howse's head, and his clothes burst into licking flame. He dropped stiffly, body locked in a posture of running. The stench and reek of scorched flesh and hair filled their nostrils.

"My, that *was* a big-time surprise," Kane remarked mildly.

Domi blinked repeatedly, unwilling to lower her

pistol, as if she couldn't believe her prey had escaped her by dying.

"The same thing will happen to us if we leave the field," said Brigid grimly.

"What caused it?" Grant asked.

She shrugged. "A negative charge coming into contact with a positive one, more than likely."

"So we're trapped," said Kane darkly. "Like flies on flypaper."

They scanned the skies and saw the lights of the Deathbird growing larger. "And here comes the swatter," Grant stated.

For a long, tense tick of time, all eyes turned upward, fixed on the blinking running lights of the black chopper. All four people retained exceptionally vivid memories of two former land-to-air battles with the gunships.

"No point in trying to use the Dragon," Grant commented dourly. "The targeting and launch systems are electrically controlled."

"If they want us dead," said Brigid, "they can just hover out of range of our handblasters and use their own missiles to blow us to pieces."

Kane eyed the armor of the vehicle critically. Though thick, it couldn't withstand a prolonged bombardment of 57 mm high-ex warheads. "And if they want us alive?"

"They can just trap us here until troops arrive to take us into custody." Brigid untabbed her hood and pulled it down. "I have a feeling this will be one of your all-time favorite one-percenters."

Kane smiled without mirth, then his eyes narrowed with a sudden thought. Removing his own hood, he inquired, "You said the shock field is like a carpet?"

Brigid nodded. "Or a voltage-conducting net."

"And even if we managed to reach the Land Rover, we couldn't start it?"

"Not if we parked within the field's effect perimeter. And even if we didn't, we couldn't leave the field without ending up like—" she nodded toward the blackened, smoldering scarecrow "—Howse."

Grant removed his gaze from the approaching Deathbird. The sudden gleam in his dark eyes showed he had caught Kane's train of thought. "If the field is like a net, why can't we tear holes in it and interrupt the flow of current?"

Brigid's lips pursed contemplatively. "Since sand is an extremely good conductor of electricity, the carrier field wouldn't need to be close to the surface. It's probably buried deeply. The grens we have don't have the power to punch much beyond the topsoil."

Kane whirled toward the 75 mm deck cannon. "I wasn't thinking about grens."

Bolted below the breechloader of the heavy weapon, Kane found the artillery shells he was looking for. He shoved his Sin Eater back into its holster, knowing he wouldn't be able to unleather it again until—or if—they left the shock field.

Carefully, Kane removed three of the projectiles from the belt-feed mechanism, cradling them in his arms. They were heavy, approximately twenty pounds apiece. They clinked together and Grant winced in apprehension.

''Don't worry,'' Kane told him. ''They're antistructure. It'll take a hell of a kick to set off one of these.''

Domi hefted her Combat Master. ''This has a hell of a kick.''

Kane smiled thinly. ''My thoughts exactly.''

The two-foot-long streamlined shells had perforated cartridge cases allowing for a proportion of the combustion gases to escape the rear of the cannon as backblast. Without the mounted howitzer's breech to vent the backblast along certain parameters, he could only guess at the radius of the shell's explosive power.

The outline of the Deathbird acquired sharper shape and definition, its searchlight beam cutting a white swath toward them. Kane began clambering over the side of the hovertank. ''Let's not be such convenient targets until we know if they mean to chill us or capture us.''

Grant, Brigid and Domi vaulted off the combat deck. Grant shook his right hand repeatedly, as if it pained him. ''Damn Sin Eater won't unleather.''

''The shock field is dampening the holster's electric motor,'' Brigid told him.

They pressed up against the tank's hull, waiting and watching. The chopper took up a hovering position several hundred yards away, about twenty yards in altitude, far outside the range of their handblasters.

The search beam swept over Howse's body, then

tracked along until it haloed the tank. The color of the light suddenly shifted, from white to yellow.

"Here we go," Brigid declared flatly. "They've got their stroboscope working. That means they want us alive if possible."

The color of the light washing over the tank changed to red, then yellow, and shifted to a greenish violet. The strobing pattern covered the entire spectrum of visible light. The stroboscope was the method employed to pacify unwilling organ donors. When the light strobed fast enough, the vibratory cycle synchronized with normal brain-wave patterns and the witnesses lapsed into trances. A form of pseudo-epilepsy occurred, triggering the photic-driving response.

The flickering, strobing cycle increased in speed and brilliance. None of them looked at the light directly. Brigid said quietly, "They may be too far away for it to be efficient. I guess they figure there's no harm in trying."

"Not to mention it's like a flare, fixing our position for another patrol," commented Kane.

Squinting her light-sensitive eyes against the flashing radiance, Domi raised her Combat Master, rested the barrel on her forearm and squeezed off a single shot to no effect.

"Don't burn any more rounds," Grant told her acidly. "They're at least a hundred yards out of range."

He glared at the Deathbird as it hung mockingly in the sky.

"Why would they want us alive?" Kane wondered aloud.

"If not as a source of genetic material," Brigid declared, "then for information. Where we've been hiding, how we've eluded capture for so long."

"After what we just did to this place," Grant stated flatly, "revenge is probably a factor, too."

Kane recalled the blank, passionless faces of the hybrids he had seen and doubted Grant's comment. Visceral emotions did not seem to be part of the new human race.

"If we hoof it, nuke-shitting Bird will just follow us." Domi's voice held a note of frustration and anger.

"The hell it will," Grant said in a tone hard with conviction.

Resting the barrel of the Barrett rifle on a projecting flange of the hovertank's skirts, Grant seated the stock firmly against his right shoulder. He pulled away his hood so he could breathe easier.

"I make the range out to be around seven hundred yards," Kane said.

"More like nine hundred," retorted Grant dismissively.

Kane did not respond. He stepped away from Grant, gesturing for Domi and Brigid to do the same. The man needed no distractions.

Grant placed his eye against the twenty-power scope and centered the crosshairs on the Deathbird's tinted foreport, above the flickering stroboscope. He preferred a clean shot at the fuselage since the massive wrecking power of the .50-caliber round would obliterate the delicate inner workings of the machine. But, under the circumstances, the cockpit would have to suffice.

Taking a deep breath and holding it, he called on his training, achieving a form of autohypnosis known as the Mag mind, a technique that emptied the consciousness of nonessential thoughts. It allowed his instincts to take over. The sounds around him faded to nothing, and he closed his awareness even to the presence of the three people behind him.

The image of the Plexiglas port behind the scope's crosshairs leaped into clear, sharp focus. He squeezed into the trigger pull. The crack of the sniper rifle shattered the brooding night air. He moved his shoulder expertly, taking the recoil, not otherwise shifting position. Through the sniper scope, Grant saw a white star appear on the Plexiglas.

The Deathbird performed an abrupt, almost frantic figure eight from west to east, banked sharply to starboard, then veered wildly up and away. Lifting his head from the rifle, Grant announced quietly, "Tagged him."

He couldn't be sure if the steel-jacketed bullet had penetrated either the pilot or the gunner when it pierced the cockpit, but the black chopper maneuvered clumsily, listing from side to side. Vanes and rotors beating the air, it lost altitude, gained it and flew away from them. Within seconds, its running lights merged with the stars and the Deathbird was lost from view.

Although everyone strained their ears, they did not hear the sound of a crash.

Shouldering the rifle, Grant turned to face his companions. His expression was set in a deep scowl, which meant he was exceptionally pleased with himself. "Time to go home."

The four people broke into a sprint, Kane stumbling slightly under the weight of the artillery shells. Sand hissed and grated under their feet.

Eyes on their backtrack, Domi said, "Nothing else. Bird gone to nest."

"Don't get too happy." Grant panted. "They may have an ace on the line waiting for us."

Kane was too busy trying to maintain a steady pace to respond, but he silently agreed with Grant's assessment. The crew of the Deathbird wasn't tracking them for one of two reasons—they expected them to be flash-fried when they left the shock field, or they had turned their apprehension over to someone, or something, else.

As they topped a gently rolling dune, Kane's eyes picked out a humped irregularity in the terrain two hundred or so feet ahead and to the right. The Hussar Hotspur Land Rover rested where they had left it, covered by a neutral-colored tarpaulin bearing a pattern of black camo stripes designed to approximate shadows. For good measure, Domi had scattered uprooted scrub brush around the vehicle.

The four people stumbled to halt. Grant gulped air before wheezing, "The question is if we're parked on the field or not."

"If we are, we won't be able to start it," Brigid said, not even breathing hard. "If we aren't, we won't know that because we'll get cooked."

Kane laid two of the shells at his feet and hefted the third one, moving his arm back and forth as if preparing to launch a javelin. Then he whipped his right arm and upper body forward.

The shell arrowed through the air, arced down and landed point first in the sand, less than thirty feet away. "We need to ignite the propellant." Turning to Grant, he asked with a grin, "Think you can hit the primer pin from here?"

Grant glowered at him for a moment, realized he was striving to be funny and brought the Barrett to his shoulder. He sighted through the scope and shifted the barrel a fraction to the left.

Kane began, "I think we'd better—"

Grant squeezed the trigger. The report of the shot was immediately swallowed up by the thunderclap detonation of the artillery shell. The explosion dazzled their eyes, stunned their ears, the concussion slapping them flat and coating their bodies with a fine layer of pulverized sand granules.

Through the tongues of flame, the clouds of smoke and grit, Kane glimpsed a giant blue spark. It popped like the handclap of a giant.

Kane snorted grains of dust from his nasal passages. "—move back a little," he finished.

Chapter 6

Grant cursed in surprise, his right arm jerking convulsively. The Barrett rifle flew from his right hand, knocked away by the barrel of his Sin Eater as it sprang into his palm.

"That obviously shorted out the field," Brigid said, her voice husky from inhaling dust. "The holster's actuator is working again."

Domi picked herself up and examined her blaster, working the slide mechanism. Kane arose, grabbing the other two shells. "Let's not stand around admiring Grant's marksmanship."

As they skirted the smoking crater the explosion had punched in the desert floor, they saw tiny blue flashes dancing and arcing at the bottom of it. The hole was at least four feet deep, and Kane saw a ragged metallic mesh sandwiched between the layers of the sandy soil. He briefly wondered if the defense measure dated back to the twentieth century or was a postskydark addition.

They reached the Land Rover and yanked off the camouflage trap. The Hussar Hotspur was one of two overland wags kept and maintained in the Cerberus redoubt. The six-wheeled vehicle was outfitted with three-inch armor plate, a barricade remover and metal-shuttered windows. A number of gun ports perforated its dull gray chassis.

The four people climbed aboard the Land Rover, Domi taking up a position in the rear cargo compartment, opposite the four 50-gallon airtight containers of diesel fuel bracketed to the bulkhead.

Kane slid behind the wheel, Grant taking the shotgun seat and Brigid climbing in the back. The V-8 turbocharged engine caught on the first try, throbbing with a muted power. Engaging the gears, Kane steered the wag in the same direction they had come early that morning.

On all sides of them they saw a trackless sea of sand overlying rock and gravel, a barren wasteland rimmed by craggy hills. The Hotspur skirted the rolling dunes. The ground looked solid but it was deceptive. Even the wag's six wheels might not be able to free them if they bogged down in a dry quagmire.

They rolled in silence for a few minutes at a moderate speed, all of them alert and peering through the ob slits, Kane constantly checking their backtrail in the side mirrors. He didn't turn on the headlights, relying on the uncertain illumination provided by the moon and the stars. The terrain began to incline gradually as it approached a gully, which slanted down to the old streambed they had followed earlier.

Kane was looking into the mirror and didn't see the vehicle rocketing into view over the crest of the ridge ahead of them until Grant growled, "Fucking fireblast."

The open-topped ATV had huge knobby tires and

an extremely broad wheel base. An M-60 machine gun was mounted on the roll bar, giving the wag a top-heavy appearance. The four black-coveralled men, all armed with spidery-looking assaults, clung to seat straps as the vehicle jounced full-tilt over the terrain. All of them wore goggles to protect their eyes from the powdery dust, their lower faces concealed by strips of cloth. The wag traveled at such a high rate of speed its tires left the ground when it topped the rise and it flew for twenty feet until it hit the sand on a course that would intersect the Land Rover's.

"Rent-a-Road-Warriors," Domi sneered.

"Now we know why the Deathbird tried to keep us pinned down," Brigid remarked, sounding not in the least fearful. "They were waiting for this group to get here. Took them long enough."

"Better late than never," Kane grunted.

The barrel of the M-60 spit a tongue of flame. The machine gun trembled as the cartridge belt writhed. Little spouts of dirt sprang up well to the right of the Land Rover. The overstimulated triggerman had fired before he had established the correct range.

Kane used the heel of his hand to wrench the steering wheel in a hard half circle, the tires flinging up a thick plume of loose gravel and sand. The cloud blotted them from the triggerman's aim for a moment.

Kane wrenched the wheel in the opposite direction, and the Hotspur fishtailed, spewing up another wave of dust to blend with the first. As he hoped, the driver of the ATV slackened his speed rather than charge blindly into the choking cloud. Kane sent the Land

Rover barreling past it. He glimpsed the gunner swinging the M-60 around, following the engine roar. He couldn't clearly see what he was shooting, but two lucky rounds slammed into the Hotspur's armored coachwork.

Glancing into the side mirror, Kane saw the red flashes of at least two assault rifles winking in the dust swirl. Bullets banged loudly against the back door of the Hotspur and ricocheted away with keening wails.

"They're not using AP rounds at least," Grant observed.

Domi positioned herself to return the fire, poking the barrel of her pistol out through the aft gun port. She squeezed off three rounds in such rapid succession they sounded like one extended report.

In the mirror, through the dissipating and settling curtain of grit, Kane saw the head of one trooper seem to dissolve in a red mist. The M-60 machine gun continued to hammer, and the bullets smacked the rear end of the Hotspur with flat clangs.

Domi cursed and ducked instinctively. "The bastards are finding the range now."

"How long do you think they'll keep this up?" Grant asked Kane.

"Until they catch us or we chill them. We can probably outdistance them, but it'll take a while and increase the odds of a lucky shot blowing one or more of our tires. And we only have the one spare."

Grant nodded, as if he expected the answer. Turning in his seat, he called out, "Domi, lay some eggs on the trail."

Showing her teeth in a savage grin, Domi opened the war bag and brought out a couple of grens. She eyed their diameter, comparing their size to that of the rear gun port, and selected a V-60, a gren small enough to be covered even by her childlike hand. Rising to her knees, she unpinned the little sphere and pushed it through the opening.

The driver of the ATV didn't see the bouncing ball through the floating backwash of grit left in the Hotspur's wake, but it detonated several dozen feet in front of the wag.

A fireball bloomed, hurling up rocks and dirt. The driver reacted reflexively, swerving to the left, the big tires finding traction on the scattered bushes and gravel. The ATV slowed somewhat, but continued the chase.

"Shit," hissed Domi in disgust. "Now they'll be expectin' 'em."

Hitching around in her seat, Brigid watched Domi inspect a canister-shaped RG-34 high-ex gren, revolving it between her thumb and forefinger. The gren was considerably larger than the V-60. Experimentally she tried to fit its base into the port.

Anxiously, Brigid said, "That looks like a tight fit."

Nodding absently, Domi worked the gren's circumference halfway through the opening. "I'll pull the ring, then bash it the rest of the way through." She demonstrated by slapping the air with the flat of one hand.

She called to Kane, "Slow down some, let 'em catch up."

Kane eased the pressure on the gas pedal as Domi peered around the RG-34 jammed into the port, gauging the distance. Then, with a swift motion, she snatched the safety ring free with her right hand and prepared to thrust the palm of her left against it.

The Land Rover's front tires caught a deep rut, and the vehicle jounced violently upward, slewing the rear end around. Kane fought the wheel for control as the shocks and springs screamed in protest.

Domi screamed, too, frantically. She fell heavily against the bulkhead, her hand swiping the gren instead of slapping it, knocking it sideways within the rim of the port. Clawing out, she managed to get her fingers around it before another brutal jolt bounced her straight up from the deck, slamming the crown of her head against the roof. She fell onto her back, arms and legs asprawl, but with the gren slipping through the fingers of her right hand. She flailed wildly for it, like a juggler afflicted with Saint Vitus' dance, but the RG-34 eluded her efforts to recapture it.

Lunging over the back of the seat, Brigid shot out her right arm, her hand literally scooping the canister out of the air. In one continuous movement, she twisted around, leading with her whipping arm, and hurled the gren out of the passenger window less than an inch from Grant's ear.

It exploded in midair, not much more than ten feet

from the flank of the Hotspur. Shrapnel rattled loudly against the armor, but the ATV drove straight into the bloom of flame and concussion. The driver was in the process of avoiding the deep rut that had nearly tipped over the Land Rover, and he steered his wag right into the epicenter of detonation.

The wag flipped, rolling end over end, strewing the ground with glass fragments and body parts. The troopers catapulted from the ATV like rag dolls, all except for the driver. He was skewered by the steering column, which had been punched through his chest by the force of the explosion.

The wag's fuel tank then ignited, the secondary detonation engulfing the bodywork in a mushroom of roiling flame. The ATV disintegrated in a shower of hardware, both of its axles wrenched loose and cartwheeling in opposite directions.

Kane slowed the Hotspur, but he didn't stop it. He gazed at the settling wreckage reflected in the mirror and commented, "Good job, Domi."

He was completely unaware of how and why the gren had done its deadly work. Grant had an inkling and he eyed both Domi and Brigid suspiciously. Dryly, he repeated, "Yeah, good job."

The two women waited until he turned around before exchanging wan smiles.

Kane guided the Land Rover into a twenty-foot-wide streambed. Pebbles rattled beneath the wheels and chassis as he hugged the high sides of the banks to avoid the softer areas. When the channel swung in a wide curve along the back side of a ridge, Kane released his pent-up breath in a long exhalation of relief.

"That's all the pursuit we can expect," he declared confidently. "We got away with it."

He struck the steering wheel with the heel of one hand and laughed. "We got away with it! We kicked the barons in the collective balls and we're still alive to brag about it!"

Grant crooked a skeptical eyebrow. "When we're back in the Darks with this shithole behind us, then mebbe I'll feel like bragging a little."

Leaning forward, Brigid said with mock severity, "Kane can't wait to perform a superior dance in front of Lakesh, since he came up with this op over his objections."

She tapped the back of his head smartly, like a teacher reprimanding an unruly student. "Don't get too full of hubris, Kane. The fates don't like it."

Kane grinned. "Yes, ma'am. I'll just hold it until we get back to Cerberus."

He started to say something else, but his eyes suddenly narrowed. The grin fled his face, and his shoulders stiffened. Leaning forward, he stared intently through the ob port. Brigid and Grant followed his gaze.

Far away, at a hundred yards, flowing at an oblique angle to their course, was a ripple in the streambed—a moving ripple, as though something, a very large something, slid and burrowed just beneath the surface.

Watching the motion of the sand, they saw the ripple swerve in a half curve and move toward them.

"Oh, for God's sake," Kane groaned in angry exasperation. "*Now* what?"

Kane didn't brake, but he took his foot completely off the accelerator as, with little puffs of dust, the ripple inscribed a course down the center of the streambed. The growing furrow looked almost the width of the Land Rover itself. His throat constricted with the tightness of fear. He—all of them, for that matter—had heard accounts of the *Ourboros obscura,* the legendary giant mutie worm of the Southwestern deserts. But they were legends, campfire tales dating back to the anarchic century following skydark when many species had been distorted by the effects of nuclear radiation.

The ripple came to a halt less than fifteen feet from the barricade remover of the Hotspur. Even through the tires of the wag, they felt the ground vibrate and heard a thudding, throbbing moan. The streambed acquired a split, and bright light sprayed out, a wavering funnel of luminescence. With a geyserlike eruption of sand, a dully gleaming armature of metal burst up from the ground, surrounded by wisps of pulverized rock. It rose directly in the vehicle's path like an impossibly large, fleshless cobra.

Fifteen feet long and as big around as Grant's body, it resembled a serpent made of segmented metal joints, hinged in several places, coated with rivets instead of scales. Where the head should have been spun three blades that emitted a high-pitched buzzing whine. Their general shape reminded Kane of Oriental hand fans, but each blade was the diameter of the Land Rover's tires. Even though they spun with blurring speed, he saw the glinting metal teeth that studded them were arranged with such precision they allowed a perfect meshing with one another. The teeth looked to be twice the length and breadth of his hands.

Brigid blurted, "Some kind of slab saw! Probably made of a tungsten steel and vanadium alloy."

Kane fought his first impulse to tell her to shut up. Stomping on the gas pedal, he yanked the steering wheel sharply to the right, swerving around the armature and the rotating metal teeth.

"What the fuck is that thing?" Grant roared.

No one answered him. Behind the armature swelled a metal dome, rising from the burrow cut through the streambed. Sand and pebbles sifted down from it in rivulets. The convex dorsal surface bore oddly faceted contours lending it a resemblance to a gigantic fluted drill bit. Nearly the length of the Land Rover, the main body was supported by scoop-shaped treads. Foot-long blades of metal rimmed the scoops, like claws. The glare from the orange headlights splashed through the ob ports, forcing them to squint.

Hissing and roaring, it lumbered out of the ground, a far more fearsome monster than the *Ourboros obscura* could ever be.

Chapter 7

"It's an excavating machine!" Brigid cried.

Even over the engine noise of the Hotspur, they heard the hissing of hydraulics and the deep rumble of motors. The armature thrust forward, and the teeth of the trio of saw blades struck the Hotspur's coachwork with an agonizing screech. It sounded like fingernails dragging across a chalkboard but magnified a thousandfold. Sparks showered as the teeth sheared through the armor of the Land Rover's driver's side. The vehicle lurched, almost tipping up on one side.

Domi fired a tri-burst from her Combat Master through the side-door gun port. Bright little flares sprang up around the steel column, accompanied by dull clangs. She fired a single shot, then another burst. The bullets hammered ineffectually against the armature and the machine's dark bulk. The behemoth rolled on, not checking its speed. Ricochets buzzed and one struck the hood of the Hotspur, a finger's width from the open ob port, causing both Kane and Grant to recoil.

"Lay off!" Grant shouted at her. "Your slugs aren't penetrating!"

The machine heaved itself farther out of the ground, the scoops churning the dirt to a powdery loam. With a steady thud of pistons, the armature straightened out, pushing the Land Rover at an angle against the bank of the streambed, dislodging rocks and sand in miniature avalanches. Kane kept working the accelerator, the gearshift, trying to break free. Sand plumed from beneath all six tires, rubber squealing and smoking.

The saw blades bore down against the Hotspur's armored hull, steel shrieking as the teeth bit deeply. The interior filled with the cloying smell of superheated metal. Domi screamed something frantic as the inner wall of the cargo compartment suddenly acquired an inward-bulging seam, then a split.

Red rage replaced Kane's fear. "Son of a *bitch!*" he snarled.

Without a word, he let up on the gas pedal, groped beneath his seat, then flung open the vehicle's door. Both hands were filled—his right with his Sin Eater and the other with an artillery shell.

Brigid plucked at his sleeve. "What are you doing?" Her voice was high and wild.

Kane shook her off and stumbled when he set foot on the ground, recovered his balance and cast one of the shells directly in front of the left-hand claw scoop. In the split second before the treads buried it, he fired his Sin Eater at the primer pin.

The range was far less than point-blank; it was foolishly, suicidally close. A hurricane of hot air struck him in the face, driving his breath painfully back into his nostrils and mouth. An intolerable white glare blinded him. The explosion was so overwhelmingly loud he heard only the first fraction of a second of it before he went deaf. He wasn't even aware of riding the crest of a tidal wave of concussive force and dirt as it tumbled him up and over.

Kane didn't lose consciousness, but he lost awareness and all feeling in his body. He felt a pounding as of immense hammers against the sides of his head. His awareness slowly returned in bits and pieces. He heard a strange bass hum, as of a musical note refusing to fade.

A heavy shadow, like an black umbrella, filled his dazzled vision and in his nostrils was the chemical stink of high explosive. He tasted blood and realized it slid from his nostrils.

The numbness in his limbs receded, and Kane felt a deep boring pain in the middle of his back and the center of his chest. His body felt like one big bruise that started at the top of his head and ended at the soles of his feet. By twisting his head slowly, he saw he lay on his stomach on the rock-strewed roof of the Hotspur. For a second he had no idea of how he had come to be there. His stupefied mind sluggishly replayed the sequence of events of the past few seconds—the backblast swatting him up, slamming him against the bank of the streambed, before he fell face-first atop the vehicle. He felt the patter of pebbles raining down all around him.

Jarred and nerve-jangled, he braced his shaking hands against the hull and pushed himself to his knees. He realized he could see and that what he had interpreted as a shadow was a mushroom of thick black smoke hanging above a litter of scrap metal. An instant later he recognized the heap of metal as the excavating machine. Both headlights were shattered and dark. The main body tilted sideways on its skewed treads.

He made a feeble move to climb down from the roof, then Grant, Domi and Brigid were standing below him, reaching up to help him down. All of their faces wore similar expressions—fear mingled with relief and anger.

"I'm all right," he said before he realized he hadn't heard anyone ask any questions. In fact he didn't hear anything. His ears suddenly popped, and not until then did he understand he had been deaf. When he heard the voices of his three companions, he wished his hearing were still impaired.

"Crazy stupe bastard!"

"What did you think you were—?"

"Coulda chilled us all!"

Kane's eyes flinched away from their furious faces. Brigid in particularly looked profoundly shaken. "You're hemorrhaging from both nostrils and your left ear," she told him grimly.

"You're goddamn lucky—*we're* goddamn lucky—the blast was squeezed downward." Grant swung around to look at the remains of the machine and shook his head in disbelief. "You crazy stupe bastard."

The machine lay half in, half out of a steaming crater. Despite its fixed metal rigidity, it reminded Kane of a giant burst-open tick. Smoke poured from the splits in the hull. Although the saw blades were still embedded in the Land Rover's side, they no longer spun. The armature had been snapped in half, and Kane saw only a couple of hard kicks would be required to loosen the saw's teeth.

On unsteady legs, Kane stepped forward to get a better look. "It worked, didn't it?" His voice sounded faraway, muffled by many layers of cotton wadding. The bass musical note still rang faintly in his head.

"Are you sure you're all right?" Brigid demanded.

He nodded.

Domi's face twisted in a porcelain mask of outrage. "You won't be when I get through with you. Why didn't you warn us about what you were going to do?"

He shrugged, and the motion sent a spasm of pain lancing through his neck and shoulder muscles. "Not enough time. I was moving on instinct."

"Moving on ego and anger more like it," Brigid snapped. "You'd been congratulating yourself on how well this mission had turned out. And when that—" she waved toward the wreckage "*—thing* showed up, something you hadn't expected or anticipated, it was a blow to your pride. You weren't about to let it stop you."

"It could've killed us all," he said firmly, trying not to allow the pain radiating out from his chest to show on his face.

"Yeah," Domi spit disdainfully. "So could've you."

"That's enough," Grant interjected sternly. He favored Domi with one of his scowls. She returned it with a crimson-eyed glare. She didn't look away, but she said nothing more.

They moved closer to the machine, alert for any signs of movement among its scattered parts. Brigid said, "According to Lakesh, burrowing machines like that were used to construct COG facilities back in the twentieth century."

"What is it now?" Grant wanted to know. "An underground security wag?"

She didn't answer. Regardless of its original function, it was a true juggernaut of destruction.

Kane gave the machine an apprehensive survey. "Think the damn thing was remote-controlled, or was an operator inside it?"

"Doesn't matter," Grant muttered darkly. "Why does this shit always happen to us? We can't just have blastermen in tanks and choppers after us—no, we've got to have shock fields and giant digging machines and holographic assassins and Russian jolt-brains dropping whales on us."

"I guess it goes with the territory we've staked out," Kane said absently.

Grant made a spitting sound of derision. "Then I'm signing over my piece of it to the first stupe who wants it."

Kane had heard him voice similar sentiments before so he didn't take him seriously. Besides, he sympathized with Grant's frustration over the life of high strangeness they had led for the past months. It was no coincidence the road to that life had begun inside the Archuleta Mesa facility.

He turned away. "Let's see what kind of damage we have."

"The wag's," Brigid asked sarcastically, "or yours?"

Kane had taken only a couple of steps when he heard a metallic creaking. He spun back around. A top section of the machine's hull rose upward and to the side, allowing a hissing halo of vapor to escape. He and Grant leveled their Sin Eaters at the hatch.

As the mist thinned, a blurred figure appeared. It was human-shaped, but excessively slender and small of stature, less than five feet tall. It fell rather than climbed down from the machine and lay on its back in the furrowed earth.

Grant, Domi, Kane and Brigid moved in swiftly but cautiously. A female hybrid lay there, her compact, tiny-breasted form encased in a silvery-gray, skintight bodysuit of a metallic weave. Her huge upslanting eyes were of a clear crystal blue, her pale delicate features smeared with soot and grease. The silky blond hair topping her domed skull was matted with blood flowing from a laceration on her scalp.

She wore a tubular plastic holster on her right thigh. In her hand she held a slim silver wand about three feet long, its tapered tip shivering and humming.

She tried to point the infrasound weapon at them, but Domi swept it from her hand with the barrel of her Combat Master.

The female stared up at them unblinkingly, placidly. She looked so delicate, so elfin, Kane had difficulty accepting she had operated the huge excavating machine. She seemed more like a mannequin than a living creature.

The crystal-blue eyes flitted from one face to the other, but they showed no recognition or emotion whatsoever.

"Brave little bitch," Grant grunted.

Domi sneered. "Got no feelings like us."

Brigid edged closer to the woman and asked, "Are you badly hurt?"

In a faint, high-pitched child's voice, she replied, "Secondary trauma to the occipital area of my skull. Blood loss seems minimal, although I suspect I'm suffering from a concussion. Several ribs are broken, but as yet my lungs have not been punctured. I shall survive."

Domi's lips curled in a silent snarl. She aligned the bore of her blaster with the female's high forehead. "Hell you will."

Brigid knocked the barrel of the Combat Master aside just as Domi squeezed the trigger. The .45-caliber bullet dug a gouge in the dirt less than two inches from the hybrid's head. Her big eyes did not so much as blink.

Domi glanced in ruby-eyed rage at Brigid. She opened her mouth to shout at her, but Brigid snapped, "Stand down, Domi. Nobody gave you an order to fire."

Domi gestured in frustrated fury. "She not even human—"

"Stand *down,*" Grant barked.

With a wordless utterance of disgust, Domi lowered her blaster. Resentfully she whispered, "Not even human."

"Neither are you, according to the barons," Brigid shot back.

Kane regarded the hybrid female impassively. "Are there any other surprises along the route you can tell us about?"

Her thin lips twitched in what might have been an attempt to smile. "Would you believe me if I told you?"

"Probably not, but answer the question anyway."

"No. There is much damage in the facility. Valuable personnel and matériel have been lost. This machine was deployed out of necessity."

She cocked her head at him quizzically, a gesture that reminded him of Balam, the strange entity who'd been held captive at Cerberus. "Are you happy to know this, that your savage act has severely and adversely affected our efforts to depopulate the Earth?"

"As a point of fact," Kane answered stolidly, "I am extremely happy to know this. And this savage act against your kind, against the barons, is just the first among many. Are you frightened to know that?"

"No," she said in a soft, papery whisper. "It saddens me."

Grant shifted his feet impatiently. "Let's get the fuck out of here. We've got a lot of miles to cover before daybreak."

They did as he said, returning to the Land Rover.

Kane and Grant worked the teeth of the saw blades free of the hull, both dismayed by how deeply the armor was scored. Grant fingered the gaping gash and gusted out a deep sigh. "What a night."

Kane allowed Grant to take the wheel. As they rolled around the wrecked machine, he noted how motionless the hybrid lay. He wondered briefly if she had downplayed the extent and severity of her injuries, and then he wondered why he even wondered about it.

Her confirmation about the destruction wrought in the Archuleta Mesa should have triggered a celebratory mood among the four of them. Instead all were silent, lost in their own thoughts.

Despite his best efforts to rekindle his earlier joy of victory, Kane knew that this first blow, one among many, would soon be answered in kind.

Chapter 8

The headwaters of the Jhelun swirled with blood. The screams of drowning people blended with the rushing of the current to make a babbling cacophony of terror.

Lakesh placed his feet carefully on the backs of the desperately thrashing flood victims, using them as stepping-stones to cross the river. He did not look at their faces, but he saw them all the same. Men, women, children, animals, some of whom he recognized. They were neighbors, colleagues, friends, even the entire faculty of the cybernetics department of MIT.

But since he had to get to the other side of the Jhelun River to visit his mother, he had no choice but to use the drowning people as stepping-stones. He felt a little badly about using them, but it was the only way to achieve his goal. They didn't mind; they were dying anyway.

As he put his weight on the back of a man who looked like a distant cousin, he lost his footing. The man floundered beneath him, pitching Lakesh into the river. The crimson-tinged waters closed over his head, and he fought back to the surface, a shriek of pure terror bursting from his throat. The current swept him like a cork with the other dying people, carrying him away from his home.

A coil of braided silk was tossed from the far bank and splashed down near him. Though his vision was obscured by the bloody water, he grasped it by instinct. Lifting his head clear of the surface, he saw his loyal mother resolutely tugging on the silk, the hem of her colorful sari dipping into the river but somehow not getting wet. She smiled at him, determined to bring her only son to dry land.

His surge of relief was replaced by cold horror when a grinning Salvo popped up and began sawing at the silk with a combat knife. The line parted, his mother howled in anguish and the bloody surface of the Jhelun swallowed him.

Lakesh awoke from his nightmare, a yell starting up his throat. His body made a blind, instinctive lunge for the bank and it was only when his hands struck the smoothly planed wall that he realized he was not in Kashmir, and a sheet covered his face, not water.

He pawed the sheet away and leaned against the pillow on his bed, then used the bedclothes to wipe the cold film of perspiration from his forehead. By squinting, he barely made out of the glowing numbers of his wall chron. It was close to 5:00 a.m., which meant he had slept uninterrupted for nearly six hours, something of a record for him.

Lakesh made a sound somewhere between a sob and a laugh, then pushed himself up to a sitting position. He fell victim to a coughing fit. When it passed, he felt light-headed and slightly nauseated.

The meaning of the dream was no mystery. He had a fair understanding of psychology and psychiatry, despite knowing they were disciplines that constantly changed their minds.

Generally, he did not remember his dreams unless they were particularly vivid, and then he rarely dissected their imagery. He knew they were shadows from his past, skulking out of his subconscious when he slept. Therefore, he tried to get by on as little sleep as possible. Only when he was awake could he keep the ghosts in their graves and avoid from contemplating how much like a ghost he was himself.

Lakesh's stomach was twisted in knots, and he got to his feet, stumbling across his quarters to the bathroom. He filled the sink with cold water and plunged his face into it repeatedly, blowing like a whale. After half a dozen immersions, the nausea receded a bit.

When he lifted his head from the basin and saw his reflection in the mirror, he felt a shock but it was faraway and by now familiar. For the first three years after his resurrection, he was always discomfited by the sight of blue eyes staring out at him from his own face.

Although the advance of the glaucoma had been halted during his century and a half in cryostasis, it had returned with a double vengeance upon his revival. The eye transplant was only the first of many reconstructive surgeries he underwent, first in the Anthill, then in the Dulce installation. Although the transplanted eyes were free of disease, they had grown weak over the past fifty years.

After his brown eyes were replaced with new blue ones, his leaky old heart exchanged for a sound new one and his lungs changed, arthritic knee joints had been removed and traded for polyethylene.

Although the operations had definitely prolonged his life, they had not been performed out of Samaritan impulses. They were done to extend his usefulness to the Program of Unification.

By the time all the surgeries were complete, the mental image he'd carried of his physical appearance no longer coincided with the reality. From a robust, youthful-looking man, he had become a wrinkled cadaver. He was old, far older than he looked, and he looked very old indeed. His glossy jet-black hair grew back as a thin gray patina of ash that barely covered his head. The follicles of his facial hair were dead, and he could never regrow the mustache he had once taken so much pride in.

His once clear, olive complexion had become leathery, crisscrossed with a network of deep seams and creases that bespoke the anguish of keeping two centuries worth of secrets. Lakesh could take consolation only in the fact that though he looked very old indeed, he was far older than he looked. He told his reflection, For a man on the high side of two hundred, you're a real babe.

Returning to the bedroom, he put on his eyeglasses, dark rimmed with thick lenses and a hearing aid attached to the right earpiece. With the glasses in place, he knew he resembled a myopic zombie, particularly with the way his white bodysuit bagged on his scarecrow frame.

Lakesh left his quarters and emerged into the twenty-foot-wide corridor made of softly gleaming vanadium alloy that ran the length of the redoubt's first level. He made for the operations center, but some errant impulse turned him down a side passageway. He stopped before a door bearing a keypad rather than a knob.

He hesitated for just a second before tapping in the six-digit code. With a harsh electronic buzz, the lock solenoid slid aside and he pushed the door inward. He stepped into the wide, low-ceilinged room and looked around warily. It was the first time he'd visited the place in two months. Most of the furnishings consisted of desks and comp terminals. A control console ran the length of the right-hand wall, glass-encased readouts and liquid crystal displays flickering and flashing. A complicated network of glass tubes, beakers, retorts, Bunsen burners and microscopes covered the black-topped lab tables.

Upright panes of glass formed the left wall. A deeply recessed room stretched on the other side of them. Although there was no longer a reason for it, the room was dully lit by an overhead neon strip, glowing a dull red.

Despite the gleaming chromium, glass and electronic consoles, the room exuded the atmosphere of a cobwebby attic in an old abandoned house, holding the accumulated bric-a-brac of lost dreams.

It had never occurred to him during Balam's three-

and-a-half years of imprisonment in the glass-walled cell he would miss the creature when he was gone. Of course, it never occurred to him he would ever be gone. Lakesh hadn't thought that far ahead.

After a couple of years, he had ceased to view the entity as a prisoner or as a source of information about the Archon Directorate. Instead, Balam became a trophy, a sentient conversation piece, like a one-item freak show.

In hindsight it was fairly apparent that Balam had chosen to remain in the Cerberus redoubt for reasons of his own. He had used his psionic abilities to manipulate Banks, his former warder, into initiating a dialogue when he probably could just as easily have manipulated the man into releasing him.

Of course, there was only one place for Balam to go, and he could not get there by himself. He needed Kane and Brigid Baptiste to take him there.

Lakesh tugged at his long nose thoughtfully and turned to leave. There were some nights when a terror borne of suspicion crowded into his mind. It was possible, though perhaps not probable, that Balam had manipulated them all into setting him free, practicing the artful deception his people had directed against the human race for thousands of years. Even now Balam could be scheming and plotting anew, safe in his subterranean sanctuary of Agartha, a world away in Tibet.

It certainly wouldn't have been the first time Balam and those of his kind tricked and lied to their human allies—or pawns.

Repressing a shudder, Lakesh left the room. When it came to Balam and the so-called Archons, the only thing he could be certain of was that he could be certain of nothing.

Lakesh walked to the command center of the redoubt. The long high-ceilinged room was filled with comp terminals and stations. The control complex had five dedicated and eight-shared subprocessors, all linked to the mainframe behind the far wall. Two hundred years ago, it had been state-of-the-art, with experimental error-correcting microchips so minute they even reacted to quantum fluctuations. Biochip technology had been employed when the installation was built, with protein molecules sandwiched between microscopic glass-and-metal circuits.

On the opposite side of the center, an anteroom held the mat-trans chamber, its brown-hued armaglass walls as translucent as ever. Lakesh did not even glance at the indicator lights of the huge Mercator relief map of the world spanning one entire wall. Pinpoints of light shone steadily in almost every country, connected by a glowing pattern of thin lines. They represented the Cerberus network, the locations of all functioning gateway units across the planet.

Banks manned the main ops console, and he greeted Lakesh with a joviality completely inappropriate for the time of day.

"All systems green and green," the young, trimly built black man reported cheerfully.

"And the biolink signals from the transponders?" Lakesh asked gruffly.

Banks waved a hand toward a monitor screen upon which four white icons throbbed and pulsed. "Sound as old-style dollars."

Everyone in the redoubt had been injected with a subcutaneous transponder that transmitted not just the bearer's general location but heart rate, respiration, blood count and brain-wave patterns. Based on organic nanotechnology, the transponder was a nonharmful radioactive chemical that bound itself to an individual's glucose and the middle layers of the epidermis. The signal was relayed to the redoubt by the Comsat, one of the two satellites to which the installation was uplinked.

The telemetry transmitted from the transponders belonging to Kane, Brigid, Domi and Grant scrolled upward. The computer systems recorded every byte of data sent to the Comsat and directed it down to the redoubt's hidden antenna array. Sophisticated scanning filters combed through the telemetry.

"Their current locations?" asked Lakesh.

Banks's face registered embarrassment. Haltingly, he answered, "I don't know for sure, sir. I haven't been briefed on the triangulation tracking program."

Scowling, Lakesh came to his side, reached around him and began tapping the keyboard. "It's about time you learned how and why we have these systems here."

Banks said nothing as Lakesh punched in the sequence. He did so very quickly, and he knew the young man couldn't follow it. A topographical map flashed onto the monitor screen, superimposing itself over the four icons. The little symbols inched across the computer-generated terrain.

"Good," Lakesh grunted. "They're on the move, already over the border. If they drive straight through and don't decide to stop at Sky Dog's village, they should be back here by tomorrow evening at the latest."

Banks nodded and ventured, "Do you think they were successful, sir?"

Lakesh didn't respond for a long moment. He hadn't allowed himself to contemplate the outcome of the mission. He was simply gratified Kane, Brigid, Domi and Grant were alive, and judging by the lack of spikes in the transponder signals, in good health.

The mission had originated with Kane. Its tactics and strategies were worked out over several days with Brigid and Grant. The only input Kane had accepted from Lakesh was intel, and he'd been unable to provide much of that. The territory surrounding the Archuleta Mesa installation was unknown, and even the few satellite pix dredged out of the database had offered little in the way of useful intel. The other satellite to which the redoubt was uplinked was one of the Vela reconnaissance class. It carried narrow-band multispectral scanners that detected the electromagnetic radiation reflected by every object on Earth, including subsurface geomagnetic waves. The scanner was tied in to an extremely high-resolution photographic relay system. The thermal imagers indicated subterranean activity, but that came as no surprise.

Only one sequence showed anything other than a

bare and sere landscape. Something resembling a slice of black pie hovered briefly over the desert terrain, then shot out of sight so rapidly it almost seemed to vanish. Computer enhancement of the image accomplished very little, except to prove the wedge was an aircraft, something all of them suspected anyway. Although Lakesh speculated it was a prototype of the Aurora, he could offer little more than its name and its probable capabilities.

Lakesh hadn't been completely shut out of the mission, but Kane made it obvious the op was a done deal and any contributions other than hard data were unwelcome.

Lakesh resented his high-handed manner, but being an essentially honest man, he couldn't deny the man's attitude was a classic example of quid pro quo.

He responded to Banks's question more harshly than he intended. "I have no idea. And don't call me sir."

Banks nodded and looked away.

Suddenly ashamed of his patronizing attitude toward the young man, Lakesh slowly reviewed the triangulation program with him. Unlike Cotta, Bry, Wegmann and Farrell, Banks was not a tech-head. He was currently in training to serve as a tech, but comps and electronics were not his field of expertise. Lakesh had arranged for his exile from Samariumville for two reasons. One was his training in biochemistry. The second, and by the far the more important, was the strong latent psionic talents that had shown up on his career placement tests. Both attributes had proved invaluable during the three-plus years he had served as the warder for Balam. His telepathic ability was strong enough to screen out Balam's attempts at psychic influence, except for the one instance when he was able to insinuate himself into Banks's sleeping mind.

But now that Balam was gone, Banks needed to be trained in another area, several if possible. He was also under the tutelage of DeFore, the redoubt's resident medic, learning to be her aide. Auerbach, her former assistant, languished in a detention cell on the bottom level of the installation, where he had been confined since his participation in a scheme to murder Kane, Brigid and Grant had been uncovered. His defense that he hadn't intended to kill Brigid left everyone unmoved.

True enough, Auerbach had been seduced, duped into taking part in the conspiracy by Beth-Li Rouch. She was dead now, drowned by Domi, and Auerbach was held accountable not only for her actions but also for his own.

No one knew what to do with the man. The vote taken among all of the Cerberus personnel provided no clear-cut resolution. Lakesh figured Kane would have simply executed him if he didn't himself have firsthand experience with Beth-Li's persuasive gifts.

If the decision had been solely Lakesh's, as all such decisions had been until recently, the traitor would have been executed. But making such choices was no longer within his exclusive purview. The mini-coup d'état staged by Kane, Brigid and Grant a short time before had seen to that.

Lakesh hadn't been unseated from his position of authority, but he was now answerable to a more democratic process. At first he bitterly resented what he construed as the usurping of his power by ingrates, but over the past month he had felt the burden of responsibility ease from his stooped shoulders. Now he felt almost grateful. Almost, but not quite, because he had been coerced into sharing his command.

Almost every exile in the redoubt had arrived as a convicted criminal—after Lakesh had set them all up, framing them for crimes against their respective villes. He admitted it was a cruel, heartless plan with a barely acceptable risk factor, but it was the only way to spirit them out of their villes, turn them against the barons, make them feel indebted to him.

This bit of explosive and potentially fatal knowledge had not been shared with the exiles. Grant's grim prediction of what the Cerberus personnel might do to him if they learned of his methods still echoed in his memory: "I think they'll lynch you."

Lakesh smiled sourly at the notion. Grant had spoken partly in jest, but a nugget of truth gleamed there. For an instant, he saw a vision of the Cerberus exiles, marching on his quarters, waving torches and pitchforks, hauling him to a makeshift gallows out on the mountain plateau.

Banks saw only the smile and, misinterpreting its meaning, said earnestly, "I'll get it right, sir."

"I know you will. And will you please stop calling me sir?"

Regardless of how the scope of his responsibilities had been reduced, Lakesh still had plans in the works. Actually, the curtailing of his authority allowed him to return to a couple of projects that he had back-burnered, and to properly implement them, he needed all staff with the slightest bit of technical aptitude at the top of their game.

Lakesh's current project involved a communications linkup with the Comsat satellite to both personnel out in the field and the Cobaltville computer systems.

During his many years as the senior archivist in the ville's Historical Division, he had made it a midrange priority to collect as many passwords and encryption codes to the ville's computers as possible. The undertaking hadn't been particularly painstaking, inasmuch as the dedicated systems were not equipped with sophisticated security lockouts.

Once he had been more or less forced to permanently join the group of exiles in Cerberus, the problem lay in what to do with the codes. All the villes had a form of wireless communication. The primary obstacle was finding an undetected method of patching into the channels in such a fashion that allowed hacking into the computers, too.

Recently Bry had come up with a solution that seemed workable and involved using the redoubt's satellite uplinks. Bry's design had yet to be tested, but so far his work progressed smoothly.

A minor aspect of that same project involved the cross-referencing and indexing of the vast amount of information Lakesh had smuggled out of the ville on hard disks. The objective was to find weak areas in Cobaltville defenses and baron-sanctioned operations in the Outlands that could be exploited. A faint recollection about a mining operation in Utah niggled at the fringes of his memory.

Despite it all, Lakesh needed goals, needed marks to hit, projects to keep his mind occupied; otherwise he would be haunted by his guilt-inspired dreams. He could not afford to dwell on the past, but more and more often it seemed to be clutching at him with spectral fingers.

Lakesh returned his attention to Banks and the triangulation procedure he was trying to master. They went over it several times until he was certain Banks had memorized the proper sequence. He patted him on the shoulder. "Now you've got it."

Suddenly, lights flashed and needle gauges wavered on the primary mat-trans console. In the anteroom, a humming tone droned from the gateway chamber.

Both Banks and Lakesh jumped in surprise. Banks snatched his hands away from the keyboard, as if he feared he had hit the wrong button. Snapping his head around, Lakesh stared at the Mercator-relief map. His eyes focussed on a single light, blinking steadily, and tried to fix its location. The tiny flashing bulb represented the transmitting gateway, somewhere in the far west. Swiftly he flipped through his mental file of functioning units in that vicinity, and for a stretched-out period of time, drew a complete blank.

The main reason for his mental confusion was pure shock. Long ago he had altered the modulations of the Cerberus gateway unit's transit feed connections, so its transmissions were untraceable—with one notable, fairly recent exception.

Recalling that exception kept his memory from working properly, and the bright flares, like bursts of heat lightning on the other side of the armaglass walls of the chamber, distracted him further. The low hum climbed rapidly in pitch to a hurricane howl as the device cycled through the materialization process.

"What's going on?" Banks demanded fearfully, pushing his chair back from the console on squeaking casters.

Lakesh gave the single blinking light on the map another searching look and reached for a desk intercom. "We've got an unscheduled materialization and an uninvited—"

Then a realization struck him full force, like a cataract of icy water. He froze, mouth open, finger poised over the intercom button. He remembered what unit the light represented.

Staring at the flares of energy on the other side of the brown armaglass, Banks blurted, "Who can it be?"

The young man's half-shouted question unfroze Lakesh sufficiently to thumb down the call button. "Armed security detail to operations! *Stat!*"

He heard his voice echoing hollowly out in the corridor. A designated security force did not exist as such in the redoubt. All of the personnel were required to become reasonably proficient with firearms, primarily the lightweight SA-80 subguns. The armed security detail Lakesh summoned would be anyone who grabbed a gun from the armory and reached the control center under their own power.

The electronic wail from the jump chamber faded, dropping down to silence. The bursts of energy behind the translucent slabs disappeared. The light on the map stopped blinking, indicating a successful transit had been achieved.

Lakesh repeated the call for a security detail, doing his utmost to control the frenzy of fear threatening to consume him.

Within a minute, DeFore rushed into the complex, wielding one of the SA-80 autoblasters. The stocky, bronze-skinned woman fumbled to keep her pink terry-cloth robe closed at the same time and did a poor job of it, exposing an ample amount of cleavage. Only one of her feet was shod—in a heelless floppy slipper that was supposed to resemble a buck-toothed rabbit.

DeFore's usually tidy hair hung in disarrayed ash-blond wisps. Her liquid brown eyes were surrounded by puffy flesh. She telegraphed fear, anger and impatience at the same time. Despite the gun, she did not present a formidable impression and under other circumstances Lakesh might have been inclined to laugh.

She demanded loudly, "What the hell kind of

emergency are we having at five-thirty in the goddamn morning?"

Lakesh stepped toward the anteroom, gesturing for her to follow him. "That's what we're about to find out."

DeFore sidled cautiously around him, refusing Banks's offer to take the subgun. They circled the big table in the room and approached the jump chamber. As they did so, Cotta raced into the control center dressed only in boxer shorts and, like DeFore, brandishing an SA-80. His black hair stood up all over his head. Breathlessly he said, "Farrell ought to be here any second. He came into the armory as I was leaving it."

He and DeFore took up cross-fire positions on either side of the unit, blasters held at hip level. Lakesh stepped up to the platform and gripped the door handle. "No matter who—or what—is in there, no shooting except at my order."

The two armed people acknowledged his words with curt nods. Farrell sprinted in, panting and wild-eyed, but at least he was dressed in a bodysuit. He pointed the barrel of the SA-80 at the gateway, but Lakesh waved him back.

Carefully, Lakesh disengaged the lock mechanism, lifted the handle and swung open the heavy door on its counterbalanced hinges. Most of the mist produced by the quincunx effect's plasma bleed-off had dissipated, so the figure slouched over against the far wall was easily discerned. Identification wasn't so easy.

A man-shape sat huddled on the hexagonal floor

plates, his extraordinarily long arms wrapped about his disproportionately short legs. Beneath a tangled mat of coarse black hair, beady dark eyes blinked in confusion. His blunt-featured, dark-complexioned face held a dazed expression. He wore a one-piece bodysuit of drab olive green. Even standing up, he couldn't have been much more than four feet tall, if that.

When he shifted his bare feet, Lakesh saw how dirty both of them were—and how each one sprouted four long toes and a very long big toe that projected out at a fort-five-degree angle near the heel. It resembled not so much a toe as a thumb, tipped with a horny, bevel-edged nail.

The little man gazed calmly up at Lakesh and extended his right foot as if he were inviting him to shake it. Gripped tightly within the curled toes, Lakesh saw the oblong shape of an implode grenade. His prehensile toe rested atop the blinking detonator button.

In a high, piping voice, the transadapt asked, "Is Miss Brigid at home?"

Chapter 9

Raking her wet hair out of her eyes, Brigid murmured wistfully, "I wish I were home."

Domi lifted her head from the surface of the stream and spit water in an arcing jet toward the bank. "Where's home for you? Hightower in Cobaltville? Cerberus?" Her tone held a bantering note, but a slightly mocking edge was there, too.

Brigid didn't quite know how to answer the question, so she pretended to concentrate on resisting the tug of the current. She and Domi floated in the broad, meandering stream that curved through the hill country twenty or so miles inside the Colorado border. The Land Rover had crossed back shortly before dawn and they decided to hide the wag under the spreading boughs of aspen trees for a few hours. If an aerial search had been launched from Dulce, they figured the Deathbirds wouldn't be dispatched until daybreak. So far, nothing had appeared in the bright blue canopy of the early-morning sky but high, fleecy white clouds.

Domi and Brigid decided to wash off the grit and dirt they had accumulated over the past day and night and so they trooped down to the stream to bathe. The water was cool, but not quite cold enough to be uncomfortable.

Domi stripped naked and plunged in without a second thought, paddling around in childlike pleasure, submerging and backstroking.

Brigid stayed fairly close to the bank and kept her underwear on. The decision was not made out of modesty, but if necessity demanded it, she preferred not to run or fight in the nude.

"So," Domi persisted, "where's your home?"

Brigid visualized the little two-room flat in the residential Enclaves of Cobaltville that had served as her home from infancy until ten months ago. Of course, it hadn't really been a home. Like all the other flats in the living towers, it was only a place to stable the ville elite, the contributing citizens. No issues of ownership needed to be addressed. Every comfort derived from Baron Cobalt's largesse, but it was all on loan.

She had been forced to leave behind every personal possession when she fled the ville, not that she had very many of them.

Her quarters in the Cerberus redoubt were not much larger, but they were certainly more comfortably appointed. She had her pick of anything in the installation's storage rooms, from two-hundred-year-old clothing to a videotape library. And, most importantly, she enjoyed complete and unrestricted access to the database.

"I suppose I mean Cerberus," she said at length. "What about you?"

On her back, Domi floated farther out in the stream,

her small but perfectly shaped breasts pointing to the sky. "What about me?"

"Where do you consider home? You've lived in more places than I have."

Domi grinned impudently. "Home is wherever I sleep, eat and break wind."

Brigid turned her moue of distaste at the old Roamer bromide into a smile. "Pretty simple set of standards."

"I'm a simple girl."

Domi was that, true enough. She was born near the predark town of Cuprum in Hells Canyon, Idaho. Guana Teague, Pit boss of Cobaltville, spotted Domi on one of his periodic forays into the Outlands and was smitten by her exotic looks and spitfire personality.

In return for smuggling her into Cobaltville, she gave him six months of sexual servitude. When Teague tried to change the terms, she cut his throat and escaped the ville with Kane, Grant and Brigid.

"Hey, you two." Kane appeared on the bank, his eyes masked by sunglasses. He wore clothing of dark, tough whipcord, the Sin Eater holstered to his right forearm. "Aren't you clean enough?"

Lying back languorously in the stream, Domi pursed her lips and squirted water at him. "You and Grant could do with a scrubbing, too."

Kane did not respond to the observation about his personal hygiene. "Come on out. We need to start rolling again if we want to hit home by tomorrow."

Domi stood up, water cascading from her naked

limbs and body. The bright sunlight struck sparkles from the droplets, and Brigid couldn't help but be reminded of a water sprite, one of the elemental nymphs from mythology who took human males as lovers.

She waded through the shallows toward Kane, completely at ease with her nudity. Despite the scars marring the pearly perfection of her skin, particularly the one shaped like a starburst on her right shoulder, Domi was beautiful.

Because of the dark lenses of his glasses, Brigid couldn't tell if Kane was gazing at the girl. Certainly he had seen her naked before—the entire redoubt had, particularly during her first few weeks at Cerberus. The outlander girl wasn't accustomed to wearing clothes unless temperatures demanded them, and then only the skimpiest concessions to weather, not modesty.

She passed Kane and he didn't turn his head to watch her. Brigid wondered if he would have if she weren't there. She sneaked a glance at the crotch of his tight trousers to see if she could spot a telltale bulge, but Kane turned slightly away, gazing at the sky.

Brigid followed Domi onto the bank, wringing water from her thick mane of sunset-colored hair. "If we cut cross-country instead of sticking to the roads, we might be able to shave a half day from our travel time."

Kane didn't answer, but he quickly shifted position

to hide the evidence of arousal straining at the fabric of his pants.

"And if we're lucky," she continued quickly, "get back to Cerberus by sunset tomorrow."

She felt a warmth rise to her face and realized a faint flush was spreading over her cheeks. She realized that with her wet brassiere stretched taut across her breasts and her equally wet panties outlining every fold and crack, she might as well be as naked as Domi. Kane had seen her nude before, but under decidedly nonerotic circumstances. It was possible his reaction was due to Domi, but she doubted it.

Gossamer scraps of memory, more like impressions, ghosted through her mind, of Kane pressing against her, of his hands on her breasts, of his hard length sliding into her—

Brigid stepped quickly past him, moving to where she had left her clothes. Those impressions weren't memories of events that had actually happened, at least not in her reality. They were the ghostly residue of their experiences on parallel worlds when their minds possessed the bodies of their alternate-universe selves, their doppelgängers.

Neither she, Grant nor Kane had clear recollections of those mirror realities any longer. Even with her eidetic memory, she could only consciously recall disconnected fragments, and they seemed like half-remembered dreams from long ago. But the subconscious was a different matter altogether, and in those dream scenes she glimpsed the Kane and Brigid of the parallel casements making wild love.

With an effort, she slammed shut the mental file drawer and quickly got dressed. "How are you feeling?" she asked.

"Head still rings a bit," he replied with a rueful smile. "My chest and back ache. But other than that, I feel fine." He paused and inquired, "Are you still mad at me?"

Buttoning her khaki shirt, Brigid retorted, "Not as furious as I was, but I'm still working on a high level of irritation. What you did was really reckless."

"I know. I wasn't thinking."

"That's a bad habit I thought you'd broken these past few months."

He shrugged. "We'd done so much and come so far, I wasn't about to let a goddamn mechanical mole stop us. I thought it was worth the risk."

Brigid stepped into her boots, kneeling to lace them with sharp, impatient movements. "I don't recall you asking if the rest of us wanted to share that risk."

Steel slipped into Kane's response. "Risk was part of the entire op, Baptiste. We calculated the factors before we left the redoubt."

"You're missing the point, Kane—another bad habit I'd hoped you'd broken. You went tearing off on your impulsive course of action without consulting the team. It was more than foolhardy—it was kamikaze."

"Kamikaze?"

"A Japanese word that essentially means a suicide charge."

Straightening, she gazed unblinkingly into his face.

"If you truly believe you're better suited to be a leader than Lakesh, then you need to adopt some of his caution. Just because your head-on approach worked this time doesn't mean you were right. It means you were lucky."

Kane's jaw muscles bunched, and the tendons in his neck stood out. Then he grimaced in pain and gingerly rubbed the base of his neck. With effort, he turned the grimace into a wry half smile. "All right," he said with an exaggerated weariness, "will you accept an apology?"

She matched his smile. "As long as a promise to think before you act goes along with it."

"I'll promise to try. Bad habits are hard to break, you know." Kane's smile widened, holding a hint of a challenge. "And it'll depend on the circumstances."

Brigid repressed a sigh of annoyance. Kane's impulses were as sudden as they were unpredictable, and those impulses had forced her into the roles of convicted criminal, exile and now a revolutionary.

She hadn't known Kane before he'd approached her with a mystery on a locked computer diskette. She hadn't really solved the mystery, but she had unlocked the diskette. Once that had been discovered, she'd been marked for termination. Only Kane's skills had gotten them free of Cobaltville, but it was her knowledge that had placed them in the Cerberus redoubt.

At the time Brigid hadn't realized she was already involved in Lakesh's scheme to turn her into a exile. He put those wheels into motion by covertly slipping her a copy of the *Wyeth Codex,* a journal of sorts by Mildred Winona Wyeth, one of the enduring legends of the Deathlands.

Born in the twentieth century, Wyeth had slept through the nukecaust and skydark in cryonic suspension. She was revived after nearly a hundred years by another semimythical figure of the Deathlands, Ryan Cawdor. Wyeth joined Cawdor's band of survivalists who journeyed the length and breadth of postholocaust America. At some point in her journeys, she found a working computer and recorded many of their experiences and adventures, telling the truth as she'd understood it back then.

The truth, as Brigid came to learn, had become far more strange and horrifying over the next hundred or so years. But she had also learned that the truth was not an absolute.

Kane tilted his head back, scanning the sky again. "Clear skies."

"You don't sound happy about that," Brigid said, tucking in her shirt.

"I'm not. It's weird. You'd think we'd see at least one Deathbird."

She said dryly, "The curious incident of the dog in the nighttime."

Kane frowned toward her. "What dog incident?"

"The dog did nothing in the nighttime. That was the curious incident."

Kane was by now accustomed to her enigmatic remarks but he was no less irked by them, particularly since they all seemed to center on dead zones in his education. He always felt that he was playing straight man to one of her academic performances.

"Sorry," Brigid said. "It's a piece of dialogue from an old detective story. The point of it being that because a guard dog didn't raise an alarm when a crime was committed, it led to the apprehension of the criminal."

Pretending he understood, Kane nodded. "So you're saying in your usual long-way-around way that because there's no sign of pursuit, there's a deeper meaning at hand."

"More or less."

Contemplatively, he said, "We may have caused so much destruction, nobody at the installation can be spared to hunt for us because those few who survived have their hands full with damage control."

She paused, as if unwilling to voice other possibilities.

Kane anticipated what she intended to say and declared, "And on top of that, we may have wrecked the bioengineering section."

Brigid nodded. "It's a strong possibility. And the implications are—"

Kane cut her off with a sharp tone, "Until we have all the facts, we won't know the implications of anything."

Momentary irritation glittered in Brigid's jade eyes, but she didn't allow it to flare into anger. She understood why Kane didn't want to discuss the possibility of total destruction of the Archuleta Mesa complex. His father's fate was still unknown despite the incendiaries they had touched off during their first incursion to the installation. The odds that his father had survived their initial penetration were exceptionally remote, but Kane was by nature a percentage player and even a one percent chance provided a feeble ray of hope.

The devastation caused by the crash of the Aurora was certainly more widespread, and even if his father's cryostasis canister had come through the gren explosions intact, this last wave of devastation might very well have engulfed it.

Kane exhaled and tried to smile. "Sorry. It's not like he was really alive anyway, is it? I guess I'd half hoped that one day I'd go back, unfreeze him and have him healthy and whole."

Softly, Brigid said, "I know that, Kane."

Grant's lionlike voice rose in a shout above the foliage screening the stream's bank. "Hey! Company's coming!"

They jogged toward the parked Land Rover. Grant stood at the edge of a ragged wall of shrubbery, peering through a set of microbinoculars. Domi, still naked, crouched near him, fisting her Combat Master.

"Get some clothes on," Kane snapped at her. Then to Grant he demanded, "Who is it?"

"Outlanders, looks like," he answered. "Come to fetch water."

"Let me see."

Grant handed him the binoculars, and Kane squinted through the eyepieces, tightening the focus. He saw a half dozen people trudging through the high grass, several of them carrying buckets. Their ragged togalike garments exposed scabbed and pustuled flesh. Several of the men had eyes covered with milky cataracts. A couple of scarred and stick-thin children led the blind men by the hands.

Nausea surged through Kane's belly. "Not just outlanders," he grated. "Dregs."

He sensed his companions stiffening, reacting with the same revulsion he felt. Dregs were the outlanders shunned even by other outlanders. One of the legacies of the nukecaust was a fixation on health. Ville doctrines revolved around purity control, and an important aspect of the unification program had been the extermination of all human deviates, particularly muties.

Dregs weren't muties, although they had been classified as such a hundred or so years before. Though not mutated, the Dregs were diseased, the lepers of the postskydark world. As Magistrates, the standing order for Grant and Kane when out in the field was to chill Dregs on sight. Even now, Kane felt the tug of his conditioning.

Only Domi expressed any compassion. "Poor bastards," she whispered.

"They're headed this way," Grant pointed out. "How do you want to deal with them?"

Anger blazed redly in Domi's eyes. "Leave 'em be. They can't hurt us."

Quietly, matter-of-factly, Grant stated, "If they see us, and if we're being hunted, and if they're questioned—"

Domi interrupted hotly, "Fucking 'forcers won't ask Dregs shit about shit. They'll just chill 'em."

Clearing her throat, Brigid said, "Besides, they're probably very good at hiding from Mags and what not. Who knows, they might have seen something that could be of use to us."

Kane lowered the binoculars. "I agree. But keep your triggers set." He cast a sideways glance at Domi. "Will you *please* get dressed?"

Domi scowled, then threw him a go-to-hell grin. "Distracting you, am I?"

Kane rudely turned his back on her.

By the time the group of Dregs pushed its way through an opening in the hedgerow, Domi had put her clothes and, like the rest of her companions, stood near the Hotspur with studied ease. At first it appeared the Dregs would not see them, then a girl leading a blind man looked in their direction, did a violent double take and uttered a wordless shriek of terror.

The ragged people stumbled to a halt, buckets dropping from their hands. Those with vision gaped wide-eyed. The stench of their unwashed bodies and necrotic tissue made Kane want to gag, but he said pleasantly, "Good morning. Go on about your business. We mean you no harm."

The Dregs eyed the blasters apprehensively. In their world, only one type of people carried advanced firearms, particularly the Sin Eaters.

One of the men, tall and rangy with a face resembling old leather in both color and texture, squinted toward them. He murmured a few words to his people, and they calmed down somewhat. He gazed at Kane, then Grant and Brigid for so long and so keenly Kane began to feel uncomfortable.

He was on the verge of repeating his request that the Dregs go on about their business, this time making it an order, when the man asked, "May I approach?"

His voice sounded surprisingly well-modulated, his diction perfect. After a moment's hesitation, Kane nodded his assent. The man strode cautiously toward them. "My name is Ethan."

His bony right hand slid beneath his rags, and as one, three blaster barrels snapped up to cover him. "Careful Ethan," Grant rumbled menacingly.

The man came to a stop and slowly withdrew his hand from beneath his clothing. A large square of stiff paper, folded in half, was pinched between a grimy thumb and forefinger. He extended it toward them. Kane's flesh crawled at the notion of coming in contact with anything touched by a Dreg.

Domi stepped forward and took the soiled and frayed paper from Ethan. She unfolded it and Grant, Kane and Brigid looked at their own faces. Kane had seen the three grainy photographs before, when a group of swampies in Louisiana had tried to collect both his head and the reward placed on it.

The head-and-shoulders shots had been reproduced from ID pix taken in Cobaltville years ago, when his face was clean-shaved with short, crisp, neatly combed hair. His hair was much longer now and certainly not combed.

The pix of Grant showed the same square-jawed

and weather-beaten face, but without his down-sweeping mustache.

The third photo was of Brigid, and of the three of them she was the least changed. No copy accompanied the photographs.

"That's you, isn't it?" Ethan asked hopefully. "You're them, aren't you?"

"And if we are?" Kane challenged.

Ethan interpreted Kane's terse question as a confirmation. He turned toward his companions, exclaiming, "It *is* them! The baron blasters!"

Kane's eyes widened in surprise, then slitted in suspicion. He echoed, "Baron blasters?"

The term Ethan applied to them was old, deriving from the warriors who staged a violent resistance against the institution of the unification program. To hear that appellation applied to him and his friends made Kane distinctly uneasy. His ville upbringing lurked very close to the surface, and he had been taught that so-called baron blasters were worse than outlaws—they were agents of chaos, terrorists incarnate, devoted to maintaining a state of bloody anarchy.

Intellectually Kane knew the doctrine was sheer dogma, but emotionally his initial reaction was the same as if he had been called a backstabbing slagger.

"We're not baron blasters!" Grant blurted angrily.

With his lantern jaw thrust out pugnaciously, the big man presented the very image of wounded dignity. Between the two of them, Grant still had the most difficulty accepting his criminal status.

Ethan regarded them speculatively. "Aren't you Grant and Kane, the Magistrates who humiliated, then escaped Baron Cobalt? Haven't you caused the barons much distress and upset? Didn't you chill Baron Ragnar? Aren't you fighting to throw off the heel of the tyrants?"

They could have answered yes to all but one of the questions the man put to them. They weren't responsible for the demise of Baron Ragnar, but a denial seemed pointless. Because Kane and Grant had been seen and identified in Ragnarville shortly after the baron's assassination, they were named as the culprits.

Kane didn't feel inclined to explain to Ethan how a holographic computer program had actually done the deed and very nearly killed all of them, as well. It wasn't exactly easy for him to understand, and he'd lived through it—barely.

While Kane groped for something to say, Brigid asked, "Have you seen any wags on the road or aircraft in the sky today?"

Ethan shook his head. "All we've seen in the past month is a freight caravan heading toward Cobaltville from the ore mines in Utah."

A faint line of puzzlement creased Brigid's high forehead. "Freight caravan?"

"Yeah," Grant said brusquely. "It's where the ville gets the raw materials for smelting and manufacturing."

Kane dredged his memory, recalling old Mag Intel

section reports. "The baron used to deal with a trader called Chapman."

Ethan's ravaged features twisted into an expression of distaste. "That's the one. A right vicious bastard he is, too. Seen him more often the past six months than before."

Kane added the bit of information to his mental file folder of potentially useful knowledge.

"Anyway," Ethan continued, "if you are being pursued, you've eluded the hunters once again."

Domi handed the picture back to him and asked, "How do you know about us—about them?"

Ethan touched his mouth and then an ear. "News travels far in the Outlands. Perhaps not quickly, but by word of mouth. The distance it travels may surprise you. Even though the Mags say you are dead, nobody believes it. Every settlement talks of you, how you strike from nowhere and then vanish, leaving the barons and the Mags to gnash their teeth. You have given hope to the hopeless."

Kane smiled wryly at the melodrama. He didn't doubt tales of their actions had spread far, but more than likely legend had cloaked the truth, fable supplanting fact.

"All we need now is a set of silver bullets to hand out," Brigid murmured.

Kane didn't understand the remark and he didn't feel like asking for clarification.

"Do you have any words of inspiration I may pass along?" Ethan's eyes shone with expectation.

Grant, Brigid, Kane and Domi all exchanged

glances. Heaving the broad yoke of his shoulders in a shrug, Grant ventured, "Don't believe everything you hear?"

Ethan nodded in satisfaction. "That we shall do, and I shall convey the message not to believe anything the villes say about you."

Bowing his head, he touched his chest, then his lips in a gesture of respect. "It was an honor meeting you. Good fortune to you, now and forever."

Ethan led his people away, although a few of them seemed to have difficulty tearing their gazes from the living legends standing before them. Grant ran a hand over his jaw. "Figures that the baron would want to circulate the story we're dead."

"Yeah," Kane agreed, watching the Dregs trudge down to the stream. "Public relations so nobody can ever think it's possible to turn on the barons and live to talk about it."

"More than that," said Brigid. "The baron is hoping that if we think *he* thinks we're dead, we'll get careless."

The same notion had occurred to Kane. Not too long before, a Magistrate assault force had been dispatched from Cobaltville to investigate the possibility they were hiding in the Cerberus redoubt, even though Lakesh had taken great pains over the years to establish the belief that particular installation was hopelessly unsalvageable. However, when the search for them among all of the redoubts began in earnest, it was inevitable Cerberus would be investigated simply by a process of elimination.

Using a refurbished war wag, Kane, Grant and Domi had joined forces with the band of Amerindians permanently encamped near the foothills of the Darks to drive off the Mags. They had managed to keep secret their participation in the battle, but it was yet another blow to Baron Cobalt's monumental vanity. That defeat would be a gnat's bite in comparison to the blow to his ego the baron would suffer when news of the attack at the mesa reached him.

The thought made Kane simultaneously happy and apprehensive. Although he had come to accept that the members of the baronial hierarchy were not semi-divine god-kings, they still held the reins of power and could array vast forces to extinguish even the most feeble flame of defiance.

Kane had feared Baron Cobalt would command an overwhelming assault against Sky Dog's people but now he had provided all the barons with something far more frightening to worry about than avenging the defeat of a Mag squad.

All this passed through Kane's mind in a second. He turned toward the Land Rover. "Let's get back on the move."

Grant eyed the sky anxiously for a moment. "Still clear."

"Storm clouds are building," Kane replied curtly.

Grant squinted at the vast blue expanse above them, then glanced questioningly toward Kane. "Where?"

Kane gestured to the southwest. "Back the way we came. I have a feeling it'll be the worst storm since skydark. If we're lucky, we can outrun it. For a little while."

Chapter 10

The initial reports filtered in sporadically, fragments of pure panic that had to be assembled like a jigsaw puzzle. By midnight, the dispatches were more coherent, forming an image that was emotionally devastating and utterly mind-staggering.

Guende stood at the window, gazing at the first colors of dawn as they splashed the sky with shifting pastel tints. Normally, the sight of sunrise buoyed his spirits, filled him with a certain hope. Yet he dreaded this one because it meant more damage and status reports from Dulce would be arriving.

The massive round tower of the Administrative Monolith thrust three hundred feet up into the new day, its facade of white rockcrete reflecting the colors of the rising sun, far above the fifty-foot-high walls surrounding Cobaltville. At night, the light pouring from the slit-shaped windows could seen from miles away, a not so subtle message that the will of the baron never slept.

The monolith stood proud and haughty, symbolizing to all and sundry that order had replaced the barbarism of postskydark America. Every level of the tower was designed to fulfill a specific capacity; E Level was a general construction and manufacturing facility; D Level was devoted to the preservation, preparation and distribution of food; and C Level held the Magistrate Division. On B Level was the Historical Archives, a combination of library, museum and comp center. The archives housed almost five hundred thousand books, discovered and restored over the past ninety years, not to mention an incredibly varied array of predark artifacts.

The work of the administrators was conducted on the highest level. Guende stood at a window on A Level, thinking that despite the tower's gleaming white facade, it was rooted in muck, rising from the Tartarus Pits. Down there swarmed a heterogeneous population of serfs and slaves in everything but name.

All Guende could see of the Pits was the glow of lanterns and the flicker of torchlight. Tartarus was wired for electricity, but the power was cut at midnight and not restored until 0800. He didn't need to see the Pits to know they seethed with outlanders and slaggers and cheap labor.

Above the Tartarus Pits stretched the complex of residential Enclaves. Each of the four towers was joined to the others by pedestrian bridges. Few of the windows in the towers showed any light, so there was little to indicate that the interconnecting network of stone columns, enclosed walkways, shops and promenades was where nearly four thousand people made their homes.

In the Enclaves, the people who worked for the ville divisions enjoyed private apartments, one of the privileges of those favored by Baron Cobalt. Seen from above, the Enclave towers formed a latticework of intersected circles, all connected to the center of the circle from which rose the Administrative Monolith, like the hub of a wheel. And here, in the top spire of the monolith, far above even the Enclaves, the baron reigned.

The baronial oligarchy revived the long-forgotten trust in any form of centralized government. Long generations after the descendants of the nukecaust survivors had forgotten the deadly legacy of predark politics, the citizens were once again prepared to accept law and order.

Nearly ninety years before, Unity Through Action became the rallying cry that had spread across the Deathlands by word of mouth and proof of deed. The barons offered a solution to the constant deprivation and fear—join the unification program and never worry or fear or think again. Humanity was responsible for the arrival of Judgment Day, and it must accept that responsibility before a truly utopian age could be ushered in.

All humankind had to do to earn this utopia was to follow the rules, be obedient and be fed and clothed. And accept the new order without question.

For most of the men and women who lived in the villes and the surrounding territories, that offer was enough, more than enough. Long-sought-after dreams of peace and safety had at last been transformed into reality. Of course, fleeting dreams of personal freedom were lost in the exchange, but such abstract aspirations were nothing but childish illusions.

Guende heard the ruffling of paper behind him, but he did not turn. Baron Cobalt had been ruffling paper almost constantly for the past five hours, reading dispatch after dispatch. Rather than draw the baron's attention away from the reports, Guende tried to make himself as inconspicuous as possible.

For a small, middle-aged man like himself, with mouse-colored hair that matched the hue of his drab bodysuit, it wasn't difficult. He almost wished the baron would forget he was even there, but that was not likely. As one of the baron's personal staff, it was his duty to simply stand there and wait.

Baron Cobalt's private-audience chamber was so completely soundproofed that the ears grew weary of trying to catch a whisper of outside noise. No one ever came to the baron's chamber unbidden. Only Guende's status as a member of the Cobalt Trust entitled him to be alone with the ruler of Cobaltville.

Very few people even knew what Baron Cobalt looked like. It was part of a tapestry of mystique, deception and deliberate misinformation. Guende studied the baron's reflection in the mirror.

Sitting inside the curve of a small, horseshoe-shaped desk, Baron Cobalt's excessively slender body was encased in a one-piece dark golden bodysuit, which accentuated the pale gold color of his skin. His narrow, hairless skull was so elongated that it resembled an upside-down teardrop. Very small ears were set low on the sides of his head. His face seemed to consist primarily of delicate brow arches, prominent cheekbones and a very long, very sharp chin. The eyes were large, slanted and the big irises were a beautiful yellowish-brown.

He was not tall, and in fact, he looked even more fragile than Guende. It wasn't the strength of his body that mattered; it was the power of his will. That and his position more than compensated for his physical shortcomings. What he willed to be always came to pass—at least, that was the general belief.

Now Guende had his doubts. Baron Cobalt's expression did not alter; his thin slash of a mouth did not so much as twitch as he read over the latest batch of dispatches. The baron read each sheet of hard copy quickly, turning every absorbed page facedown on his desk. Guende watched how his huge eyes flicked back and forth over the dense columns of copy.

Guende had skimmed a few of them when Kearney, the Mag Intel shift commander, brought them up, but he'd only gleaned the skimpiest overview of the situation. Even so, he could think of only one word that accurately described it—*disaster.*

During his eleven years of service, Guende had unquestioningly obeyed the baron's bidding, seen to the implementation of his desires, even his whims, and insulated him from the tedious day-to-day business of keeping the ville running smoothly. But Baron Cobalt could not be insulated from this catastrophe—none of his brother barons could, either. The destruction wrought in Dulce struck at the very heart of what—if not who—the barons were.

Guende saw Baron Cobalt suddenly stiffen in the process of turning over a sheet of paper. The thumb and inhumanly long forefinger of his hand pinching it by the corner suddenly trembled. Up until that moment, the baron had devoted almost exactly the same amount of time to reading each dispatch. Now his eyes widened in disbelief. Then, carefully, he set it aside, separating it from the others.

"Guende." The baron's usually musical voice held a flat, dead note.

Guende turned. "Yes, my lord?"

"Bring Abrams to me."

His aide hesitated before saying mildly, "My lord, Abrams is confined to detention, awaiting a tribunal. He has been stripped of his rank and privileges and is not fit to even crawl in your presence." Guende's words held no particular emotion, as if they were delivered by rote.

Baron Cobalt nodded. "So I recall. Thank you for reminding me. Come here, please. I wish to point something out to you."

Guende crossed the room, obeying the baron's hand gesture to come around the desk and stand beside him. His eyes flitted over the dispatches, and he caught only the most fleeting glimpse of movement from Baron Cobalt before a sun of pain went nova in the vicinity of his groin.

The agony was so unexpected, so overwhelming, Guende could do nothing but cry out and bend double. It seemed like a very long time before he realized the baron had secured a crushing grip on his testicles.

Through tear-filled eyes, Guende saw Baron Cobalt's face floating within inches of his own. His delicate features were contorted, his perfect little teeth bared, his golden skin suffused with furious blood.

Guende struggled to keep the bile rising in his throat from spewing out of his mouth. He clamped his jaws shut on it and a deep groan of agony. Through the thundering of his pulse in his temples, he heard Baron Cobalt's sibilant whisper, "I know where Abrams is."

His long fingers tightened on Guende's scrotum. "I commanded you to bring him to me, not to remind me of where he is!"

Guende uttered a gagging, raspy "I will obey, my lord—"

Baron Cobalt's fingers opened, and Guende staggered backward, still doubled over, hands instinctively cupping his crotch. He shambled out of the office on rubbery legs. Out in the corridor, he stumbled over to a potted ficus plant and hung his head over it until he was sure he wasn't going to throw up.

The deep, hot pain blazing out from his testicles ebbed in intensity. He didn't think he was seriously injured—at least he prayed not—but he decided to stop by the medical section at his earliest opportunity.

Taking deep, regular breaths, Guende straightened and started striding down the hall, doing his utmost not to walk spraddle-legged. By the time he entered the magnificent foyer, his gait was steadier. Glittering light cast from many crystal chandeliers flooded every corner of the entrance hall. A baronial guardsman passed him, giving him a contemptuous sideways glance. Guende ignored the big man in his white, impeccably tailored uniform jacket, tight red trousers and high black boots, though it wasn't easy. It was whispered that the guardsmen were not born, they were made—the products of genetic engineering. They were allegedly far stronger and faster than normal men. However, despite their Herculean physiques, they weren't invincible. Two of the breed had been killed here in the hallowed halls of Alpha Level a few months ago.

Because of his pain, Guende had no intention of taking the elevator down to the cell block on C Level and fetching up Abrams personally. He went looking for Kearney and found him approaching from an adjacent reception area carrying another sheaf of reports from the Intel section.

If the baronial guardsmen practiced the religion of arrogance, then Kearney was its high priest. Six feet eight inches tall, Kearney brushed his straw-colored hair back from his forehead so severely it looked like a blond skullcap. He wore the long black Mag duty coat in the Administrative Monolith for no other reason than it made him look even bigger and more impressive. With his face carefully arranged in a grim, unsmiling mask, the man was the epitome of swaggering Magistrate ego.

Wordlessly, he thrust out the dispatches to Guende, towering over him by at least a foot. Guende took the reports and said, "The baron wants to see Abrams. Bring him here."

One of Kearney's pale eyebrows rose. "I thought he was out of favor."

Normally an unassuming man in appearance and manner, Guende was surprised by the unexpected rush of anger that flooded through him. "It doesn't matter what you think, you puffed-up asshole! The baron told me and I'm telling you. You're not part of administration yet, so you haven't earned the right to have thoughts. Just do it!"

Kearney was not in the least intimidated. A corner of his mouth quirked in a patronizing smile. He made a deliberately laconic show of turning around and marching back in the direction he had come.

Guende watched him go and licked his dry lips. He had diverted his rage at the baron toward the Mag officer, and that wasn't like him. Nor was feeling angry with Baron Cobalt. But his lord, his master, his deity had never violated his dignity before, even though such violent outbursts had become more common as of late.

Matters had been turning sour in the villes for the past ten months or so, and the trouble could all be traced back to the night Kane was inducted into the Trust. Each of the nine villes in the continent-spanning network had its own version of the Trust. Less than an organization and more of a secret society, it was the only face-to-face contact allowed with the barons, and the barons were the only contacts permitted by the Archon Directorate.

The Trust acted more or less as the protectors of the Directorate, and the oath of allegiance revolved around a single theme—the presence of the Directorate must not be revealed to humanity. If their presence became known, if the technological marvels they had designed became accessible, if the truth behind the nukecaust filtered down to the people, then humankind would no doubt retaliate with a concerted effort to wipe them out—or the Directorate would be forced to visit another holocaust upon the face of the earth, simply as a measure of self-preservation.

Kane, whose father had been a member of the Trust, was recommended for recruitment by Salvo, his former Magistrate Division commander. Guende vividly remembered the night of Kane's initiation ceremony when he learned the secret truth of humanity's past, present and future from none other than Baron Cobalt himself.

Kane accepted the offer to belong to the elite that literally ruled society in secret. But after that, everything went to hell on a slide. Guende was never briefed on exactly what happened in the twenty-four hours following Kane's induction into the Trust. He knew Kane escaped Cobaltville with Brigid Baptiste, a seditionist awaiting execution, and his partner of many years, Grant. Salvo was badly injured trying to stop the escape, and a few Magistrates were killed.

Guende next saw Kane only a day later when he, Abrams and Ojaka accompanied Baron Cobalt to the Dulce facility for his annual medical treatment. Kane had attacked and hurt him, but not as badly as he'd hurt Abrams. The former administrator of the Magistrate Division had been permanently lamed.

But all of that was just prologue to a subsequent raiding party into the very heart of the Administrative

Monolith. Kane and Grant not only killed a pair of the baronial guard, but they also abducted Lakesh and Salvo.

Upon examination, there seemed no reason for the kidnapping of Guende's fellow members of the Trust. In the intervening months, no ransom demands had been made in exchange for their return. It was as if the two men had fallen off the face of the Earth.

Reports of Kane, Grant and Baptiste sightings increased, coming in from all over. The obvious conclusion was they were using the forbidden mat-trans units to jump from sealed redoubt to sealed redoubt. A cooperative undertaking among the nine barons to inspect all of the installations in their territories resulted only in false trails—and violent attacks on two barons.

To complicate the situation, Kane and Grant's acts of terrorism had triggered a rebellion of the kind not seen in ninety years. Over the past couple of months, caravans of precious metals and ores were hijacked by frightfully well organized and armed raiders, who struck, killed and disappeared. Although none of the few survivors of these attacks described anyone resembling Grant and Kane as being involved, the suspicion was definitely there.

The clacking of boot heels on the polished floor tiles announced the arrival of Kearney, who escorted Abrams down the corridor. Abrams looked like a parody of his former self, an actor who had made himself up to only vaguely resemble the real man for the purposes of cruel satire. His normally ramrod carriage was slumped; his iron-gray beard and hair were unkempt and matted. His face still sported raw patches from half-healed burns.

A pair of nylon cuffs bound the man's wrists in front of him. He wore a soiled and ill-fitting orange bodysuit, the color identifying him as a prisoner but not yet a convict. If he had been sentenced either by a tribunal or the baron himself, the bodysuit would be yellow. Criminals marched down to the termination chamber on E Level always wore the yellow bodysuit.

Abrams dragged his right leg, grimacing whenever he put too much weight on it. Without his cane, his gait was unsteady and uncertain. Kearney shoved him forward impatiently and Abrams staggered, nearly falling.

Despite the words Guende had used to describe the man to the baron, seeing him stripped of his pride and treated like the lowliest slagjacker in the filthiest squat of Tartarus awakened pity in him—and outrage.

Stepping forward, Guende snapped, "Stop. Take those cuffs off him."

Kearney pulled Abrams to a rough halt by the collar of his bodysuit. A sneer crossed the tall man's features as he loomed over the much smaller man. Guende met that stare without blinking.

Uncertainty flickered briefly in Kearney's eyes, and Guende easily imagined what passed for thought in the man's mind. Regardless of his height, his strength and the fact that he was allowed up to Alpha Level, he was still only an errand boy. The older and much smaller Guende was a member of the baron's personal staff. That seniority and all it implied penetrated Kearney's armor of arrogance. He slipped the cuffs from Abrams's wrists without so much as a mutter.

"Go back to your section," Guende ordered him. "Don't come back up here unless you have more reports to deliver."

With that, Guende turned his back dismissively on the giant Mag. He waited until he heard the man's heavy footfalls receding down the hall before he spoke. "One of yours, Abrams. A true cretin."

Abrams nodded. "Just another blunt instrument. Thank you for intervening."

They began walking down the corridor side by side. "What does Baron Cobalt want with me?" Abrams asked.

Slapping the sheaf of dispatches against his thigh, Guende replied, "A situation has developed at the Dulce facility. Very, very bad. I don't know many of the details, but evidently it's a catastrophe."

Abrams nodded gravely. "Catastrophe seems to be the standard nowadays."

Guende knew he was making a cryptic reference to the reason for his confinement, and again he felt a surge of compassion for the man. In a low, subdued tone, Guende said, "I fear it will only worsen unless something equally catastrophic is done."

Abrams's eyes cut toward him, widening in consternation, then recalling the vid spy-eyes on the ceiling, he cast his gaze downward.

Guende walked with him until the door to the

baron's suite came into sight. He stopped and allowed Abrams to trudge past him. Before the man was out of earshot, he leaned forward and whispered, "We must talk further of planned catastrophes, old friend."

Chapter 11

Standing before Baron Cobalt, Abrams said contritely, "You wished to see me, my lord." Despite his tone, he held his head high, meeting the baron's aureate gaze unflinchingly.

Abrams did not ask a question, so Baron Cobalt did not voice an answer. Instead he extended a sheet of paper toward him. Abrams took the dispatch, seeing the words printed on it but not really absorbing them. Then his eyes skimmed over one word and traveled back to it. He forced himself to focus on it and the context in which it appeared.

After a moment, he said hoarsely, "Kane again."

"Kane again," the baron repeated flatly. "Or rather, Kane always."

Baron Cobalt tilted his head to one side and regarded Abrams appraisingly. "The one recent exception being in your defeat at the foothills of the Darks. He wasn't involved in that, was he? The savages didn't need his help."

Abrams lifted his gaze from the paper. Stonily, he said, "My lord is mistaken."

Baron Cobalt's eyes narrowed. "Indeed. How so?"

"We never reached the foothills before we were set upon."

"Nevertheless, you and your Magistrate squad did not achieve the mission goals. You did not investigate Redoubt Bravo in the mountain peaks. A horde of barbarians routed you, took your vehicles and weapons, forced you to make a long foot march back to Cobaltville."

"I've never said otherwise," retorted Abrams. "Nor have I ever denied my culpability in the matter. I failed you."

An almost imperceptible edge slipped into his voice. "However, I will remind the lord baron I advised against the mission. We did not have adequate intelligence of the territory. If scouts had been sent out first, we might have learned that the Indians had a fully armed and operable war wag. We could have taken measures. Instead, we rolled right into a trap."

Baron Cobalt pitched his tone to a silky whisper. "Am I to apprehend you hold me responsible for your defeat, for being bested by barbarians?"

"Only insofar as we were obeying your wishes." Abrams shrugged, as if the matter were no longer of any importance. "With the element of surprise, they were simply too much for us. We weren't prepared for such stiff resistance. Are you planning another incursion?"

Baron Cobalt shook his head. "Not at the moment. There are more immediate concerns than avenging your ignominy."

"The situation at Dulce being one of them." Abrams spoke with no particular emotion.

"Just so. It's possible, perhaps even likely, what

happened there may eventually spell doom for the barons. How does that make you feel?"

"Right now, my lord," answered Abrams earnestly, "the possibility doesn't disturb me at all. Without the Aurora aircraft, you no longer have an efficient method of harvesting fresh genetic material. From what the dispatch stated, the damage to the medical facility itself may be total."

Abrams paused and a cruel smile creased his lips. "Without the annual treatments to detoxify your blood, filter out the impurities, to infuse your deteriorating genetic structures with untainted material, the barons will do more than simply age. The new humans will sicken and die. Just like the inferior old humans they rule."

Baron Cobalt sat in silence, not blinking or even appearing to breathe.

Abrams continued, "And since you revealed to me the Archon Directorate does not truly exist, you can't rely on their help to maintain control. After ninety years of order and regimentation, the end of unification is in sight. Your reign will soon be over. I only wish I could be alive to see it."

He spoke calmly, confidently, and maintained a steady gaze upon Baron Cobalt's face. The baron did not blink or so much as move during Abrams's blasphemy.

Finally, the baron shifted slightly in his chair. "You are the only member of the Trust in whom I have confided that information."

Abrams nodded. "I suspected as much. Then you

must kill me. It will not stave off the inevitable, but silencing me will buy you time.''

The baron uttered a weary sigh. ''I do not wish to merely buy time, Abrams. Nor do I wish to silence you.''

The affected cruel smile instantly vanished from Abrams's face. ''My lord?''

In a smooth, conciliatory voice, Baron Cobalt said, ''I did not have you brought to me so I could taunt you, Abrams. I realize I may have been too hasty, too harsh in my judgment of your failure. I confess I was very angry when you returned without all the ordnance or personnel you took with you. We have lost a great deal of equipment over the past year, including the two Deathbirds. Only recently have we replaced them from our armory.''

The baron's large eyes softened. ''I did not have sympathy for your ordeal or your own anguish over the loss of your men. The term 'harrowing' does not do justice to your suffering, does it?''

''No, my lord, it does not.''

Long fingers idly brushing over the stack of reports, Baron Cobalt went on. ''If my theory regarding the nonexistence of the Archon Directorate is true—and so far nothing has occurred to disprove it—then what binds all the villes together is based on superstition, no less, no more.''

Abrams nodded. ''That is so.''

''Therefore, if the tie that binds us is false, so is our sense of unity. The villes need not be equal in power and resources—or ambition—any longer. Has that not occurred to you?"

"It has," admitted Abrams. "I've had plenty of time to think about it in my cell."

Baron Cobalt chuckled, and though musical, the sound did not warm Abrams's heart. "And perhaps you've had plenty of time to consider that you don't know everything about the baronial hierarchy."

"I never thought I did. I know only as much as you allowed me to know."

The baron nodded as if satisfied by the response. "Just so. I have two missions in mind and I require you to help me see them through to completion."

Abrams's mind raced with speculation, with exultation, but he maintained his reserved pose. "What are those missions, my lord?"

"The first, but not the most immediate in importance, is a matter of revenue."

"Revenue?" echoed Abrams in surprise.

"As you know from your position as Magistrate Division administrator, Cobaltville receives ore shipments from contract mines in Utah."

"Yes. We had no choice except to trade once our mines played out. I'm also aware the caravans have been the targets of very efficient raiders."

"What you don't know is that there is more than ore in those shipments."

Abrams angled an eyebrow. "May I ask what?"

"You may ask," the baron answered, a laugh lurking in the back of his throat. "But I won't tell you, not yet. As I said, that matter is of secondary importance. I want the raids stopped, but that task need not occupy your immediate attention. There is something else that takes paramount priority."

Abrams waited expectantly.

Slowly, Baron Cobalt asked, "Would you be surprised to learn that the Archuleta Mesa installation is not the only one that contains both an advanced medical facility and a method of harvesting fresh genetic material?"

Abrams felt his eyebrows crawl toward his hairline. "As a point of fact, my lord, I would be."

The baron frowned slightly. "It is the one place forbidden to the barons, shrouded in so much secrecy it is a taboo we all share. But like the Archon Directorate, I suspect that taboo is a sham."

Baron Cobalt paused, his thin lips compressing as if he tasted something sour. "The installation is within my territorial jurisdiction, but I have never so much as glimpsed it. I intend to claim it, Abrams. Once I have secured it, Cobaltville will be the barony to which all the other baronies pay homage. I will dictate the terms of the medical treatment of the entire baronial oligarchy, as well having the exclusive monopoly on genetic material."

The baron pitched his voice to a low, almost intimate croon. "If you are forgiven your errors, extended clemency and restored to your former station, would you be interested in helping me see these undertakings to fruition?"

Abrams stared silently, momentarily speechless.

Stroking his beard, he replied, "I suppose I would be, my lord."

Baron Cobalt nodded. "Then it is done. You are pardoned."

"To which undertaking do you wish me to devote my attention first, my lord?"

"Obviously, securing the installation I spoke of. I have compiled a briefing jacket on its location and its history and I wish you to look for more data regarding it. After which, return with a strategy and a plan. As for dealing with caravan raiders, you should appoint one of your officers to head that particular mission."

The baron eyed him speculatively. "Do you have anyone you can trust with the responsibility?"

Abrams squared his shoulders, his spine stiffening. He was casting off the role of disgraced prisoner and assuming the mantle of a Magistrate with a mission. In a clipped, formal tone, he said, "Yes, my lord baron."

The image of the hulking, disrespectful Kearney popped into this mind. He pictured the man's shock when he called him into a briefing. He visualized terrorizing him, running roughshod over his arrogance, forcing him to genuflect and fulfill his every whim.

Smiling thinly, Abrams announced, "I have just the man who will serve that purpose."

Chapter 12

Kane looked at the dark peaks backlit by the fiery glory of the western sunset and murmured, "Land of the Shining Mountains."

Grant squinted toward him. "What?"

"Sky Dog said that's what his ancestors called Montana."

Grant's reply was uninterested and indifferent. He returned his attention to coaxing the Land Rover up the road.

The old two-lane blacktop was steep and treacherous, and the greater the elevation the more painstaking their climb became. The road stretched up from the foothills and plunged deep into the Bitterroot Range before turning into a twisting, rugged hallway. It skirted dizzying abysses on one side and foreboding, overhanging bluffs on the other.

The journey to the mountain plateau was always nerve-racking, so much so that Grant insisted he be the one to drive, not wanting to trust his life to Kane's sometimes impatient piloting. Brigid and Domi sat in the back seat. The albino girl dozed quietly, not in the least disturbed by the violent jolts or the whine of the overstressed V-8. Brigid resolutely stared at her lap.

They had lost a little time down below, clearing away then recamouflaging the narrow track cut through the rockfall that blocked the highway as it entered the foothills. Some months back, they had used an explosive to trigger an avalanche and thus make the road impassable to all but the most foolhardy of intruders, and then only those who cared to make the trek on foot.

In the interim, an alliance had been struck with Sky Dog and his band of Sioux and Cheyenne living out on the flatlands. With their help, a narrow and easily disguised path had been forged through the fall. The undertaking had required a week of hard labor and the judicious use of demolition charges, but the warriors were eager to help. If it hadn't been for Grant, Kane and Domi, a squad of Magistrates would have slaughtered the entire settlement. The Amerindians also received a fully operable war wag in the bargain.

Despite their gratitude, the tribespeople had yet to completely overcome the superstitious regard in which they held the mountain range, colloquially known as the Darks due to their mysteriously shadowed forests and deep, dangerous ravines.

Neither Kane nor anyone else who lived in Cerberus cared to tear away the veil of frightful fable that shrouded the peaks. Enduring myths about evil spirits lurking in the mountain passes to devour body and soul was a form of protective coloration that jack—not even ville scrip—couldn't buy.

"We should be in range," Grant said to Kane

tensely without taking his eyes from the road. "Give 'em a ring."

Kane picked up the trans-comm from the seat. Thumbing up the cover of the palm-sized radiophone, he pressed a key, held it up to his ear and spoke into it. "This is Rover. Do you read me, Cerberus? Acknowledge."

The range of the comms was generally limited to a mile, but in open country, in clear weather, contact could be established at two miles. Kane repeated the request, and after a moment, a voice filtered through the unit, shot through with so much static, Kane wasn't sure who spoke. Finally, he recognized the voice as Bry's.

"Reading you, Rover. What's your ETA?"

"Not long now."

"Do any of you require medical attention?"

"For once, no. Tell Lakesh that we—"

Bry interrupted. "We have a situation here, Rover. Please expedite your arrival." His voice dissolved in a series of crackles and pops.

Irritably, Kane folded down the unit's cover. "I wish Bry would hurry up and patch our comm frequencies into the satellite linkup. It'd make things a lot more efficient when we're out in the field."

"So would fixing this damn road," Grant growled.

Brigid leaned forward, saying in dry amusement, "Once the barons are overthrown, our first order of business will be to restore the Department of Transportation and Roadwork."

"He didn't seem too interested in finding out about how the mission went," Kane said.

"Probably because Lakesh didn't come up with it," replied Grant. "He wants to fight this war his way."

Kane nodded reflectively, remembering all the times he had told Lakesh that a war that was already lost could not be fought. A new one had to be waged. It wasn't until recently, when he learned that the Archon Directorate did not exist, that he had actually devoted much thought to the meaning behind his own words.

He couldn't really fault Lakesh, particularly in view of the fact he was the man who came to the pivotal conclusion that the Directorate was but a cunningly crafted illusion. Even so, Lakesh seemed reluctant to accept the findings of his own detective work, despite Balam's essentially having confirmed his suspicions. Kane wasn't sure if Lakesh's doubts sprang from a distrust of Balam or simply the fact he wasn't prepared to directly confront the barons.

Not that it really mattered at this point. Lakesh's self-assumed position as the final authority in the redoubt was no longer absolute.

The Land Rover, all six tires gripping the cracked asphalt, topped another rise, turned another bend and Grant exhaled a deep sigh of relief as the road widened to a huge plateau.

The mountain plateau concealing the Cerberus redoubt was a masterpiece of impenetrability and inaccessibility. Two centuries before, trained labor and the most advanced technology available had worked to ensure that no one—Russian, Iraqi or taxpaying American citizen—might even suspect it existed.

The tri level, thirty-acre Cerberus facility had come through the nukecaust intact, since it had been built according to specifications for maximum impenetrability, short of a direct hit. With its vanadium radiation shielding still in good condition, and powered by nuclear generators, Cerberus could survive for at least another five hundred years.

The multiton vanadium sec door folded aside like an accordion as the vehicle drove onto the tarmac. They saw Farrell standing just inside the door. The middle-aged man with a shaved head had recently grown a goatee and affected a gold hoop earring after watching a predark vid called *Hell's Angels on Wheels.*

Waving his arms, he flagged them down. He gave the ugly scar in the Hotspur's hull only a cursory glance as Grant slowed down. Speaking loudly in order to be heard over the throb of the engine, he said, "Lakesh wants you in the control center." He pointed toward Brigid. "Especially you."

"Why?" she asked.

Farrell opened his mouth, closed it, shook his head. "We've got an intruder."

"What's the threat assessment?" Kane asked.

"Triple red," Farrell answered blandly.

Grant glowered at him in angry surprise. "Then why does Lakesh want Brigid?"

Farrell made a helpless gesture with his hands. ''It's something you'll have to see for yourself.''

All of them stared at the man, speechless with surprise for a long moment, then they piled out of the Land Rover. Domi slept on, curled up on the seat. As Farrell climbed in behind the wheel, Kane asked him uneasily, ''How can there be an intruder up here? Did he walk?''

Farrell said flatly. ''No. He's still in the mat-trans.''

He steered the wag into the twenty-foot-wide corridor, toward the vehicle depot adjacent to the armory. As Grant, Brigid and Kane entered the redoubt, Grant said, ''I thought it was impossible for anyone to jump except us to this gateway, accidentally or on purpose.''

That was certainly Lakesh's often stated claim. However, they all remembered the one fairly recent exception to the rule. Kane threw down the lever to close the sec door. He glanced at the large, garishly colored image of a froth-mouthed black hound emblazoned on the wall near the door. Three stylized heads grew out of a single, exaggeratedly muscled neck, their jaws spewing flame and blood between great fangs. Below the image, rendered in an absurdly ornate Gothic script, was the word *Cerberus*.

The ferocious guardian of the gateway to Hades seemed an appropriate totem and code name for the project devoted to ripping open gates in the quantum field.

They strode quickly to the operations center, wending their way down aisles between the comp stations.

Bry, seated at the master ops console, gave them a lopsided smile when they entered. In the ready room, they saw the armaglass door to the jump chamber hanging ajar. It was flanked by Cotta and Banks, both brandishing an SA-80 subgun. Although the bores of the blasters were pointed at the floor, the faces of both men registered relief at their approach.

"Where's Lakesh?" Kane asked.

Cotta jerked his head toward the mat-trans unit. "In there with our guest. DeFore is with him, too."

Grant and Kane's Sin Eaters automatically snapped into their hands. The big-bored, Mag-issue hand-blasters were less than fourteen inches long at full extension. When not in use, the stocks folded over the top of the weapon, lying along the frame, reducing their holstered length to ten inches. The forearm holsters were equipped with sensitive actuators. They activated a flexible cable in the holster and snapped the weapons smoothly into the hand, the stocks unfolding in the same motion. Ingeniously designed to fire immediately upon contact with the index finger, the Sin Eaters had no trigger guard or safety. Since the guns fired upon touching the crooked finger, both men kept their fingers stretched out straight.

Eyeing the weapons apprehensively, Banks said, "There's no immediate danger. He's been here for nearly thirty hours."

Neither Kane nor Grant holstered his blaster. Cautiously they stepped up onto the platform and peered into the chamber. Lakesh and DeFore stood over a small man squatting against the far wall. The foil packages of several self-heat rations lay crumpled up around him. At the moment, he was drinking from a water bottle gripped by his left foot. His dark eyes slitted when they rested on Grant and Kane. When Grant saw the gren clutched within his right foot, he uttered a wordless grunt.

Kane's reaction was not so restrained. "A goddamn transadapt, one of Sindri's crew of trolls!"

The little man lowered the water bottle and squeaked, "Fuck you, big 'un."

"What the hell is he doing here?" demanded Grant.

Without looking at him, Lakesh replied calmly. "He came over a transit line around dawn yesterday. He's refused to say from where exactly or why or even leave the platform. He threatened to use that grenade if we tried to force him out. He'll only talk to Brigid."

"I'm here," she said, shouldering between Kane and Grant.

The transadapt's swart face split with a huge welcoming grin, exposing discolored stumpy teeth. "Hi, Miss Brigid. Do you remember me?"

She regarded him keenly and found with a sense of dismay she could not find his face in her memory. "I'm afraid I don't."

The little man tapped the crown of his head. "My name is Leland. You conked me real good on Cydonia, hit me with Sindri's cane."

Brigid nodded in recognition. "Now I recall you. Did Sindri send you here?"

Leland nodded. "He needs help, an' he said to tell you he's sorry and to give you this."

He inserted dirt-encrusted fingers into a breast pocket of his coverall, oblivious to the bores of the Sin Eaters staring at him like hollow eyes. He brought out a small, slip-sleeved CD-ROM and held it up toward her. "Look at this. It'll explain everything."

As he spoke, Leland's words slurred slightly. His black eyes bore a glassy sheen.

DeFore said quietly, "He's suffering from the increased atmospheric pressure and richer oxygen content."

Bending down, Brigid took the disk, eyed the gren and said in a level tone, "If you want my help, I'll need you to disarm that gren."

Leland blinked, as if surprised about the presence of the device clutched within his toes. "Sorry. Almost forgot about it."

His toe-thumb tapped the primer button, and the blinking light went out. He opened his toes, and the metal ovoid rolled clinking over the floor hexagons. Grant and Kane began a forward lunge toward Leland, intent on immobilizing him, but Brigid spread her arms and held them back.

"Knock it off," she said crossly. "What are you going to do, double-team a man not even half your size?"

"Those transadapts are stronger than they look, remember?" Kane shot back a little defensively, but he came to a halt.

Grant reached down and scooped up the gren, eyeing it closely. "A DM-54 implode with an electronic detonator, manufactured around 1999. The proverbial handful of hell. Damn rare. I doubt we have more than a dozen in the arsenal."

He cast Leland a suspicious stare. "There were no weapons in the Cydonia Compound, so where'd you get this?"

Leland only glared at him.

"I imagine he got it from the same source that supplied our dozen," Lakesh commented quietly.

Grant swiveled his head toward him. "What do you mean?"

Lakesh shook his head and addressed Leland. "Do you feel secure enough to leave the chamber now?"

Leland blinked expectantly at Brigid. She said reassuringly, "You're safe. Consider yourself our guest."

Kane snorted scornfully, but Leland ignored him, pushing himself erect. He walked across the jump chamber, listing slightly. The knuckles of his hands nearly dragged on the floor plates. Grant stepped aside as Brigid led the little man out into the ready room. "Is there anything you want?"

"Need to go to the head," Leland piped. "Been at least three days since I took a leak. It's starting to get serious."

Brigid asked Banks, "Would you mind showing him the proper facilities?"

Banks quirked an eyebrow, first at her then at Leland. He smiled. "Once the nursemaid of aliens, always the nursemaid of aliens, I guess. My lot in life."

Handing the SA-80 over to Cotta, he started off across the room. "Come with me, Leland."

Leland shambled after him, muttering sullenly, "I'm no alien. I may be a Martian, but that don't make me no alien."

Kane, Grant, Lakesh and DeFore emerged from the mat-trans unit. Turning to face them, Brigid lightly tapped the compact computer disk against the palm of one hand. "I guess there's no longer any need to wonder if we'll ever hear from Sindri again."

Chapter 13

Kane had figured that if he and his partners ever collided with Sindri again, it would be through happenstance. It hadn't occurred to him Sindri would dispatch an emissary in order to actively seek out their aid. In his more tolerant, fair-minded moments, Kane admitted to himself it was almost their fault they had met Sindri in the first place.

While exploring an anomaly in the network of functioning mat-trans units, Lakesh, Brigid and Kane found the corpse of a transadapt killed by a Mag squad. A post-mortem performed upon the troll revealed he was not a mutant or a hybrid but a human being modified to live in an environment with a rarefied atmosphere and low gravity.

After a bit of investigation, Lakesh traced the quantum conduit used by the transadapt to a point in outer space—a predark space station on the far side of the moon known as *Parallax Red.*

Kane, Grant and Brigid jumped to the station, which was overseen by an ingenious gnome of a man calling himself Sindri, after the master forger of the troll race in Norse mythology.

Sindri impressed them all with his wit, his charm and his probing intellect. They were particularly impressed by the startling story he told about *Parallax Red* and its connection to a human colony on Mars. Originally *Parallax Red* was a covert joint undertaking between America and Russia, under the authority of the Totality Concept's Overproject Majestic. Envisioned as an elite community with a maximum population of five thousand, the station was intended as a utopia for the best of Earth transported to space. And not only did it establish a permanent military presence in space, but it also provided a staging point for launching deep-space exploratory craft.

Once Project Cerberus began mass-producing the mat-trans gateways as modular units, conventional spacecraft were rendered obsolete, since the gateways allow instantaneous movement of personnel and matériel back and forth from Earth. Additionally, experiments were conducted regarding the teleportation of gateway components through space along carrier-wave guides, which allowed travel to the inner planets of the solar system without using conventional spacecraft.

Construction of the Cydonia One Compound on Mars began in late 1990. Earth-normal gravity was maintained in the compound by using a network of synthetic-gravity generators. The descendants of the first Martian colonists were engineered to adapt to the planet's environment. Thus was born the first generation of "transadapts," capable of existing in very cold temperatures and drawing oxygen from a thinner atmosphere. The load-bearing function of the spine and legs was altered, with the legs becoming a second

pair of arms. The transadapts were engineered to have a relatively short life span, with few living past thirty years. The transadapts were developed in secret in the Cydonia Compound using raw genetic material provided by people taken forcibly from Earth—an ugly twist on the UFO-abduction myths.

However, because of the chaos engendered by the nukecaust and the damage the space station sustained, both the fledgling colony and *Parallax Red* were forgotten. The personnel of the station had no choice but to move permanently to Mars, where they formed a caste-based society built on the labor of the transadapts.

As the twenty-first century became the twenty-second, the transadapt population of the Cydonia Compound continued to grow, eventually outnumbering the human population by well over three to one. Only their much shorter life spans prevented them from completely controlling the colony.

Genetic testing determined Sindri was the offspring of a transadapt mother and human-colonist father. As an adult, Sindri discovered a crisis in fertility was looming, and he urged an exodus back to Earth before the entire human population of the colony became extinct. Rather than accepting Sindri's proposal, the dwindling number of human colonists used a medical treatment disguised as necessary vaccinations to make the transadapts barren.

Sindri led an open, bloody revolution against the human population of Cydonia. At the end of a month, all of the human colonists and three-quarters of the transadapts had perished by violence.

Delving into the compound's computer database, Sindri found the location of a hidden mat-trans unit and its one active jump-line—the *Parallax Red* space station. He and a group of his people occupied it, restoring atmosphere to part of it.

Still obsessed with transplanting the survivors of the Martian colony to Earth, Sindri realized their only chance for survival was to successfully hybridize their genetic structure with those of native Terrans, so the women at least could reproduce. When Kane, Grant and Brigid arrived on *Parallax Red* via the gateway, Sindri saw them as both fonts of information about Earth and the salvation of the transadapts.

Though his plans for genetic hybridization were unsuccessful and his space station almost destroyed when Kane, Brigid and Grant escaped back to Cerberus, Sindri was undaunted. The day following their return to Cerberus, the ingenious dwarf had sent them, via the mat-trans unit, his signature walking stick. The theatrical gesture told them he was still alive and could overcome their security locks.

Lakesh still had no idea of how he managed to do it. Since that day, several months ago, all of them had wondered at one time or another if they would confront him again.

Curiously, despite what Sindri had planned and had done to them, Kane couldn't dredge up much genuine hatred for him. Brigid had referred to him as a warped little man with ambitions to challenge God. He was certainly that, but he had also proved himself to be a cunning adversary operating on his own skewed code of honor.

Also—though Kane would have never admitted it to anyone—he felt a grudging admiration for the little madman and his childlike enthusiasm for wreaking havoc.

At the master console, Brigid inserted the CD-ROM into the drive. Light flashed and pixels crawled across the four-foot VGA monitor screen, then images flickered, overlaid by a strobing blue glow like the sputter of dying neon.

Crashes of static mixed with unintelligible voices screaming and shouting. Then came the unmistakable staccato crackle of autofire.

The flickering pattern coalesced into a scene dimly illuminated and shot through with snowy pixel patterns. Barely visible was a wide corridor sheathed in dully gleaming metal. Shadow shapes glided along it.

Pinpoints of flame twinkled, and again came the hammering of blasterfire. A blur of images skittered across the screen as if whoever held the camera ducked and dodged. A well modulated voice with a sonorous tenor quality to it filtered through the speaker. ''Fall back, fall back!''

Kane recognized the voice and felt his spine stiffen.

The viewpoint panned sideways and stopped with a lurch, bobbing unsteadily up and down. An extreme close-up of a man's face filled the screen, viewed from slightly below. His thick, dark blond hair was swept back from an unusually high forehead. The tape accurately recorded his big eyes of clear, clean blue, wide and wild now with fear and with other emotions deeper than mere fright.

"The high pissant himself," Grant growled.

Kane had seen Sindri's chiseled features alight with laughter and twisted with rage, but never contorted into the expression of terror he saw on the screen. Since there was no other object in the scene by which to judge perspective, it wasn't apparent the man was only a shade more than three feet tall.

Seeming to stare right into the control center directly at Brigid, Sindri half shouted over the gunfire in the background, "Miss Brigid, I make this appeal to you in the hope you will urge your companions to render me aid."

Absently, Kane noted how little puffs of vapor accompanied Sindri's words, as if he spoke from a meat locker.

"I realize none of you have any reason to care about what happens to me and my people, but what we've stumbled onto here will directly—and tragically—affect the lives of everyone in the world."

"Where is 'here'?" Brigid murmured. She cast a swift glance at the Mercator-relief map.

"We've been running and fighting for our lives for the past two days. I don't know if this recording will even reach you, but I'm sending Leland to the gateway with it and I pray he makes it through."

The blasterfire increased in both volume and intensity. Sindri looked feverishly over his shoulder. High-pitched voices rose in a babble of panicked shrieks and shouts.

"They're making another move to cut us off!" Sindri blurted. "They're not people—"

The image shifted swiftly to show a view of the corridor. Due to the poor lighting and the shaky camera work, only blurred dark figures appeared on the screen. They ran, dodged, triggered blasters. Cordite smoke floated in flat planes like scraps of dingy chiffon.

Kane made out two stunted, dwarfish bodies sprawled on the floor. Blood, black in the dim light, oozed across the alloy. Standing figures moved into view, wielding what appeared to be AK-47 assault rifles. They wore dark coats and trousers, their white shirts gleaming against the gloom like ghosts.

Behind them a figure gestured, but the shouted orders couldn't be heard over the drumming of autofire and the screams of the transadapts. For a splinter of an instant, Kane glimpsed flaccid lips and eroded flesh.

Abruptly, blackness swallowed the image, but not before he discerned the silhouetted contours of a woman's bosom.

Releasing her breath in a prolonged sigh, Brigid looked toward the Mercator map again. No lights blinked anywhere on its surface. "Where did this happen?"

Lakesh's response was an almost inaudible rustle. "South Dakota."

Grant swiveled his head toward the old man. "What redoubt is there?"

"It isn't a redoubt, not exactly...." His voice trailed off.

Brigid pushed her chair back from the console, eyeing him suspiciously. "I don't recall an indexed gateway unit there."

Lakesh nodded, eyes behind the lenses of his glasses at once vacant and haunted. "That's because it's not part of the Cerberus network."

"But you *do* know where it is," Brigid declared.

Lakesh leaned forward. "Give me a playback."

Brigid frowned slightly at Lakesh's blatant stonewalling, then touched the keyboard. Images once more flickered across the monitor screen. When it backtracked to the scene in the corridor, Lakesh said, "Normal play."

Brigid did as he requested. The indistinct image of the woman in the background reappeared. Lakesh said tensely, "Freeze it there. Digitally augment and enhance."

By stroking the appropriate sequence of keys, Brigid enlarged the figure. Not much could be done about the poor illumination, but the computer program highlighted features and reduced interference.

Brigid manipulated the keys until a three-quarters view of the woman's profile filled the screen. Her face was lovely, well molded and contoured with soft, full lips and the one visible eye a deep blue.

"That's not the same woman," Kane objected.

"We saw her from a different angle." Brigid's fingers continued tapping the keyboard, and in slow, fitful jerks the woman's head turned. The program automatically reduced the shadows obscuring the image until it achieved a full frontal view.

Brigid bit back an exclamation of horror. Grant winced. Lakesh did not react at all.

The right side of the woman's face bore dark, roughened skin sagging like wax exposed to intense heat. The corner of her mouth dipped down like a dewlap, and her eye was lusterless and milky. Her hair on that side did not flow—it sprouted from her head in stiffened tendrils between bald patches through which the inflamed scalp showed.

The vision of feminine beauty juxtaposed with deformity was so unsettling, so bizarre that Kane asked uneasily, "Are you sure that thing is working like it's supposed to?"

Brigid didn't answer, staring transfixed at the distorted image, so Kane turned to Lakesh. "That can't be right, can it?"

Inhaling a deep breath, Lakesh tore his gaze away from the screen, took two faltering back steps, turned around and vomited.

Chapter 14

After that, no one cared to linger around the master console. Over his croaking protestations, DeFore led Lakesh away to the dispensary. He claimed he was fine, but everyone saw the clammy film of sweat glistening on his face and the unsteadiness in his legs.

Brigid ejected the disk and frowned at it. "Seeing that woman—or whatever she was—stressed him out."

"He's seen as bad as that before and probably been responsible for worse," Grant remarked darkly.

"What the hell kind of trouble has Sindri gotten himself into?" Kane demanded. "And why would he think we'd give a shit about it?"

Before Brigid could venture a guess, Banks returned to the control complex with Leland. A relieved smile creased the troll's face. Worriedly, Banks said, "We just passed DeFore and Lakesh. Is he sick?"

"We don't know," Brigid answered. She gestured to a chair several yards away from the puddle on the floor. "Leland, sit over there. I want to ask you some questions."

"Okeydoke." Obligingly the little man shambled over to the chair and hopped up onto it. He gazed up at Brigid with something akin to adoration shining in his eyes.

"I hope you don't hold that crack on the head against me," she said.

"Oh, no. I deserved it. I was half-drunk because of too much oxygen." He shifted his gimlet gaze toward Kane. "Sindri said you made that happen, monkeying around with the airflow."

Folding his arms over his chest, Kane shot back, "Sindri was right. If it wouldn't have killed us, too, I'd have cut off the oxygen supply to the entire compound. Consider your ugly little ass fortunate."

Leland clenched his fists and feet, favoring Kane with a gargoyle sneer of defiance. To Grant he said, "And you killed Elle."

"I didn't mean to," Grant responded dispassionately. "Casualties of war. What was she to you?"

Leland shrugged negligently, as if he had lost interest in the topic. "She gave me blow jobs sometimes."

Kane noticed Brigid wince and he had trouble repressing a shiver of revulsion himself as the memory of the bulldog-faced transadapt woman drifted through his mind. A new thought struck him. According to the autopsy performed on the troll they found in Redoubt Papa, the male transadapts didn't have conventional reproductive organs....

His revulsion returned twofold, and he chased the grotesque thought away.

Brigid regarded Leland gravely. "Where is Sindri?

What place were you in? How did you get there? And why?''

Leland answered the questions in reverse order. ''We'd been tryin' to find another place to live. Sindri keeps sayin' Cydonia ain't our real home. He says Earth is, 'cause that's where our ancestors came from.''

He rubbed his splayed nose. ''Sindri found the right buttons to push in the comp on the space station to take us places.''

''Buttons?'' inquired Grant.

''You know, on that quantum thingamawhatsit.''

''The quantum interphase mat-trans inducers,'' Brigid said. ''He found the destination and target-lock coordinates for the gateways. Is that what you're saying?''

Leland nodded. ''Yeah. So Sindri and a bunch of us climbed into the one on the station and went away. Then we were in the other place.''

''Where was this other place?'' Kane asked.

Leland shivered and he hugged himself. ''Don't know. But it was cold there, different kind of cold than on Mars. Damp cold goin' right to your bones. Dark place, too. Always felt like you were bein' watched even if you didn't see nobody. Some parts of it stank, like meat goin' bad.''

Leland paused, then stated, ''Sindri called the place a stockpile, but he called it somethin' else once. Can't remember offhand.''

''A COG facility?'' Brigid supplied.

The transadapt nodded. ''Yeah, that's it. He said

something else, something do to with bugs. Don't know why, though. Anyhow, we explored around... it's big, biggest place I ever seen. Guess we were there for a couple of days afore we found the bang-bangs."

"Bang-bangs?" Kane echoed in confusion.

Leland lifted his right hand, folding all but his thumb and forefinger against the palm. "You know."

"Blasters," Grant rumbled. "You found an armory."

"Yeah. There was bang-bangs of all kinds in there, like the one I brought here. Even some vehicles. Lotta stuff I didn't know anything about. Sindri sure was happy, though, especially when he found the comp system. He played with it for a long time, and the longer he played with it, the happier he got. He said there was something else in that place a lot bigger than the bang-bangs. So we set off to find it."

Leland took a breath, and the tip of his tongue touched his leathery lips. "We didn't get far afore them...*things* jumped us."

"What things?" Brigid asked.

Leland shook his head. "Don't really know, not exactly. Never got a real good look at 'em. They were big 'uns like you, but Sindri said they were monsters. They had bang-bangs—blasters—and they knew how to use 'em better than we did. We had blasters from the armory, but it was the first time most of us had ever seen 'em.

"They chased us all around, back toward that quantum thing where we first got there. They killed at least five of us, and I don't think we nailed a single one of them."

Leland sighed, eyes intent on Brigid's face. "You know the rest. We got back to the quantum thing, and Sindri sent me here with the tape."

He stopped speaking, drumming his dirt-encrusted heels on the legs of the chair. Kane said dryly, "Straightforward enough story. I wonder why I don't buy it."

Glaring at him from beneath his sloping brow, Leland declared, "Sindri ain't lyin'."

"Mebbe not," said Grant. "But he's a master at withholding some of the facts. What did he mean when he said what he found there would affect the lives of everyone?"

"I don't know," Leland responded. "Guess you'll have to go to that COG place to find out."

"Right," Kane stated sarcastically. "That tape is bait, pure and simple, to lure us into a trap."

"No," the little man snapped with surprising vehemence. "He told me you were his only hope. He's gotten in over his head and he wants bygones to be bygones. He needs you."

In agitation, Leland jumped down from the chair and reached for Brigid's hand, clutching it within his calloused palm. Gazing up at her beseechingly, he said, "If it was a trap, I wouldn't go along with it. Sindri told us you were gonna keep us from goin' extinct, but—" Leland cast a venomous glance toward Kane "—he spoiled it. I wouldn't mind leadin' him or that other big 'un into a trap, but not you."

Kane rolled his eyes ceilingward, just barely able to suppress his gag reflex.

Gently, Brigid pulled her hand away. "We'll need to discuss this." She nodded toward Banks. "Go with him and he'll find you quarters."

Leland hesitated. "Not much time. I need to get back. I been here longer than I thought I would already."

"I understand that," Brigid replied patiently. "You won't have to wait much longer."

Reluctantly, Leland turned and left with Banks. Kane dry-scrubbed his hair in frustration. "I don't see much need to discuss this. Sindri used us, experimented on us, he damn near raped you, not to mention how he nearly chilled me and Grant on the space station."

Brigid nodded reflectively. "It's not Sindri. It's where he is."

"South Dakota?"

"Yes. And there's only one COG facility there."

Grant regarded her with an ironically arched eyebrow. "We're all waiting."

She drew in a slow breath and released it. "The Anthill."

ALL OF THEM HAD HEARD Lakesh make passing references to the immense installation within Mount Rushmore more than once. But from his few casual comments, Kane at least had received the impression the so-called Anthill had been abandoned long, long ago.

According to Lakesh, when he determined to build the resistance movement against the unified baronies by secretly reactivating the Cerberus redoubt, he filled most of its arsenal with ordnance stockpiled in the Anthill. All of that had been accomplished slowly, over a period of at least thirty years, and Kane assumed Lakesh had been able to loot the place at will because no one remained in the installation to stop him.

Rather than stand around in the operations room and argue the point, Kane and Brigid sought out Lakesh while Grant went to unload their gear from the Land Rover. When Bry demanded who was going to clean up the pool of vomit, Kane told him to fetch Auerbach up from detention and give him a mop and bucket.

They found Lakesh in the dispensary, sitting on the edge of an examination bed. A thermometer jutted out of the corner of his mouth, and DeFore stood next to him, holding his wrist and timing his pulse.

"I tell you I'm fine," he mumbled around the glass stem beneath his tongue.

"Hush," she commanded.

"How is he?" Kane asked.

"Hush," DeFore ordered again, concentrating on the stopwatch in her free hand.

Kane complied and stood waiting, hands clasped behind his back. Only recently had he and the medic reached an accord so they weren't active adversaries any longer. Still and all, they certainly weren't friends. At least she went to greater efforts to disguise her dislike of him—or rather, what he represented to her. In her eyes, as a former Magistrate, he embodied the strutting arrogance of ville law enforcement, glorying in his baron-sanctioned power to deal death indiscriminately.

She also believed that because of his Magistrate conditioning, he had difficulty reconciling his past with his present, causing acute psychological conflict, and at one point she had diagnosed him as suffering from post-traumatic stress syndrome. She hadn't felt he could be trusted. Inasmuch as he hadn't killed himself or anyone else in the redoubt, DeFore had backed off as of late. In return, Kane extended to her more respect and a professional courtesy.

The bronze-skinned woman released Lakesh's wrist, pulled the thermometer from his mouth, eyed it and announced, "Your temperature is normal, but your pulse is fast and a little irregular. I can't find anything physically wrong with you."

"That's because there isn't, as I've been telling you for the past ten minutes." Lakesh's reedy voice held a note of complaint. "I just had a shock, an emotional reaction."

"That's what we figured," Kane said. "The question is why."

"Did you recognize that woman?" Brigid asked.

Lakesh squeezed his eyes shut, as if trying to blot the image from his mind. Faintly he said, "In a way."

"That's no answer." Kane's voice sounded as sharp as a whip crack.

Opening his eyes, Lakesh met Kane's steely blue-gray stare unblinkingly. With slow deliberation, he repeated, "In a way."

He looked toward Brigid. "Did you get a backstory from Leland?"

Nodding, she repeated almost verbatim every word Leland had spoken. With her eidetic memory, it was easy, though she omitted the details about Leland's relationship with Elle.

When she was done, Lakesh eased himself down from the table. "Fits in with what we know about Sindri."

"Actually," Kane corrected, "it fits with what Brigid, Grant and I know. You never met the sawed-off son of a bitch."

Lakesh walked toward the dispensary's exit. "That may change, friend Kane. That may change."

Kane blocked his way. "Or it may not. Brigid says Sindri is in the Anthill."

Lakesh nodded. "Yes, I believe he is."

"You've mentioned the Anthill before," Kane continued. "The largest of the Continuity of Government facilities, even bigger than Redoubt Zulu in Alaska. It was where you dozed through the nuclear winter and at least a hundred years after. But that's about all you ever said about it. I don't recollect you saying the place was still functional and inhabited."

"I don't recollect you asking if it was or wasn't," Lakesh retorted.

Brigid put in mildly, "The database doesn't have much information about it, either. I checked shortly after we first got here. There is some construction history, some specs, but that's all. It's almost as if the more pertinent files had been—'' she paused, then added ''—deleted.''

Lakesh did not respond to the observation. He pushed past Kane without a word.

Kane felt a flash of anger, the same old resentment at the man's high-handed ways that had enraged him since the day they'd met. Grabbing Lakesh by the arm, he spun him around and growled, ''You don't call all the shots around here anymore. And that includes withholding information.''

With a studied, haughty calm, Lakesh replied, ''I have no more information regarding the current status of the Anthill than you do. But I intend to rectify that.''

Surprise overwhelmed Kane's anger. He released the old man's arm. ''You're planning a mission to the Anthill?''

''A personal one, friend Kane.''

''You intend to jump in there alone?'' he demanded.

''I'd prefer company, but whether I have it or not, I *am* going.''

As he made for the door, Kane started off after him, but Brigid put out a restraining hand. In a low voice, she said, ''Let me talk to him.''

Kane hesitated, then nodded curtly.

She caught up to Lakesh in the corridor, but he didn't acknowledge her presence. Conversationally she told him, ''That aircraft you called the Aurora—Grant shot it down.''

Lakesh muttered something indistinct, as if she had just informed him she intended to rearrange her underthings drawer. They walked side by side, Brigid telling him quietly of the events at Dulce. Only once did Lakesh react and then with an absentminded grunt.

Irritated, Brigid said, "What we didn't know is that they were breeding dinosaurs in there, too. Just when we figured we were home free, a troop of velociraptors showed up, armed with gren launchers and riding unicycles."

Lakesh turned a corner, heading toward his office. Wearily he said, "There's no need to test me in such a foolish fashion. I've heard every word you said."

"You don't seem very interested in them," she retorted, nettled.

"I fear I have other matters completely occupying my mind and heart at the moment. I can't spare the attention of either."

He started to open the office door, but Brigid put her hand on the knob. "That's obvious. What isn't are the reasons why."

Not meeting her penetrating emerald gaze, Lakesh said in a rustling whisper, "They're personal."

"Not in this place. You saw to that a long time ago, at least as far the rest of us are concerned. Are you claiming an exemption?"

Finally he turned his head and looked at her. Despite the thick lenses of his glasses, she was dismayed to see the pain swimming in his rheumy blue eyes. It was more than just pain; it was a soul-deep anguish.

"I am," he stated with his characteristic firmness.

Although she felt empathy for him, Brigid replied coldly, "Then you're not going anywhere. I'll confine you to quarters or put you in a detention cell. Auerbach will be glad to have some company."

Lakesh blinked owlishly at her, as if he couldn't believe his ears. "You wouldn't dare," he rasped.

"Try me," she challenged.

The man's shoulders abruptly sagged, not so much in resignation as in exhaustion, as though the burdens he had carried for so many years suddenly had become too much for him to bear. At that moment he looked every second of his 250 years.

Speaking softly and sympathetically, Brigid said, "Lakesh, I'm asking you to tell me what's going on with you. What do you know about the Anthill? Who is that woman on the tape?"

Lakesh opened and closed his mouth, groping for something to say. He shook his head sadly. "I want to tell you, but I'm afraid."

"Of what?"

"That after you hear me out, you'll hate me."

It was her turn to blink at him. "Why would I hate you?"

Lakesh uttered a noise somewhere between a sigh and a groan. "Several months ago, when I revealed to Kane my involvement—he called it tampering—in the details of his birth, you asked me how many other people's lives I'd arranged in like fashion."

She reviewed her memories of the incident to which Lakesh referred. "Yes. You only said, and I quote, 'What you're really asking is if I arranged yours.' You didn't give me an answer."

Lakesh nodded miserably and cleared his throat. "That woman on the tape is your answer."

Chapter 15

Brigid faced Lakesh across the top of his small desk in his Spartanly furnished office. She did her best to tamp down her rising impatience. "You can't just toss off a remark like that and then tell me to forget you said it. You know better than that, Lakesh."

Pushing his glasses up on his deeply grooved forehead, Lakesh used his gnarled knuckles to massage his eyes. Quietly he said, "Dearest Brigid, with all the surgeries I underwent, I wish some of my memories had been removed in the process. There are many things I wish I could forget."

"And the woman on the tape is one of them?"

"Yes," Lakesh husked out.

"Explain."

"I—" Lakesh's words blurred into inaudibility. He stopped rubbing his eyes and buried his face in his hands.

Brigid gazed at him, perplexed and more than a little disturbed. In a softer, more reasonable tone she said, "Lakesh, if that woman has some kind of connection to me, you owe me an explanation. You came clean with Kane." She didn't need to add, *After he gave you no choice.*

Voice muffled and quavering, Lakesh replied, "My

involvement with Kane's genetic makeup was impersonal, a matter of applied science."

"He didn't think so," Brigid pointed out.

"No," admitted Lakesh. "And neither will you."

The matter they alluded to was a sore point not just with Kane but Brigid, as well, and she understood Lakesh's reluctance to discuss it again. In his drive to buy off his guilt for what the postskydark world had become, a world he'd helped to create, the man had stopped just short of playing God.

By using the Archon Directorate's own fixation with genetic purity, Lakesh had attempted to create a breed of superior humans. Kane was his only true success, and in the process of his creation, Lakesh had triggered a deadly feud that extended across two generations. By his own confession, Lakesh was a physicist cast in the role of an archivist, pretending to be a geneticist, manipulating a political system that was still in a state of flux.

Although he expressed remorse over what his machinations had wrought, Lakesh hadn't stopped there. A few months before, he'd arranged for Beth-Li Rouch to be brought into the redoubt to mate with Kane, to ensure that Kane's superior qualities were passed on. Mating him with a woman who met the standards of Purity Control was the most logical course of action. Without access to the techniques of fetal development outside the womb, the conventional means of procreation was the only option. And that meant sex and passion and the fury of a woman scorned.

Kane had refused to cooperate for a variety of reasons, primarily because he felt the plan was a continuation of sinister elements that had brought about the nukecaust and the tyranny of the villes. His refusal had tragic consequences. Only a thirst for revenge and a conspiracy to murder had been birthed within the walls of the redoubt, not children.

More than once, the notion had occurred to Brigid that Lakesh might have tampered with her DNA in the same way he had done with Kane. She had never raised the issue with him.

Now that the question had been posed, Brigid wanted an answer. "Would it help if I promised to keep whatever you tell me strictly confidential?"

Lakesh swallowed hard, his Adam's apple bobbing beneath the wattles of his neck. "I don't know if it would help. But I do owe you an explanation."

Reseating his eyeglasses on the bridge of his nose, he attempted to meet her penetrating green gaze. "I believe I know who the woman on the tape is—or was, two hundred years ago. I never allowed myself to seriously consider she was still alive. The idea seemed preposterous, but at the same time I always felt the possibility, if not the probability was there.

"I'll tell you the story from the beginning, and I ask you to be patient with me. I've never spoken of this with anyone other than myself—and then only in the most private, dark moments of my soul."

Brigid did not react to the old man's melodrama; she had grown accustomed to it by now.

Lakesh took a deep breath, placed his hands flat on

the desktop and straightened up in his chair, as if he were drawing on hidden reserves of strength. He began to talk, quickly and without hesitation, trying to get out as many words as he could before his courage faltered.

"I really, truly loved only once in my life, Brigid. I was so devoted to my career, to pursuing the holy grail of science, that I had no time for love."

Brigid nodded in understanding, knowing how Lakesh's extraordinarily high IQ earned him a scholarship to MIT at age sixteen and a Ph.D. in cybernetics and quantum mechanics at nineteen.

"I've already told you how I went to work for the Totality Concept's Dulce installation when I was but twenty, where I eventually was appointed overseer of Project Cerberus. This redoubt was the Cerberus headquarters, and it was in this very room where I first met Dian, when she reported for duty."

Lakesh's reedy voice softened, and his eyes took on a vague, faraway sheen as if he pierced the mists of the past. "She was a biochemist, studying changes in organic matter that traveled the quantum pathways opened by the gateways. Needless to say, she was very bright and very beautiful. She saw through my shyness. And even more refreshing, she wasn't intimidated by my position as project overseer.

"I in turn saw through her clinical facade. Although she had a very regimented mind, able to keep emotions and intellect separate, she was also warm and compassionate. Her soul was lonely and so was mine. It was inevitable our spirits would recognize each other as kindred.

"I was surprised by how deeply she touched me. By that time I thought I was pure cerebration, a sterile intellect. The strongest emotion I experienced was irritation if my secretary hadn't prepared my tea exactly the way my mother had done."

A wan, bitter smile tugged at the corners of Lakesh's lips. "In the parlance of the era, I was a total geek, right down to my plastic pocket protector. I'd had very little intimate contact with women and I had developed health problems—my heart, for one—which affected my self-esteem.

"At first I kept my distance from Dian, but she sought me out. She pursued me. The concept of such a young, beautiful and bright woman actually desiring my company did wonders for my ego. She wasn't simply trying to ingratiate herself with me. I knew otherwise. I *felt* otherwise.

"As you know, in mid-2000, most of the overseers of the varied Totality Concept divisions were all headquartered in the Anthill. Dian was assigned to join the staff of Project Invictus, out in the Guadalupe desert of California. I cheerfully admit to using my influence and pulling a few strings to have her transferred to the Anthill with me."

He paused, shook his head and murmured, "I wish we had both stayed behind here in Cerberus. Our lives would have been shorter, but at least we could have shared them in relative peace. However, with the crazed chaos of the Anthill—"

"Chaos?" Brigid echoed quizzically.

Lakesh shook his head again, this time in frustration. "Realization of the true magnitude of the plan to reshape the Earth in a new, ordered image finally hit the personnel there. Many of them were so filled with horror, so consumed with guilt, they preferred death to survival."

He chuckled, but it had no true mirth in it. "I would have gone just as mad as the rest of them in that place if it hadn't been for Dian. We clung to each other for some small assurance that things still made sense. But eventually, even that wasn't enough.

"With the Anthill's resources strained to the breaking point and with so many of its personnel becoming unmanageable, it was proposed that some of us volunteer to enter stasis for an appointed period of time. I discussed it with Dian. We quarreled about it, the only thing we ever argued over. She was loath to give up her work in altering human biology. I was just as loath to go into stasis sleep without her.

"But I and others like me were the targets of persuasive pressure, mainly by General Kettridge, whose power in the Anthill was near-absolute.

"Though I gave in, I couldn't convince Dian to join me. So we had one last, sadly beautiful night together."

Lakesh's eyes brimmed with tears, and he blinked them back. One spilled down his seamed cheek. "I never saw Dian again. At least, not the Dian I knew and loved."

Brigid eyed him questioningly. "Explain."

In a creaky voice, Lakesh replied, "This is difficult for me. I agreed to a twenty-year stasis period. Can you imagine my profound shock when I next awakened and found that nearly a century and a half had elapsed? During that time, conditions had so worsened in the installation, Kettridge and his staff embarked on a radical program. Cybernetics had made great advances in the last decades of the twentieth century, and all of that technology existed in the Anthill—as well as the people who knew how to put it to use.

"Radical operations were performed on all of the personnel, evidently whether they cooperated or not. Over a period of years, everyone was turned into a cyborg, a hybrid of machine and human."

Thinking of Colonel Thrush, that ghastly blending of human, nonhuman, and circuitry, Brigid couldn't keep the disgust from her voice when she asked, "Why?"

"Fewer bellies to keep filled, more obedient to the rules. I agree it seems cold-blooded, but if they hadn't taken such measures, everyone in the Anthill would have succumbed to either illness or old age. Also, it was a way to repair damage caused by exposure to radiation, replacing the damaged tissue with synthetic flesh."

Lakesh drew in a long breath through his nostrils. "In any event, I and several scientists were revived around the same time. Those of us who needed it were operated on. After our recoveries, we were assigned to different villes and barons to help reshape the Earth in its new, secured and ordered image."

"And the Anthill? What of that?"

"As you know, its vast stockpile of predark artifacts supplied most of the technology now in use in the villes. The ordnance it held, at a conservative estimate, was the equivalent of three fully equipped military bases...not to mention the equivalent of several predark shopping malls—the big indoor ones, too, not the strip malls. After that, the Anthill became a forgotten installation."

Lakesh paused for a thoughtful few seconds. "No," he corrected himself. "A *feared* installation. Regardless of its original purpose, many of the barons viewed it as both a threat and an untapped treasure trove. But inasmuch as all the villes were standardized, equally matched in terms of technology and firepower to maintain a perfect balance of power, none of the barons dared mention what unclaimed wonders might still lie within Mount Rushmore.

"Even a word of wonder about it might be construed as a tendency toward ambition, a prelude to a territorial war. Such ambitions were strictly forbidden by the tenets of the Archon Directorate. Therefore, the Anthill became a taboo subject, no-baron's-land, so to speak."

Brigid made a "humph" sound of contemplation. "And what happens if a baron discovers what we did—that there is no Archon Directorate keeping watch from on high, prepared to obliterate any ville that threatens unity? When a baron learns that all of those doctrines were only dogma, a set of control mechanisms?''

''Then,'' answered Lakesh gravely, ''the balance of power may well become a balance of terror. We can only hope the conditioning of the baronial oligarchy is so deep they will never question the existence of the Directorate.''

Brigid nodded, trying to control her mounting apprehension. ''You said all the ordnance here in Cerberus came from the Anthill. If the place was off-limits, how did you manage it?''

A haunted expression misted over Lakesh's eyes. ''It wasn't hard for me to bypass the gateway's security lock-outs. I phased there, loaded what I needed onto the big cargo mat-trans and sent it to Cerberus. All over an extended period of time, of course.''

''There was no one living in the Anthill?''

''I wouldn't exactly call it living, but I saw signs of habitation.''

''And they didn't try to stop you?''

''No. It was as if I was allowed to take what I wanted.''

''Allowed? By whom?''

Lakesh cleared his throat. ''When I first awakened from my stasis sleep, I was aware—only for a fraction of a second—of a woman's presence nearby. That brief glimpse has given me nightmares ever since. She was so distorted, so horrifying, I convinced myself I had been hallucinating.

''Years later, when I made my secret forays into the Anthill, I sensed that same presence again. I never saw her, in fact I never saw anyone, but I felt eyes upon me. Her eyes, I fancied. I also received the unmistakable sensation that if anyone other than myself had trespassed there, they would have been killed instantly. I was given a special dispensation only because it was me. Perhaps for old times' sake."

Brigid narrowed her eyes. "Who do you think it was?"

In response, Lakesh opened a drawer in his desk and produced a small framed photograph. He handed it to her, and Brigid experienced a flash of disorientation. The pix showed Lakesh and a woman standing in front of the brown-tinted armaglass walls of the Cerberus mat-trans chamber. Except the man wasn't the same Lakesh who sat across the desk from her. If she hadn't seen the Lakesh of the twentieth century in an alternate time line, she would not have recognized him. Dark hair, mustache, big brown eyes and an ear-to-ear grin splitting his olive-complexioned face, the Lakesh of the past looked almost foolishly happy.

His arm was around the waist of a lovely blue-eyed woman. Her long blond hair with reddish highlights fell nearly to her waist in waves. Her pretty face held a happy smile that matched Lakesh's. That smile invoked a distant but distinct shock of recognition.

"That picture was taken right after the gateway here went on-line and made its inaugural transfer to another unit in another redoubt." Lakesh's voice was soft, almost a whisper.

"And this woman is Dian?"

Lakesh's response was so long in coming Brigid looked up from the photograph and almost repeated the question.

To her surprise, Lakesh's face suddenly collapsed in a pained network of furrows and wrinkles. "Yes," he said hoarsely. "That *was* Dian. Dr. Dian Baptiste."

Chapter 16

During her years as an archivist in Cobaltville's Historical Division, Brigid had perfected a poker face. Because archivists were always watched, it didn't do for them to show emotional reaction to a scrap of knowledge that might have escaped the censor's notice.

When she heard Lakesh's pronouncement, Brigid's composure failed her. She didn't gasp or drop the photograph, but she felt her throat constrict and her eyes widen. She was stunned into momentary paralysis. She couldn't take her eyes from the image of the smiling woman, now grasping why her smile had struck a chord of recognition. A cold pool of nausea quivered in the pit of her stomach.

Lakesh didn't wait for her to recover her emotional equilibrium. He plunged on, his words almost tumbling over one another in their haste to leave his mouth. "Don't jump to conclusions, please. Dian is not your great-great-grandmother—at least I don't think so. By the limb of the family tree I was able to trace through the records, she is more than likely a great-great-aunt."

Brigid finally found her voice. She said in a pained whisper, "She has my mother's smile."

"Yes," Lakesh solemnly agreed. "She does have Moira's smile."

Brigid's mother had literally disappeared from her life some thirteen years ago. One day she had returned home from her archivist's training class and Moira was gone. No note, no message. She left behind a framed photograph as the only evidence she had ever lived at all. Brigid had been forced to leave that sole memento behind when she escaped Cobaltville.

Brigid had made no inquiries into what had happened to her mother. People vanished from the residential Enclaves all the time, their flats never vacant for more than an hour. Asking about it only drew attention and suspicion.

Years later, when the Preservationists made their first covert contact with Brigid, slipping her a copy of the *Wyeth Codex,* she had found some small comfort in the remote possibility her mother was associated with the secret society of scholars.

Even that hope was dashed when she learned the group of renegades was a fabrication, a straw adversary concocted many years before by Lakesh to divert the barons from what he was really doing.

She never asked Lakesh about her mother's fate. But always on a deep, almost subliminal level, she had suspected Lakesh's involvement in her upbringing.

Still holding the photograph of Lakesh and Dian Baptiste, Brigid fastened her level gaze on Lakesh's face. She heard herself say, as if from a distance, "Is my connection to this woman the reason why you singled me out, chose me to be one of your rebels in exile?"

Lakesh couldn't meet her stare. He glanced down, groping and faltering for a response. Then he said simply, "Yes. But it's not quite as cut-and-dried as that."

"It never is with you." Her tone was hard and challenging. "Tell me about it, and save the whys and wherefores and lame justifications for later."

Lakesh's shoulders jerked in reaction to her truculent words. "As you wish. Once my position in Cobaltville was established, and I had won the complete trust of the baron, I reviewed all of the records, trying to find not just the genetic material from Dian, but also other people I had known, hoping their genotype had been selected for continuation. Dian's was indeed in storage, and her genetic characteristics had been utilized. At that time your mother had just been born. I observed her from afar, very infrequently and very, very secretly contributing to it.

"Many years later, when she reached reproductive age, I made a few small changes in the breeding-program records, altering the genetic matchups. I placed a secondary choice for your father at the top of the list."

Brigid knew child producing was considered the supreme social responsibility of ville citizens, but only the right kind of children. Therefore genetics and social standing were the most important criteria and actual matrimony was of secondary importance. A man and woman were bound together only for a length of time stipulated by a contract. For anyone to build an actual family unit was a violation of ville doctrine.

Love among humans was the hardest bond to break, so people were conditioned to believe that since all humans were intrinsically evil, to love one another was evil. That way, all human beings forever remained strangers to one another, and the concept of a family was worse than obsolete—it was seditious. When a child entered the training regimen at one of the ville divisions, the parents were required to separate so as not to interfere with their child's conditioning.

Brigid had never known her father, and her mother had never spoken of him except to say he no longer existed. She had interpreted her choice of words as an euphemism for dead. Now, a new possibility and a new chill suspicion filled her mind.

"Who was this secondary choice?" she demanded.

Without hesitation, Lakesh stated, "His name was Geoffrey Uther, one of my archivists. Shortly after the mating contract with Moira was approved, he died on a research assignment to the Outlands. His body was never recovered."

Brigid nodded speculatively. "I see. Geoffrey Uther. An unusual name."

Lakesh lifted a shoulder in a shrug. "Under the circumstances, with him dead, Moira gave you her family name rather than his."

"And his qualities were superior to those of the original choice?"

"I thought so," Lakesh said brusquely, obviously desiring to change the subject. "At any rate—"

Brigid cut him off. "As I recall, the legendary King Arthur was the son of a strange liaison between Ygerna, duchess of Cornwall, and King Uther Pendragon. Uther fell so violently in love with Ygerna he persuaded Merlin the magician to change him into a replica of the duke of Cornwall so that he might enter Tintagel Castle and her bed. Uther's men killed the real duke before the deception was discovered."

Lakesh sat silently and expressionlessly as Brigid recounted the ancient legend in a calm, contemplative voice. "The story is a mythic archetype, first recorded in 1137 by a Welshman named Geoffrey of Monmouth. I can see how recreating the myth, taking advantage of the baron's ignorance of culture, would appeal to you."

Brigid threw the framed photograph at him. It skimmed over the desk, and Lakesh avoided it only by twisting his upper body to one side. It struck the wall behind him with a jangle of splintering glass.

Coming to her feet in a rush, Brigid lunged across the desk and closed a hand around his throat. In a voice high and quaking with fury, she hissed, "You son of a bitch. How did you trick my mother into going along with that charade? Did you threaten her? What lies did you tell her? Why did you keep this from me?"

Lakesh didn't move, completely taken aback by her rage. He had seen her angry and upset in the past, particularly when she learned about the chromosomal damage she had sustained in the Black Gobi, but now she seemed engulfed by a near-homicidal anger.

Choosing his words with extreme care, Lakesh said reasonably, "Brigid, I did not threaten Moira or lie to her. Or lie with her, for that matter. Ectogenesis techniques were employed to impregnate her. As far as she knew at the time, Geoffrey Uther was a real man. She did not even meet me until after you were born.

"It was I who helped conceal your ability to produce eidetic images, which showed up on your earliest placement tests. She knew if your talent was discovered, you would be taken away while you were still an infant and trained in secret. Moira was grateful to me for my intervention. I revealed to her what I had done and why. We both agreed to keep the truth of your paternity a secret."

Brigid's grip on his throat loosened somewhat, so he went on. "It was due to that agreement I concealed the truth from you."

"And what happened to her?" Brigid demanded between clenched teeth. "Did you arrange for her to go away like you did with Kane's father—did the same thing happen to her?"

Lakesh's lips firmed in a tight line. "I swear to you I had nothing to do with Moira's disappearance. It came as much of a shock to me as it did to you. I can tell you this, though—whether she vanished against her will or by her own accord, neither the baron nor the Magistrates had anything to do with it. She was not under investigation or under suspicion of any crime, petty or large. However she did it, whatever her reasons, she disappeared from Cobaltville so thoroughly that not even my contacts could find any trace of her."

Although it required a great effort, Lakesh met Brigid's piercing stare. "I swear on my own mother's soul that is the truth."

Slowly, reluctantly, Brigid pulled her hand away from Lakesh's throat. She hugged herself, looking down at the floor. Dully, she said, "She was a nutritionist. When she stopped reporting for work, why didn't anyone come around to interrogate me?"

"I was able to deflect all inquiries of that sort, as well as pull the proper strings so you could stay in your flat. After all, I was the baron's most trusted adviser and no one dared to question my hands-off edicts pertaining to you."

"Am I supposed to thank you?"

"No," he answered. "But I want you to understand."

"In the way all daughters should understand their fathers?"

Lakesh's eyebrows rose and he forced himself to chuckle. "Dearest Brigid, transgenic cells were spliced with Moira's eggs. A mixture of enhanced characteristics derived from various superior sources. I'm not your father, although I took a very paternal interest in you. I protected you, kept you from coming to the baron's attention. Until, of course, you met Kane."

He gave her a jittery smile. "I hope that reassures you."

Dropping back into the chair, Brigid ran trembling fingers through her tousled mane of hair. She said nothing nor did she look in his direction.

"I know this is a great deal to absorb in one sitting," he persisted, "but we must return to the main topic."

"My great-great-aunt Dian," she murmured dourly. "I presume you're convinced she's the deformed woman on the tape?"

"Yes."

"And if she is, you intend to go there and do what? Rescue her? Propose to her?"

Lakesh bristled at her sarcasm. "I confess I haven't thought that far ahead. But Sindri is there in the Anthill, apparently locked in conflict with her. I'd prefer neither one killed the other. If Sindri is as brilliant as you claim he is, then he can be a valuable ally."

Brigid said curtly, "According to Leland, he stumbled onto something in a computer database there. But even though Sindri is seeking our help, he's not our friend."

"Nor a friend to the barons, either. What's that old saying—'the enemy of my enemy is my friend'? And there is another consideration."

"Which is?"

Lakesh stated grimly, "Sindri claimed he had stumbled onto something there that could tragically affect the lives of everyone in the world."

Brigid smiled a little contemptuously. "He has a

gift for theatrics. Something to which you should be able to relate.''

Lakesh ignored the observation. ''Regardless, there are things in the Anthill that fit that description.''

''Like what?''

''Small atomic devices, known in twentieth-century vernacular as backpack nukes. Not to mention an array of deadly biological agents and other...items.''

Brigid repeated, ''Like what?''

''Aren't those enough?'' he shot back, irritated. ''If Sindri isn't our friend, we cannot allow him to gain access to those weapons. The impression you gave of him was that of a child with urges for destruction for its own sake.''

Brigid couldn't argue with his comment.

''Conversely,'' continued Lakesh, ''if he fears the inhabitants of the Anthill intend to deploy them for some reason, we can't allow that, either.''

Brigid scowled at him. ''Would the Dian you know be a party to an undertaking like that?''

''No,'' he responded. ''The Dian I know is gone. The only way she could still be alive after all these years is if she were cyborganized like all the others. And if you consider how insanity spread like a virus within the walls of the Anthill—''

He broke off, squeezing his eyes shut and exhaling a shuddery breath. After a long moment, he opened his eyes and horror swirled within them. ''I am going to the Anthill. I ask you to accompany me, and I also ask you to persuade Kane to come with us. But I will hold you to your promise to keep the personal element of this conversation confidential."

Brigid pushed herself to her feet, feeling drained, emotionally enervated. "More of your secrets. And you want me to help you keep them."

"They're *our* secrets, dearest Brigid. Whatever Dian Baptiste is now, she is your family, perhaps the only family you will ever have."

Lakesh's reference to her barren condition caused her eyes to narrow. Affecting not to have noticed, he intoned, "Moreover, she is the only woman I have ever loved and more than likely the only one I ever will. Even if Sindri wasn't involved and I'd learned Dian still lived in some fashion, I would insist on going to the Anthill."

She rubbed her forehead in weariness. "Just you, me and Kane?"

"And Leland."

"Grant and Domi will want to know why they're being excluded."

"We'll tell them to stand by here in case we need to be rescued." Lakesh smiled crookedly. "That sounds reasonable, doesn't it? And it's also the truth."

Brigid stepped to the door. "Yes. And that's getting to be quite the rare commodity in this place."

Chapter 17

The Intel section of the Magistrate Division had no windows. The only light illuminating the vault-walled, spacious room was provided by flickering vid monitor screens, comp stations and various readouts. The monitors displayed black-and-white images transmitted from the residential Enclaves, the promenades and even the Tartarus Pits. In the background was the clatter of keyboards, the beeping of machines, and crisp voices of officers communicating with other villes and Magistrates out in the field.

Kearney's eyes felt like poached eggs liberally sprinkled with hot sand. As he closed in on his twentieth hour without so much as a catnap, his back ached abominably, his neck tendons spasmed like snakes exposed to high voltage and his wrist and metacarpal bones screamed with pain.

He hadn't spent so much time sitting before a comp station since the first couple of years of his assignment to the Intel section. Usually, if he needed some information or data dredged out of the memory banks, one of his fellow officers did it for him. They didn't perform the tasks out of friendship, but out of intimidation.

For a very long time, Kearney had used his imposing size and threatening manner to avoid what he considered scut work, delegating his no-glory assignments to the other Mags in the section yet assuming credit on their completion.

Once, nearly three years ago, small, swarthy Morales had asked him snidely if he was such a ball-buster why he hadn't been chosen to be a hard-contact Mag, inasmuch as he was even bigger than Grant. Kearney hadn't bothered to answer him then.

He waited until Morales was off duty, and caught him on his way to his flat. He beat him not only severely but scientifically. He did just enough damage to keep Morales out of the medical ward, but also to keep him limping and pissing blood for a week.

Kearney had learned the long-term benefits of physical violence from his father, who actually had been a hard-contact Mag. His father taught him the ideal result of beating a man didn't lie in the pain that was inflicted—it was the creation of a beaten man, both in body and spirit, that mattered most.

After that beating, Morales had never made a snide remark or even made direct eye contact with him again. He had performed any and all assignments Kearney shunted off to him without a murmur of complaint.

A few months later, Kearney practiced a variation of the technique with a woman he fancied who worked in the Manufacturing Division. When she told him she and her lover were waiting for their marriage contract to be approved, he arranged for her to be brought in for questioning on a completely fictitious charge. In the holding cell, he raped her. Then he let her go, knowing the memory of her violation would poison the act of making love for a long time to come. He took a great deal of pleasure in that knowledge.

But now even those memories brought him no joy. The fear that had possessed him for the past twenty-four hours canceled out everything, even recollections of simpler times.

When Abrams marched into the Intel section at the beginning of his shift, Kearney at first didn't recognize him. With his beard and hair trimmed and groomed, and attired in the high-collared, pearl-gray duty bodysuit, the man did not resemble in the least the shuffling, dirty prisoner he had escorted up to A level only a few hours before. Despite his cane, the only hint of the deprivations Abrams had suffered was the dark rings around his flint-hard eyes.

Those eyes had carefully surveyed every officer in the room, then fixed on Kearney. When Abrams barked his name, Kearney rushed to him and stood at attention, his stomach turning cold flip-flops.

In a clipped, no-nonsense tone, but loud enough for everyone to hear, Abrams said, "Kearney, I have a special assignment for you. It supersedes all your other duties. It is a project for the baron and my eyes only. I've selected you to head it."

Kearney's flush of pride washed away his trepidation. "I'm honored, sir."

"In fact," Abrams continued as if he hadn't heard, "not only will you head the project—you'll be its sole member."

A little of the trepidation returned, and Kearney asked, "What is its nature, sir?"

"That we will discuss in private. But first there is a small ritual to be completed."

"Ritual?" Kearney echoed. He was so puzzled he couldn't even speculate.

With a speed belying his age, Abrams whipped the metal ferrule of his cane up between Kearney's legs. Engulfed by a surge of agony, Kearney jackknifed at the waist.

Abrams slipped the hook of his cane around the nape of his neck and yanked him violently to the floor. Planting a boot heel on the back of the man's hand, Abrams slowly rested his entire weight on it. Despite the pain flaring through him, Kearney felt the eyes of all the Intel officers upon him, and he sensed their amused approval.

Dimly, through the blood pounding in his temples, he heard Abrams say dispassionately, "A wounded lion is still a lion, Kearney. And wounds heal. Even jackals know that. Past time you learned it, too."

Abrams stepped away and ordered him to his feet. Kearney accompanied him to his office, his physical pain overwhelmed by a heavy fog of humiliation. He understood that Abrams had accomplished what he had set out to do. Within a handful of seconds, his pride was ripped like a layer of dead skin to expose the beaten man that lay beneath.

In Abrams's office, Kearney learned his assignment—to sift through any and all intelligence reports regarding the ore mines and the attacks on the caravans, then present him with a unrefutable identification of the raiders and their method of operation. The administrator made it very clear he expected Kearney to devote all of his waking hours to it until he completed the assignment.

It sounded simple enough, the way Abrams phrased it, but in practice Kearney learned it was like a fiendishly complicated digital scavenger hunt. Most of the eyewitnesses were members of the caravan parties and most of them were chilled. Those who survived tended to gravitate toward Outland settlements, often in other ville territories.

By the time any Intel officers reached these settlements, the witnesses had moved on, leaving only highly dubious secondhand accounts, which were repeated by acquaintances. These reports filtered back slowly to the Intel sections of the respective Magistrate Divisions. He was forced to confront the essential inefficiency of the entire network of the so-called unified villes.

The nine baronies that survived the long wars over territorial expansion and resources had divided control of the continent among themselves, but they were supposed to be interdependent. Kearney realized just how little genuine give-and-take went on among the villes.

The fleeting notion that the caravan raiders appeared far more organized and efficient than the Mag Divisions occurred to him. Whoever led the raiders could conceivably turn his attention to the villes themselves. He tried to dismiss the concept as paranoia. Every so often, rumors floated from the Outlands about an army of the disenfranchised building strength to attack the villes. In his eighteen years as an Intel officer, not a single one of the rumors proved to have any foundation.

There were Roamer bands, marauding outlaws who claimed their depredations were acts of rebellion. But even the largest group of Roamers, led by a slagger calling himself Le Loup Garou, was nothing more than a collection of back-shooting scavengers, their best weapons only home-forged muzzle loaders. A single squad of Mags could easily eliminate the entire band—if they could be found. But Le Loup Garou's name was conspicuously absent from all the Intel reports Kearney scanned. The Roamer was not a suspect.

So Kearney, sitting before the comp terminal and reading one file after another, grappled to control a mounting frustration so intense it felt like a madness. His emotional and mental stability was further eroded by Abrams's hourly demands for status reports.

Kearney knew everyone in the big room enjoyed his torture, snickering behind their hands, wagering on how long it would take before he cracked. He wasn't sure himself anymore.

Abrams's iron-hard voice blared from the wall trans-comm for the fifth time in as many hours. "Kearney. Update."

KEARNEY'S MUTED VOICE, tone overlaid with a thick blanket of humility, filtered out of the comm unit on

Abrams's desk. "Sir, I'm reviewing the transcript of an interview with a friend of a friend of a surviving eyewitness to the last raid."

"I see. And when you do foresee having the final, comprehensive report for me?" Despite his grim, uncompromising tone, Abrams's lips creased in a smile.

A nervous cough wafted from the speaker. "Sir, I hope to have a provisional draft for you to review by tomorrow morning."

"I see," Abrams said again. He met Guende's eye and grinned, but his words dripped with sarcasm and more than a hint of menace. "I will expect your report by then. But it will not be a provisional draft, Kearney. It will be the final one that tells me everything I wish to know. I will expect it to answer questions I haven't even asked. Is that understood?"

Kearney's timid, hopeless "Understood, sir" was very nearly inaudible.

"Speak up, Kearney."

Louder, but sounding no less defeated, Kearney repeated, "Understood, sir."

Abrams released the transmit key of the comm unit and laughed loudly. Guende smiled, too, but said, "I don't blame you for victimizing the sadistic fool. But don't you think you're devoting too much time to terrorizing him? The baron gave you an assignment, too."

Abrams simply shrugged, tapping a file folder on the corner of his desk. "It's completed."

Guende pursed his lips disapprovingly. "So quickly? What was his reaction?"

"I haven't informed the baron yet. I've my own plans to make first."

The small man shivered, whipping his head around toward the spy-eye vid lens bolted to the wall just beneath the ceiling molding.

"Don't worry," Abrams told him reassuringly. "A long time ago I altered it so it plays the same image on continuous loop. If any of the internal monitor officers noticed, they never raised the issue. One of the advantages of being the division administrator."

Guende continued to stare at it, as if it were a blaster barrel trained on him. He murmured, "Who watches the watchmen?"

"In this instance," retorted Abrams brusquely, leaning back in his chair, "no one."

The small adviser blinked in discomfort at Abrams's self-possession. Under the circumstances, his attitude seemed not only premature but completely misplaced. "Baron Cobalt gave you a second chance, an opportunity to redeem yourself. It's not like you to push him."

A little flare of anger lit up Abrams's eyes. "I'm not pushing him. But by the same token, I'm not defaulting myself into believing he pardoned me out of altruism."

"Of course not," Guende agreed nervously. "After what happened in Dulce, and with the attacks on the ore shipments, he needs people he can trust."

"I don't give a damn about who is behind the caravan attacks." Abrams's brows knitted together over the bridge of his nose. "Kearney could present me with complete biographies of all the raiders and a perfect counterattack plan and I'd still reject it.''

''But if the baron finds out—''

''The baron needs me,'' interrupted Abrams. ''He can't afford to either execute or alienate any member of the Trust. Not at this juncture.''

Guende frowned. ''Why do you say that?''

Abrams lifted his right hand, four fingers extended. ''One—despite the stories he has spread about Kane, Grant and Baptiste being dead, they are far from it. Most of my Mags know this and therefore morale is at an historical low. Incarcerating me, their sole authority figure, did not help matters. I was released as a form of damage control.''

He folded his index finger. ''Two—some time ago Baron Cobalt took me into his confidence. He made me privy to secrets he has shared with no one else. He needs confidants. He has neither the experience nor the wherewithal to rule the ville completely alone.''

Abrams bent his middle finger against his palm. ''Three—and the baron has been entertaining ambitions of expanding his territory. Once again, he can't do that alone.''

Guende stared at him in baffled astonishment. Sounding scandalized, he exclaimed, ''Expand Cobaltville's territory? Infringe upon those of the other barons?''

Abrams nodded.

''That violates the entire spirit of the unification

program! The Directorate expressly forbids such actions!"

Abrams bestowed a patronizing smile upon the small man. He said, "Four—Baron Cobalt is toying with me. He charged me with the task of finding a viable alternative to the Dulce facility when in truth he knew one existed all along."

Abrams folded his fourth finger and linked his hands behind his head. "I knew damn well what he wanted me to find. I've been aware of the place for some years now."

Guende squinted toward him in bewilderment. "Aware of what place?"

Abrams grinned at the man's confusion. "The one place off-limits to the baronial hierarchy, cloaked in so much secrecy it's become almost a legend. The mother of all stockpiles. The Anthill."

Guende's squint deepened into a rictus of pain. "The Anthill? I never heard of it."

"There's no reason why you should have, my friend. Over the years, in the culture of the barons, it's evolved into a taboo. Only X-coded archives have any reference to it."

"Is that where you learned about it?"

Abrams nodded. "You know that Lakesh and a few other highly placed people in the villes were freezies, don't you?"

"Selected predark scientists who hibernated through the skydark and were revived to serve unification. Yes, I know that. Every member of the Trust knows that."

"Didn't you ever wonder where they had been sleeping for all those decades?"

Guende lifted his downsloping shoulders in a shrug. "No, it never occurred to me. I supposed it was in one of the redoubts."

"It was the Anthill," Abrams declared, "which was and is far more than a redoubt. I think it's safe to say that without the Anthill, there never would have been the unification program, perhaps not even the nine barons. It was in many ways the cornerstone for our society. Everything we have here in Cobaltville—in all the villes, for that matter—derived in some fashion from the Anthill."

The bearded man's offhand pronouncements shook Guende far more than if he had engaged in theatrics. "And Baron Cobalt wants to secure this place?"

"He does indeed. I don't blame him."

Guende cleared his throat. "What will you do?"

The burn-reddened face of Abrams stretched in a huge, immensely amused grin. "I intend to act on the advice you gave to me yesterday morning, old friend. I intend to plan some catastrophes."

Chapter 18

The hammer dropped and the big revolver bucked in Kane's hands, the bore lipping flame and thunder. The .44-caliber, 246-grain round drilled through the man's forehead, barely a half inch above his right eyebrow.

Tiny scraps of paper exploded in a spray. They were swept away by the midmorning breeze and carried over the edge of the cliff. The abyss plummeted straight down a thousand feet or more. At one time, steel guardrails had bordered the rim of the plateau, but only a few rusted metal stanchions remained. Kane had erected a man-shaped and -sized target between two of them.

He frowned at the Dan Wesson .44 pistol with its eight-inch barrel, then squinted toward the target a hundred feet away.

"I think you nailed him," said Brigid as she crossed the tarmac toward his improvised firing range.

Kane glanced over his shoulder. Unlike him, she wore the tight-fitting, one-piece white bodysuit that unofficially served as the redoubt's uniform. He was attired in a checked flannel shirt, jeans and running shoes pilfered from the stockpile of predark clothing.

She came to his side, briefly inspecting the blue-steel revolver in his hands. "Looks heavier than your Sin Eater."

"They weigh about the same. There's a lot more kick to this, though. The muzzle velocity gives it more stopping power."

"Are you thinking about trading up?"

He shook his head. "Never cared much for revolvers, double-action or not. I just think it's a good idea to get in some practice with all the different kinds of blasters we have here. Want to try it?"

She smiled wryly. "I've had my fill of musketry for a while."

"You didn't even carry a blaster out in the field this last time, much less use one. You need to find one you're comfortable with."

Brigid's distaste for firearms had been a minor point of contention between them for the last several months. For a while she had carried an H&K VP-70, then a Beretta, but she found the weight and recoil of both guns a little uncomfortable. She had opted for a .32-caliber Mauser at one point, but its range and accuracy depended on too many variables. She'd carried an Uzi for a bit, but never had to fire it.

"Not right now," she said stiffly. "I need to talk to you."

"Go ahead." Facing the target again, Kane assumed a combat stance, holding the revolver in both hands. He sighted down the Wesson's length and squeezed the trigger.

The cracking report made Brigid jump and sent echoes rolling across the mountain peak. Fingering her ears, she said sourly, "It's louder than your Sin Eater, too."

Kane peered at the target through the shifting plane of cordite smoke. "Better," he muttered distractedly. Turning to her, he said, "I'm waiting."

"Can we talk without you damaging my hearing with that thing?" Her tone was peevish.

"I guess so." He lowered the pistol. "Shoot."

Brigid frowned at his attempt at humor. "I talked to Lakesh last night, you know."

He nodded, then looked into her face and uttered an exasperated groan. "I know that look, Baptiste. He's talked you into going along with one of his fused-out schemes—like going with him to that Ant-hill place."

"Yes. He asked me to go with him. Moreover, he asked me to ask you if you'd go with us."

Kane assumed an expression of pondering the topic. "Is that all?"

"Yes."

He turned back to the target. "Tell him I said no."

Brigid knew he was being deliberately provocative, so she didn't show her annoyance. Besides, she had expected his reaction.

"He said he was going anyway, Kane. And after thinking it over last night, I agree with his reasons. I'm going with him."

Centering the blade sight of the revolver on the target, Kane said in a very disinterested tone, "No, I don't think so."

He squeezed the trigger, and the tranquil mountain

air vibrated with the eardrum-knocking crack. Kane grunted in satisfaction. This time the round punched through the target exactly where he wanted it.

As the echoes of the shot still rolled, Brigid demanded hotly, "You don't think so what?"

Letting the pistol dangle at the end of his right arm, he faced her. "I don't think you're going."

She opened her mouth to voice an angry rebuke, but he overrode her words by saying sternly, "This isn't an official op. It hasn't been put to a vote. It's another one of Lakesh's personal interests, another whim he wants us to help him indulge. We all agreed after the business with Rouch that Cerberus would operate more democratically, not like Lakesh's little fiefdom." He smiled tightly. "And those were your words, not mine."

Brigid said nothing for a long, tense tick of time, knowing he had her. Calmly, she stated, "I don't need you to remind me of my choice of phrases. But while the reason Lakesh wants to go the Anthill might be personal, it's certainly not a whim. He convinced me of that."

"Then you're going to have to convince me, Baptiste."

She brushed a breeze-tossed strand of hair away from her face. "The Anthill was the primary Continuity of Government installation, and served as the major supply depot for all of the villes during the unification program."

"So Lakesh has said," Kane interjected.

"What he *didn't* say is that there is still a tremendous amount of matériel stored in there, a lot of it very dangerous. Nuclear warheads, nerve agents, bio-warfare contagions. Do you want Sindri to get his hands on all of that?"

After a second, Kane answered, "No, I don't. But it wasn't that particular prospect that shook up Lakesh so much."

"True," admitted Brigid. "He thinks he recognized someone on the tape Leland brought."

"The two-faced woman?"

Hesitantly, reluctantly, Brigid replied, "Yes."

"Who is she?"

"I'm not at liberty to divulge that."

Kane's blue-gray eyes instantly turned cold and remote. His tone reflected that frostiness. "More goddamn secrets. The old bastard just can't stop hoarding them, can he?"

"He's lived three times as long as we have, Kane. He has more experiences."

"And he's done three times as many things he doesn't want us to find out about. I guess that woman is one of them."

Brigid kept silent, her poker face not registering either a confirmation or a denial. Privately she damned Lakesh for forcing her not only to act as his advocate for the mission, but also to obscure the main reason for it.

"He's persuaded you this is important?" Kane inquired.

"He has."

"I suppose I can run it past Grant and Domi—"

"No," she broke in curtly. "Lakesh wants only you, me and Leland to go with him."

His eyes widened then narrowed. "Two academics, a troll and me?"

Testily, she retorted, "I'm not an academic, Kane."

He smiled ruefully and acknowledged her comment with a short nod. "I stand corrected. But that still leaves only me to pack the musketry. Why does he want to cut out Domi and Grant?"

"He feels it would be best if they stood by as backup in case we need to be rescued. Besides, since Sindri wants our help, we have allies already in place there."

"Sindri says he wants our help," Kane remarked darkly. "He said he wanted our help the last time, too. I don't have to jog your memory about how that turned out."

"Not at all. I don't trust him much more than you do. That's why we can't allow him access to the weapons that may still be stockpiled in the installation."

Kane's brow furrowed as he gauged the logic of her words. At length, he made a sweeping gesture with the barrel of the revolver. "All right, Baptiste, as long as we're agreed it's a recce to see the lay of the land and make contact with Sindri. I'll take you at your word this is important."

"You have my word." She paused, and added, "I'd like your word on something, too."

"Which is?"

"That if we get into a tight spot, you'll be more circumspect than you were in New Mexico. Curb your reckless impulses, don't try to blast our way out of it. We still aren't sure who is friend or foe in the Anthill."

He forced a hard, grim smile. "Then we should feel right at home."

Quickly, Brigid briefed him on what Lakesh claimed they could expect of the conditions in the Anthill. They crossed the tarmac together, toward the open sec door.

When the redoubt was built, the plateau had been protected by a force field, powered by atomic generators. Sometime over the past century, the energy screen had been permanently deactivated, so new defenses had to be created. Although they couldn't be noticed from the road, an elaborate system of heat-sensing warning devices, night-vision vid cameras and motion-trigger alarms surrounded the mountain peak. It could be safely assumed that no one or nothing could approach Cerberus undetected—not that there was any reason to do so.

As they entered the dimly lit main corridor, Kane was struck once again by how oppressive the vast installation seemed, especially after spending the past hour outdoors. He had often tried to picture what the place had been like before the nukes flew, bustling with activity, purpose and people. Now it was full of vacant corridors, empty rooms and sepulchral silences.

"When does Lakesh want to leave?" he asked.

Brigid consulted her wrist chron. "As soon as possible. Leland's been jumping up and down to get back to Sindri, too. Let's say half an hour."

Kane spun the Wesson .44 around by the trigger guard and nearly dropped it. "Shit," he hissed.

She affected not to notice his embarrassment.

"I'll take this cannon back to the armory and pick up a few odds and ends to take with us. Including a blaster for you."

She shook her head. "Not necessary. The last three times we went out into the field, I didn't fire a single shot."

"Things change," he told her with an edge in his voice. "It's better to have a blaster and not need it than to need it and—"

"Oh, spare me," Brigid said irritably.

"I'll choose something you can handle. I'll meet you, Lakesh and Sneezy in the ready room in half an hour."

She arched an eyebrow. "Sneezy?"

He shrugged as he turned the corner. "One of the vids here was a cartoon about a princess who hooked up with seven dwarfs."

"I know," Brigid replied. "I'm just surprised you went to the trouble of watching it."

"Grant and Domi were watching it. I just sat in."

He strode down the corridor past the vehicle depot and workroom and entered an open doorway. He thumbed the flat toggle switch on the door frame, and the overhead fluorescent fixtures blazed on, flooding the armory with a white sterile light.

The big square room was stacked nearly to the ceiling with wooden crates and boxes. Many of the crates were stenciled with the legend Property U.S. Army.

Glass-fronted gun cases lined the four walls, containing automatic assault rifles, many makes and models of subguns and dozens of semiautomatic blasters. Heavy assault weaponry occupied the north wall, bazookas, tripod-mounted M-249 machine guns, mortars and rocket launchers.

He had been told that all of the ordnance was of predark manufacture. Caches of matériel had been laid down in hermetically sealed Continuity of Government installations before the nukecaust. Protected from the ravages of the outraged environment, nearly every piece of munitions and hardware was as pristine as the day it rolled off the assembly line.

After returning the revolver to its case, he surveyed another case. He picked out a pair of autopistols, both manufactured by Iver Johnson. One, a TP-22B, was fairly small and lightweight, less than fifteen ounces. However, it was chambered for .22-caliber long rounds, and though .22-cals had the penetration, they carried no real stopping power unless a target was struck in the heart or the head.

He chose the 9 mm instead, figuring Brigid wouldn't find its 26-ounce weight and six-inch length too unwieldy. It came equipped with an ambidextrous safety that would reduce the amount of fumbling-around time if the situation turned ugly.

He loaded two magazines with six Parabellum rounds apiece, then glanced over at the two suits of

Magistrate body armor mounted on metal frameworks. He eyed his suit speculatively. Though relatively light, the polycarbonate was sufficiently dense to deflect every caliber of projectile, up to and including a .45-caliber slug. It absorbed and redistributed a bullet's kinetic impact, minimizing the chance of incurring hydrostatic shock.

The armor was close-fitting, molded to conform to the biceps, triceps, pectorals and abdomen. The only spot of color anywhere on it was the small, disk-shaped badge of office emblazoned on the left pectoral. It depicted, in crimson, a stylized balanced scales of justice, superimposed over a nine-spoked wheel. It symbolized the Magistrate's oath to keep the wheels of justice in the nine villes turning.

Like the armor, the helmets were made of black polycarbonate, and fitted over the upper half and back of the head, leaving only portions of the mouth and chin exposed.

The slightly convex, red-tinted visor served several functions—it protected the eyes from foreign particles, and the electrochemical polymer was connected to a passive night sight that intensified ambient light to permit one-color night vision.

He devoted a few moments' consideration to the wisdom of wearing the armor, then decided the Mag-issue coat he had appropriated from Rhine would suffice. It offered a degree of protection against penetration weapons, and was insulated against all weathers, including acid-rain showers. Trans-comm circuitry was sewn inside the lapels, terminating in tiny pin mikes connected to a thin wire pulley. If he was cut off from Lakesh and Brigid and searched, the transceiver would pass a cursory inspection.

Lifting a crate lid, he removed four grens from their foam cushions—an implode, two incens, and a high-ex. He attached them to the combat harnesses he would wear beneath his coats. He clipped three 20-round magazines for his Sin Eater to the harness, as well.

He took his holstered Sin Eater from the hook behind his body armor and left the arsenal, carrying all the ordnance to his quarters. Once there, he dressed warmly in a heavy, turtleneck sweater, and put on fleece-lined, thick-soled boots with steel-reinforced toes. He sheathed his fourteen-inch combat knife, the razor-keen blade forged of dark blued steel at his hip.

After strapping on both the combat harness and the Sin Eater holster, he shrugged into his coat and slipped a Nighthawk microlight and his dark-lensed night-vision glasses into a pocket. The treated polymer lenses of the glasses allowed him to see clearly in deep shadow as long as there was some kind of light source, no matter how feeble or indirect.

There came a rap on the door, a knock he recognized. "Come," he called out.

Grant pushed open the door and stepped in, eyes shadowed by his drawn-down brows. "What's this about you, Brigid and Lakesh taking that troll back to the Anthill?"

"It's just a scout-out."

"Yeah," he rumbled sourly. "I remember how a lot of our own scouts turned out."

Kane tugged a fingerless black glove onto his right hand. The textured palm allowed a secure, frictionless grip on the butt of his Sin Eater. "This isn't an op. If it turns into one, we're jumping out fast."

"Then why are you going?" demanded Grant.

"Because Baptiste asked me to. She and Lakesh would just go without me."

Grant folded his arms over his broad chest and leaned against the door frame. "You could stop them."

"How, short of locking them both up? We don't need any more dissension here, not when we've finally reached a point where we can a make a difference against the barons."

"But to freeze me out—"

"You're not frozen out—you're on standby. If we're not back in say, six hours, you and Domi can come after us."

Grant snorted. "If you don't come back from dark territory, then I'm supposed to jump into dark territory after you. A hell of a strategy."

Kane rolled up the right sleeve of the coat to adjust the straps of his blaster holster. The cuff was just a bit larger than the left to accommodate the Sin Eater. "Like I said, they'd go anyway. I was asked to nursemaid them, so I am. I don't care for it any more than you do."

"And if you stroll into a trap laid by Sindri?" Grant challenged. "I was just an annoyance to him, but he put you on the top of his enemies list, remember?''

"Very clearly. And if I get my ass stuck in his trap, I'll expect you to show up and unstick it.''

"As usual,'' Grant replied with undisguised sarcasm. He stepped aside, and Kane moved toward the door.

"It's not just Sindri,'' said Kane. "There's something else, something Lakesh feels very strongly about.''

As they walked into the corridor, Grant declared, "Nothing new about that. He feels very strongly about something on the average of once a month. And then we end up being chased, shot at, blown up, buried or drowned.''

They strode along the wide passageway beneath great curving ribs of metal that supported the high rock roof. The vanadium alloy that sheathed the floor muted their footfalls.

Grant gusted out a sigh of resignation. "I guess I should know better than to try and talk you out of anything.''

"There's no need to try. It's not like this is a one-percenter.''

"Yet,'' Grant muttered.

Lakesh, Leland and Brigid were in the ready room when they entered. The transadapt slitted his eyes at Kane's approach, then glanced away.

Brigid wore a long, fur-collared leather coat with voluminous pockets. She was checking the contents of a flat case containing emergency medical supplies, including hypodermics of pain suppressants, stimulants and antibiotics. A trans-comm unit, a rad counter, the motion detector and a square metal-and-leather case holding survival rations lay on the table.

Lakesh was attired in a quilted down jacket, heavy gloves and a knit stocking cap. He wound a woolen scarf around his throat.

"Is it that cold where we're going?" Kane asked.

Brigid nodded in Leland's direction. "He says it's cold, and you know transadapts were engineered to tolerate very low temperatures."

Kane turned his attention to Lakesh, noting the tremor in his hands as he knotted the scarf. "Are you sure you're up for this, old man?"

Lakesh peered at him over the rims of his eyeglasses. "No, friend Kane, I'm not sure. But there's nothing novel about that."

"Are you packing?"

"You mean a firearm?"

"Yeah."

Lakesh shook his head. "I presumed you would more than adequately hold up that end."

Kane removed the Iver Johnson autopistol from his coat pocket and handed it to Brigid. "You can help me hold up that end with this."

Her eyes flickered with momentary irritation, but she took the blaster without a murmur of protest, slipping it into a pocket.

"I've already programmed the destination codes and autosequencer," Lakesh announced. "We may leave at any time."

Leland immediately scuttled toward the jump platform and entered the chamber. Grant looked toward a digital wall chron in the ops center. "Six hours from now?"

Kane nodded. "Right."

"Six hours from now what?" Lakesh asked a little nervously.

"If you're not back in six hours," Grant retorted, "me and Domi will come after you, loaded for dwarf."

Lakesh swallowed and stepped toward the gateway, slinging the ration case over a shoulder by its strap. "It's not a dwarf that occupies me."

Brigid slipped the motion detector over her left wrist, pinned the rad counter to her lapel and handed the medical kit to Kane. The three people entered the gateway unit. Right above the keypad encoding panel, imprinted in faded maroon letters, were the words Entry Absolutely Forbidden To All But B12 Cleared Personnel. Mat-Trans. Even Lakesh did not know what had become of the B12-cleared personnel, though he had opined they had probably jumped from the installation after skydark, desperately searching for a place better than Cerberus and doubtless not finding it.

Using the metal handle affixed to the center of the armaglass, Kane closed the heavy door behind them, the lock mechanism triggering the automatic jump initiator. The sec lock clicked and the automatic transit process began. All of them understood, in theory, that the mat-trans units required a dizzying number of maddeningly intricate electronic procedures, all occurring within milliseconds of one another, to minimize the margins for error. The actual conversion process was automated for this reason, sequenced by an array of computers and microprocessors.

The disks above and below them exuded a silvery glow, and wraiths of white mist formed on the ceiling and floor. Tiny static discharges, like miniature lightning bolts, flared in the vapor. As if from a great distance came a whine, which quickly grew in pitch to a drone, then became a howl like a gale-force wind.

None of them felt any pain, only a mild shock and then a sensation of plummeting headlong into an impenetrable sepia sea.

Chapter 19

Kane opened his eyes, feeling a mild band of pain across his temples. He lay still, his vision still fogged as he recovered from the mat-trans jump.

He felt a heavy pressure in his ears and could only dimly hear the hum of the emitter array beneath his body cycling down to shutoff. Only his sense of smell seemed to work normally, and after the first tentative whiff of air through his nostrils, he wished it were as impaired as his sight and hearing.

The air was cold, but damp and clammy, like the cloying atmosphere around a bog in the dead of winter. The chill penetrated through his clothes to his very bones, making old injuries ache.

A fetid odor permeated the air, a stench Kane associated with a slaughterhouse, or the poorly buried body he had come across once during a patrol of the Tartarus Pits. The effluvium wasn't quite dense enough to trigger nausea, but it made him want to pinch his nostrils shut.

The patterned glow of the overhead metal disks faded completely, and Kane heard his companions stirring around him. Lakesh groaned faintly and wheezed a few words in a language Kane didn't understand.

Hiking himself up to his elbows, then to a sitting position, Kane squinted around at their surroundings. The armaglass walls of the jump chamber gleamed greenish-blue, reminding him somewhat of the Irish Sea. Its size appeared to be identical to the unit in Cerberus.

Brigid sat up, resting her forehead on her knees as she endured a wave of vertigo. "All things considered, we've had worse transits," she murmured.

Even the cleanest of jumps left the brain temporarily confused and disoriented, but that was nothing compared to the time when they made a transit to a malfunctioning unit in Russia. The matter-stream modulations couldn't be synchronized with the destination lock, and Kane, Brigid and Grant suffered a severe case of jump sickness—vomiting, debilitating weakness and hallucinations.

Leland sprang to his feet, reeling dizzily for a moment, then moved to the door. He fumbled with the handle, and Kane snapped, "Hold on that, Sneezy. Wait until we're all afoot."

The transadapt glowered at him, but subsided.

Weakly, Lakesh tried to sit up, and he required Brigid's help. "Sorry," he rasped. "Haven't made a jump in several months. Give me just a moment."

Kane climbed to his feet, tottering for a second, steadying himself with a hand on the translucent glass wall. He fingered his nose. "We should've brought respirators with us."

"You stay here awhile," Leland commented, "you'll get used to it."

With Brigid's help, Lakesh staggered to his feet, swaying on unsteady legs. Although it was difficult to tell in the feeble light shining from the fixture in the center of the ceiling panels, he looked ashen and ill.

"You're not going to throw up again, are you?" Kane asked him.

Lakesh covered his nose and mouth with his scarf. "The smell—"

"I'm told you'll get used to it," Kane drawled.

Brigid shot him an angry glare, then extended her left arm, sweeping the motion detector in short arcs. "Clear."

Kane put on his night-vision glasses and tensed his wrist tendons, and the Sin Eater slapped into his waiting palm. He lifted and turned the chamber's handle, and the heavy door swung open silently and easily. As he expected, the door opened into a control room, filled with whirring consoles and dancing lights.

The charnel house odor rushed into the chamber like a tidal wave. Lakesh uttered a retching, gagging noise behind his scarf. Kane fought down a rise of bile and forced himself to breathe through his mouth. The solution wasn't perfect since a faint, vile taste coated his tongue, making him want to spit.

Brigid winced, but said nothing. "Where's Sindri from here?" she asked Leland.

The transadapt shrugged. "I don't know. We'll have to look for him."

"Didn't you use any comms?" inquired Kane.

"Uh-uh."

"Great," Kane half snarled. "And how big is this place again?"

"Big," mumbled Lakesh. "Monstrously big. But I believe I know where we are. Judging by the color of the glass, I think this is an auxiliary personnel gateway on Level Two."

"Auxiliary?" echoed Kane. "How many are in the Anthill?"

"Not counting the cargo units, three. There's another cargo gateway hidden in a cave a few miles away used to transport large, heavy items into here."

Kane grunted in interest. "Cargo mat-trans units? How big are they?"

"Big."

Brigid turned to Leland. "This is the gateway you materialized in when you made the jump from *Parallax Red,* isn't it?"

The transadapt nodded. His eyes darted back and forth uneasily. "Thought perhaps Sindri would leave somebody here to meet me."

"It could be your crew jumped back out," Kane suggested. "Back to the station."

Leland thought that over, then muttered, "Don't think so."

Lakesh stepped out first. They followed him through the control room, and Kane noted how the glass-covered gauges glistened with condensation. Passing through a doorway, they entered a high-ceilinged, narrow corridor. Lakesh stopped, looked from his left to his right, then turned to the left. They became aware of a distant, grinding rhythmic sound like the pulse beat of some great piece of machinery in need of a lubricant.

The walls of the passageway were damp, and faint tendrils of mist drifted under the ceiling. The only light was a dim bluish radiance from neon strips. The cold, shadowless illumination made their flesh look pallid and unhealthy.

"Do you know where you're going?" Kane asked Lakesh.

"More or less," he answered distractedly. "It's been well over twenty years since I last visited here."

Increasing his pace, Kane caught up to Lakesh. "Let me take the point."

"I know what I'm looking for, friend Kane. You don't."

"Which is what exactly?"

Lakesh stopped abruptly. "This." Turning and facing the right-hand wall, he said loudly, "Complex display."

Mystified, Kane glanced from Lakesh to the blank expanse of bulkhead. Lines of consternation appeared around the old man's eyes. He pulled the scarf from his mouth and repeated, "Complex display." He struck the wall with the heel of his left hand.

Suddenly a three-by-three-foot square of wall panel shimmered and became a network of throbbing lines and pulsing dots. The lines and dots were a confusing mishmash of flickering colors.

"What the hell is that thing?" demanded Kane.

"It's a map and personnel tracker, tied into a computer system. It locates everyone wearing ID badges." Taking a breath, Lakesh announced, "Locate Walt."

Nothing happened.

"Locate Clarence."

Again nothing happened.

Lakesh stood before the display and rattled off a stream of first names: Francis, Paul, Larry, Darryl, Chris, Van and so forth. The wall map did not change as far as Kane could see.

Lakesh muttered something indistinct under his breath, then stated calmly, "Locate Dian."

Whatever reaction he hoped to elicit from the computer map did not occur, and he turned away, obviously disturbed. Bleakly he said, "It's one of two things. Either the digital sensor link with the ID badges is disconnected, or there's no one left alive to wear them."

Brigid eyed the wall display. "Or no one is bothering to wear the badges any longer. After all these years of being pent-up in here, everybody should know everybody else."

Lakesh directed a suspicious sideways glance toward her, then turned and began walking down the corridor again. Kane shivered against the moist chill, estimating the air temperature to be in the high thirties, but because of the damp it felt far colder.

The repulsive stench of putrefaction seemed to ebb, although Kane wasn't certain if he, as Leland suggested, was simply growing accustomed to it.

Shallow puddles of algae-scummed water lay on the floor in places, and foul-smelling liquid dripped from overhead pipes. Beads of condensation slid down the vanadium walls.

Brigid continued making motion-detector sweeps, trying but failing to keep a few paces ahead of Lakesh. Leland tried to scamper past him, but Kane restrained the little man with a hand on the collar of his coverall. The transadapt struggled, slapping his hand away with a surprising strength, which reminded Kane of his kind's tensile-steel muscles.

"I know where I'm going," he grated.

"Good," Kane snapped. "You can stay with us and point out areas of particular interest."

The four people turned a corner and, despite the inadequate lighting, they saw shell cases glinting on the floor, bullet pocks in the walls—and smears of blood.

"This is where them crazy big 'uns jumped us," Leland muttered.

Kane paused by a large bloodstain, touching it with a forefinger. The blood had pretty much congealed, leaving only a slightly tacky surface. He recollected seeing two transadapt bodies in the tape. Judging by the volume of blood spilled on the floor, he guessed the two trolls hadn't just been wounded.

"Who took the bodies?" he asked no one in particular.

Leland shrugged, but did not offer a verbal response. Neither did Lakesh or Brigid, but Kane caught the momentary uneasy look they exchanged.

They moved on down the passageway, skirting the pools of blood. Kane sensed other presences, as if something monstrous and horrible lurked just beyond his vision in the mist-shrouded shadows. He felt watching eyes, cold and remote. The feeling ate at his nerves like acid.

Brigid seemed to share a similar sensation. She continually checked their backtrack, then the LCD of the motion detector. "Nothing," she murmured in slight surprise. "Nothing moves at all."

The corridor took a dogleg jog to the right and ended inside an enormous chamber, the alloy-sheathed walls climbed sheer to the roof, half lost in swirling fog. Hazy shapes loomed about them in the semigloom. It took Kane a moment to get a sense of perspective and absorb the overwhelming immensity of the vault, and to begin to visually catalog the shapes.

Almost as far as the eye could see in any direction were aisles and aisles of stacked boxes, crates, galvanized-steel cargo containers, high shelves, vehicles, furniture, racks of clothing, statuary, electronic gear, books and even musical instruments.

Brigid and Kane blinked, stared, blinked again, rooted in place by awe. Kane's stunned brain told him that this single chamber was nearly the size of one entire level of the Cerberus redoubt. That gave him a clue to the truly vast scale of the Anthill installation. All of Cobaltville could have fit inside the facility, the Pits included.

His eyes darted back and forth, over several broad-chassised vehicles he recognized as Hummers, to a life-size bronze likeness of a naked man seated upon a stone, chin propped up by a fist, apparently deep in thought.

He realized the room was less a stockpile than a museum of predark artifacts, representative samples of mechanics, art and popular culture. He had no difficulty understanding how the Anthill supplied the nine baronies. Nine more villes could have been established and provided with only a fraction of the items in the vault. There was treasure in such profusion that its accumulated worth defied his imagination. The artifacts waited for hands to brush off the dust of two centuries and carry them away.

Neither Leland nor Lakesh appeared to be impressed. Lakesh in particular barely gave the collection a glance. He swiftly made his way down the first aisle, Leland scuttling beside him. Kane cursed under his breath, then he and Brigid forced their numbs legs to start moving and follow the pair.

"Where are you going?" demanded Kane, unconsciously lowering his voice to a whisper.

"To the inventory terminal," Lakesh said distractedly over his shoulder.

Kane sidled between racks of clothing, noting absently the green patches of mildew staining the fabric. He knew it required all of Brigid's concentration to resist the temptation to stop and examine everything they passed. Their footfalls echoed oddly, as if they were walking not on a floor but on a layer of foam rubber.

They followed Lakesh and Leland up one aisle, down another, then up another one. Lakesh stopped so suddenly Brigid and Kane nearly trod on his heels. A computer console, apparently molded from the wall to which it was attached, curved outward in an abbreviated ellipse. Lights indicated power, and they heard the faint hum of drive units. The two monitor screens were dark.

"That's the comp Sindri used," Leland piped up.

Lakesh sat down in a castered chair before one of the two keyboards.

"What are you doing?" asked Brigid.

Stroking several keys, Lakesh waited until the screen flashed with amber light before saying, "I'm looking for the record of last activity in the database. I want to find the file that Sindri accessed that so excited him."

A drop-down menu appeared at the center of the screen. Leaning over his shoulder, Brigid scanned the options. "The last activity was recorded five days ago." She glanced in Leland's direction. "Does that sound about right, when Sindri used it?"

Leland's receding forehead creased in thought. "Mebbe. I don't know. I'm no clock watcher."

Manipulating the cursor, Lakesh scrolled down, highlighted the activity date and clicked the button to open the file. The screen wavered and the words Access Denied/Password Encoded File appeared in bloodred letters.

Lakesh hissed in anger. "The little bastard has encrypted the file!"

"Why would he do that?" Brigid asked.

Glaring at the screen as if it were deliberately

mocking him, Lakesh rasped, "Probably to keep anyone from knowing what he found."

Kane took a step forward, standing on the other side of Lakesh. "That stuff Brigid said you told her about—the warheads, the nerve gas, is it in this room?"

Lakesh shook his head. "No—or at least it didn't use to be. Such items were stored in a hermetically sealed vault on a sublevel, buried beneath Mount Rushmore itself."

"But Leland said they found bang-bangs—blasters—here," Brigid argued.

Leland nodded, turning and gesturing to a distant point. "We did, down there, in a little side room."

"How easy would it be for Sindri to get into that vault?" asked Kane.

"It wouldn't be easy at all," Lakesh muttered, pushing the chair from the console with a squeal of rusty wheels. "He'd have to pass at least three automated security checkpoints, go through retinal and fingerprint identification scans."

"And if the checkpoints no longer function?" Brigid inquired.

Lakesh's expression and tone were bland. "I don't know." He said nothing more.

Kane pulled in a deep breath through his mouth, made a face at the repulsive taste that settled on his tongue and declared, "Lead us to it, then. If Sindri's still here and alive, that's where we'll find him."

Lakesh blinked owlishly. "I don't even know if the

lifts still work. If they don't, there is no way to get down there."

"He'd find a way," Kane said grimly. "Lead on."

As Lakesh began to rise from the chair, Kane caught a sudden blur of movement at the periphery of his vision. At the same time, Brigid bleated wordlessly in surprise and pain.

Pivoting on his heel, he saw Leland stiff-arming Brigid out of his way, spinning her around so she tottered between him and Kane's Sin Eater. By the time she recovered her balance, Leland had lunged out of sight behind a cargo container.

"Shit!" Kane went after him in a long-legged bound.

Lakesh called out anxiously, "Let him go!"

Not bothering to respond, Kane turned the corner of the container. He saw no sign of the transadapt, but he heard the rapid slap-slap of his bare feet on the floor between two stacks of boxes. He sprinted toward the sound, hearing running footsteps behind him, and knew Brigid was following.

Ahead of him he heard a muffled rustling and he saw mold-green clothing swinging on its hangers. He tore them aside and the rotted fabric fell away, his mouth souring with the musty odor.

"Kane!" came Brigid's tense call.

"This way," he shouted over his shoulder.

"Don't chase him. We don't need him—Lakesh knows his way around."

Kane didn't divert his attention or waste his breath explaining to her the tactical stupidity of allowing an

X factor to run free in a potential killzone. As he dashed past the mouth of an aisle formed by two long ranks of twenty-foot-high shelves, he glimpsed a vague figure flit from sight at the nether end. If not for his night-vision glasses, he would not have seen it. Turning down the aisle, Kane ran with all the furious speed of which his finely honed body was capable.

He fumed at himself and Leland. Although one of his strides equaled three made by the transadapt, the little man still eluded him. He decided when next he caught so much a glimpse of Leland's shadow, he would open up with his Sin Eater.

The aisle opened on a fairly spacious expanse filled with heavy moving machines—yellow-painted forklifts, and two cranes from which hooks and winches dangled.

Breathing hard, he circled one of the cranes, smelling grease and diesel fuel. Then a net made of a fine metallic mesh dropped onto him from above. Fist-sized lead balls attached to the net's hem acted as counterweights, making him stagger. One of them fetched him a cruel crack on the crown of his head. His feet struck a few others, and he toppled gracelessly facefirst to the floor, entangled and thrashing.

To his pain-blurred eyes, what seemed like a horde of stunted giants materialized all around him. Giving voice to triumphant hoots and yells, they hurled themselves on top of him. Their combined weight pinned his blaster beneath his body; knobby knees pressed into his thighs, and the back of his neck, mashing his face against the floor. His flailing left arm was bent back and secured in a painful hammerlock.

Through his own panting curses he heard a lilting voice say, "No need for such rough handling. Let him breathe at least."

The pressure on the back of his neck eased, and he raised his head, peering through the mesh in the direction of a low-pitched mechanical whine. A crane's boom arm with a small, metal-railed platform at the end dropped slowly into his field of vision.

Leaning against the rail, Sindri grinned at him. "How gratifying to look down on you again, Mr. Kane."

Chapter 20

Sindri looked much the same as the first time Kane had seen him. As he stood on the elevated platform, his perfect proportions confused Kane's sense of perspective for a moment. Unlike the transadapts, his legs weren't stumpy or his arms too long or his head too big.

His dark blond hair was swept back from a high forehead and tied in a ponytail at the nape of his neck. Under level brows, big eyes of the clearest, cleanest blue regarded him in mocking amusement.

He wore a perfectly tailored, fawn-colored bodysuit. A silk foulard of blue swirled at its open collar. A gold stickpin gleamed within its folds. The cuffs of the legs had stirrups that slipped between the arch and heel of polished, black patent leather boots. He wore a fringed buckskin jacket, which Kane figured he'd found in the storehouse of clothing. Since it fit his three-foot-tall frame well, more than likely it had once belonged to a child.

The only item missing from his ensemble was his signature silver-knobbed walking stick. Regardless, he still exuded complete confidence and self-assurance.

Between clenched teeth, Kane spit, ''So this was a trap after all.''

''Knowing your propensity for direct violent action,'' replied Sindri smoothly, ''I thought it best to temporarily restrain you. But this is not a trap.''

Kane strained to lift his head and saw three transadapts, all armed identically with skeletal Federal XP-900 autopistols. Leland stood with them, a smirk on his swart features.

''Let him up!'' Brigid's curt order cut through the chill, dank air, her tone brooking no debate.

Sindri looked in the direction of her voice, and his grin widened. He exclaimed happily, ''Dear Miss Brigid, I'm so happy to see you again.''

''Let him up,'' Brigid repeated, biting out each syllable.

Sindri gestured to the transadapts crouching on Kane's net-enshrouded body. ''You know I can refuse you nothing.''

The dwarfs released their painful grips and climbed off Kane. He struggled to rise, to pull away the weighted metal mesh. ''Help him,'' Sindri directed.

A couple of the transadapts yanked away the draping net, and Kane staggered to his feet. An over-the-shoulder glance showed him Brigid standing behind him, her Iver Johnson pistol trained on Sindri. He followed suit, framing the little man in the sights of his Sin Eater. Standing on the platform, he was about two feet above the top of Kane's head. He knew the psychological ploy was deliberate.

"There's no need for that," Sindri said calmly. "I mean you no harm."

"That's what you said the last time, pissant." Kane spoke in a growl. "How'd you get back into the station after being sucked into space?"

"I had no great difficulty getting back since I never left it. Emergency fail-safe bulkheads sealed off the hull breach before I was drawn into the void. Such a fate didn't appeal to me, so I didn't cooperate with it."

Kane jerked the barrel of his blaster toward the floor. "Come down from there. I'll be damned if I'll look up to you."

Rage glittered in Sindri's blue eyes, but as quickly as it flared, it was just as quickly veiled. He forced an ingratiating smile to his lips and pulled on a control lever to lower the platform. Swinging aside a hinged section of railing, he said, "Would you mind not pointing firearms in my direction? I've had my fill of that these past few days. I only restrained you so you wouldn't be tempted to start shooting as soon as you saw me."

Studiously ignoring the bore of the Sin Eater, Sindri strode toward Brigid. Placing a long-fingered hand over his heart, he bowed before her. "I am very grateful for the opportunity to see you again, so that I might personally offer my most humble apologies. I beg your forgiveness."

Although Brigid didn't aim her pistol at him, she didn't pocket it, either. Stonily she replied, "I may accept one, Sindri, but I think it's premature for me to grant the other."

Sindri nodded in resignation. "I deserve that. I can only offer a madness born of desperation as a reason for my behavior, but not as an excuse."

Kane rolled his eyes. "Can we save the groveling for later? What the hell is going on here?"

A sudden scuff of footfalls commanded his attention. A wheezing Lakesh reeled into the area. As his eyes took in the collection of armed transadapts, he stumbled to a clumsy halt.

Sindri peered at him with narrowed eyes. "Who is this old fart?" His tone held a frosty note of contempt.

"This is Lakesh," Brigid said.

Sindri's slitted eyes popped wide with wonder. "Not Mohandas Lakesh Singh?"

Lakesh coughed. "One and the same."

Sindri stepped eagerly toward him, hand outstretched. "My apologies, sir. The file pictures I've seen of you were taken many, many years ago. You've changed somewhat."

Grasping Lakesh's hand, he pumped it enthusiastically. "It's a great honor to meet one of the premier yet unappreciated geniuses of the twentieth century. If not for the holocaust, your name would be spoken of with the same awe as Einstein, Bohr and Hawking."

Lakesh tried to repress a smile, but he couldn't quite succeed. Kane noticed how he appreciably preened at the flattery—as Sindri no doubt hoped he would.

"When I learned you still lived," Sindri continued, "I hoped I would have the opportunity to meet you."

"Learned how?" inquired Lakesh.

Brigid answered the question. "Probably when Sindri drugged and questioned us on *Parallax Red*."

Lakesh withdrew his hand. "I'm not that awesome a genius, seeing how you managed to circumvent the security locks to keep you from activating the Cerberus gateway. My compliments to you, sir."

Sindri nodded respectfully. "I wish I could say it was child's play, but it was not. However, once I grasped your fundamental approach to the quantum inducers, at least I had a starting point."

Kane demanded harshly, "Let's backburner the mutual-admiration society for a little while."

Sindri glanced toward him. "Where is the truculent Mr. Grant? I certainly hope nothing untoward has happened to him."

"He'll be along if we don't return to Cerberus in about five hours," Kane replied. "And if he does have to come, he'll be a lot more truculent than you remember."

Sindri grinned, displaying his perfect teeth. "Five hours should be sufficient time to accomplish what needs to be accomplished."

"Which is?" Brigid asked.

Sindri shrugged. "Nothing much. Just saving the world as you know it."

SINDRI AND HIS SEVEN transdapts had established a base camp in the area of the heavy machinery. Kane grudgingly admitted to himself the little man's tactics were sound. The forklifts provided mobile, bullet-proof breastworks, and the boom arms of the cranes made for excellent lookout points. The blasters in the possession of the transadapts were all automatics, compact and easy even for novices to operate.

Sindri led them to a small enclosure formed by cargo containers and crates. Moldy clothes taken from the racks served as bedrolls. The little man sat down on a box, crossed his right leg over his left and beckoned for Brigid, Kane and Lakesh to join him.

"I know what you're going to ask," he stated. "We've explored only this level and the one below. The frontal assaults have ceased, but there are still skulkers in the vault, watching and waiting for one of us to get careless."

"Frontal assaults from whom?" Brigid wanted to know.

Sindri gestured to a transadapt. "Adam, bring out our guest."

The transadapt scuttled toward the cargo container and opened the hatch. They heard the hollow thud of feet on the interior metal. Voices murmured, one rising in petulant protest.

A few moments later, Adam returned, pushing a normal-sized man ahead of him. His height, around medium, was the only thing approximating normal about him. He wore a threadbare business suit, the sleeves of the coat crudely cross-stitched to the shoulders. A red necktie hung limply from the collar of his soiled white shirt. Shoes that had once been black patent leather were scuffed, cracked and green with fungus. But it was the man's face, not his clothes, that caught and held their horrified fascination.

Brigid, Lakesh and Kane stared incredulously at the white cheekbones protruding through the peeled flesh. There was only a semblance left of the lips, which were drawn like old leather over discolored teeth. Part of the forehead was completely bare of skin and tissue, showing naked skullbone. One ear was gone and what little flesh remaining on his face seemed to be composed of a jellylike film. A ghastly overpowering stench surrounded the man like a cloud. Kane's belly lurched sideways, and he heard murmurs of revulsion from Lakesh.

"Meet Francis," Sindri said genially. "Formerly of the U.S. State Department. Or so he said, over and over."

The man did not look as if he was formerly of anything, except perhaps a shallow grave.

In a liquidy burble, Francis hissed, "More degenerates from a nation of degenerates, defiling the sanctity of our capitol."

His voice was slurred as though he had difficulty moving his vocal cords and tongue in tandem.

"We captured him two days ago," Sindri said. "Obviously he's a lunatic, but I managed to decipher some interesting tidbits about this place from his rants."

To Kane's surprise, Lakesh took a hesitant step toward the walking cadaver. In a low voice, he said, "Frank, it's me. Dr. Singh. Do you remember me?"

The man's deep-set, watery eyes surveyed him dispassionately without recognition. "If you desire a meeting, please schedule one with my secretary. However, the earliest date I can give you is after the New Year."

In a faint whisper, Brigid said, "All of his organic tissues are in an advanced state of decomposition. How can he still be alive?"

Sindri climbed off the crate. "I wondered about that, too. Look."

Grabbing Francis by the arm, he turned him around. Almost all of the rear portion of his skull glinted with a layer of metal. "His body is mainly bionic, prosthetic limbs and joints."

Twirling Francis back around, Sindri jerked up the man's sleeve. The exposed forearm was pale white in color. He rapped with a knuckle, producing a dull, solid knock. "Acrylics, ceramic and a titanium alloy. An artificial man for an artificial environment. Evidently everyone here is a cyborg to some extent or another. Quite fascinating.

"What keeps his heart pumping and his organs working isn't blood as we understand it. I considered returning with him to the Cydonia Compound so I could dissect him, but he's more valuable alive."

He grinned. "Employing the term by its loosest definition, of course."

"What kind of information has he given you?" asked Kane. "And what did you mean by saving the world? That's a hell of a reversal from your attitude of a few months ago."

"Pretty much a one-eighty," agreed Brigid.

Sindri didn't respond to the observations. "The information I received from Francis is best shown rather than verbally described."

Kane uttered a short, derisive laugh. "That's what you said on *Parallax Red.* And then we woke up on Mars."

Sindri heaved a deep sigh of exasperation. "Please, may we move beyond the leftover baggage from our first encounter? I've changed my ways. I apologized for what I did to you. I was in a desperate frame of mind and therefore undertook desperate measures. Surely, Mr. Kane, you've been guilty of reckless excess at one time or another yourself."

"Agreed. But my question still stands."

Sindri turned to Adam. "Return our prisoner to his cell, please."

Kane felt a bit less tense after the man was led from sight. "Leland claimed you found something here that scared you shitless."

Sindri frowned. "A rather vulgar simile, but essentially correct."

"We already know about the nukes and other matériel stored here," Brigid said.

A faint line of consternation creased Sindri's forehead. "Really? I know nothing about that." His eyes suddenly gleamed with sudden comprehension. "Ah, I understand now. You were less moved by my plea for help than by the fear I could access those items and deploy them for my own purposes."

"Something like that," ventured Lakesh.

Sindri shook his head. "My purpose is to find a new home for me and my people, one superior to the Cydonia Compound. Contaminating the Earth with fallout and other toxins in order to gain control of it would be a fairly Pyrrhic victory."

"We knew that," Brigid said. "We just weren't sure if you did."

Sindri scowled. "You really have the most distorted idea of me and my motivations, Miss Brigid."

"Under the circumstances, I don't think you can blame me."

The little man's handsome face went from a scowl to an expression of remorse. "No, I cannot. I deserve your suspicion—"

"And worse," interjected Kane.

"But believe me, I stumbled over plans afoot here that are far more diabolical than the scheme I wanted to hatch."

"So you keep saying," Kane snapped impatiently. "Tell us what they are, or we're leaving."

Sindri made a theatrical gesture. "Death from above, Mr. Kane, riding on the winds of doom."

Kane growled from deep in his throat. "Cut out the goddamn melodrama, Sindri. Talk or you're on your own."

Sindri turned sharply on his heel, waving for them to follow. "Come along, then. I'll explain as we go."

Neither Kane, Brigid nor Lakesh moved. "Go where?" Brigid demanded.

"To the level below, where I'll provide you with proof of what, as Mr. Kane so commonly phrased it, is scaring me shitless."

Chapter 21

After exchanging brief questioning glances with one another, Kane, Brigid and Lakesh fell into step behind Sindri. A pair of transadapts followed them. As he wended his way among the aisles of shelves and crates, Sindri said, "Keep alert. We've seen no signs of the walking dead in about twenty-four hours, but I know they're watching us."

"How many are there?" Kane asked, glancing around, feeling his nape hairs tingling.

Sindri shrugged. "I wish I knew. I can only estimate. I doubt there are more than a dozen, but there may be twice that number on the other levels."

"Have you seen a woman with them?" Lakesh asked haltingly.

Sindri glanced up at him, face drawn into lines of disgust. "She might have been a woman once. Yes, not only have I seen her—she is evidently the commander of this place. I've heard her referred to by that rank more than once."

"Does she have a name other than Commander?"

"Not that I know of. I have to confess she commands her forces well. They almost got us several times."

Sindri continued to lead them through the vast space, past pillars made of stacked crates.

"Why didn't you just leave?" Brigid asked him. "Use the gateway to jump back to *Parallax Red*? The way to the chamber is open."

"It is now," answered Sindri smoothly. "It wasn't until just yesterday. You were fortunate you arrived when you did, else you would have materialized into a cross fire."

They passed long trestle tables laden with electronic parts, obviously the guts of a number of computers.

"I saw you had encrypted a computer file," Lakesh announced. "Why?"

"The implementation of their plan depends on access to certain data," replied Sindri, "encoded commands, that sort of thing. I blocked their access to it. Granted, given enough time, the encryption keys can be broken and overridden. It was simply a delaying action."

Sindri marched toward the circular rim of a hatch cover rising from the floor. Nearby lay a metal screen of thick mesh. They saw metal rungs affixed to the shaft wall. A faint breeze wafted up, bringing with it the reek of spoiled meat.

Sindri climbed into the shaft. "Follow me."

They followed him down, the transadapts bringing up the rear. As he climbed, Sindri continued to speak, his voice echoing hollowly. "The only thing I can figure out, based on some disconnected comments made by Francis, is that some years in the past, this installation's cryogenic systems malfunctioned. They still work to some extent, but no longer with sufficient output to prevent the deterioration of their organic tissues."

The ladder descended some fifty feet, down into the elbow of an L-shaped tube. The shaft was made of a dull, nonreflective metal, featureless except for ridges where the sections of pipe were joined. It was narrow and stretched almost as far as the eye could see. Far in the distance glimmered a faint circle of light, shining like a coin seen face-on. The sickening odor became even more pronounced.

"It wasn't like this the last time I was here," Lakesh murmured to Brigid. "Whatever catastrophic failure this facility suffered, it was in the last twenty-five years or so."

Sindri led the way down the pipe, saying, "This used to be an air-circulation shaft, probably pumping chilled air throughout the installation."

They walked steadily for several minutes, the coin of light growing in size. Finally, the six people emerged from the shaft into an immense tri-leveled chamber that held banks of rusting carcasses of ancient comps. Six chrome-capped glass tubes, each one ten feet long and three feet in diameter, were positioned at equidistant points on the uppermost level of the chamber. Some of the tubes held a green liquid, while others bore cracks and were empty. Flexible metal conduits extended from the metal caps on top and bottom. The conduits snaked down, disappearing into sleeve sockets on the deck.

Kane leaned carefully over a handrail. Barely visible at least a hundred feet below, he saw a dark metal framework surrounding six gargantuan fan units. Only one of the fans moved, sluggishly revolving with a steady squeak. The ever-present grinding sound of machinery was much louder here. A chill, oil-scented breeze ruffled his hair.

"What is this place?" he asked.

"One of the main pumping stations," Lakesh answered in a muted tone. He gestured to the tall glass tubes. "Those were containers of coolant, circulated down into a conversion chamber."

Sindri strode purposefully toward one of twelve open shafts. "Let's keep moving."

All of them entered the lateral shaft. After twenty yards or so, it terminated in another elbow joint, this one crooking down. Without hesitation, Sindri swung his body over the lip of the opening. The others followed him, descending hand over hand.

The shaft ended at a passageway that stretched off to their left. This tube was much wider, and they were able to walk two abreast, passing several other openings from which blew cool, stinking air.

The tube ended at an opening, and they looked down on a miniature city, a scale model of Washington, D.C. None of the buildings looked big enough to house even the smallest transadapt, though.

In the city's center towered a pointed obelisk of stained stone, stretching upward at least twenty feet. Kane noticed that its white facade bore deep cracks that had been thickly mortared.

Confused and uneasy, he gazed out at the buildings, the streets and the parks. "What the hell was the point of building this thing? It must have taken them years."

Lakesh shook his head sadly. "A form of denial, perhaps. Building a Washington as it had been, even in miniature, reminded them of their world in the corridors of government, of the power they once wielded over the country."

"And besides," commented Sindri with a sour grin, "they had a lot of time on their hands."

With that, he jumped out of the shaft, landing on the roof of the Lincoln Memorial. He shimmied down a Doric column and gestured impatiently for the others to join him.

All of them leaped to the roof and clambered down to the floor, the transadapts as nimble as monkeys. When it was Lakesh's turn, he lost his footing and nearly toppled to the floor, but one of the transadapts used his foot to snatch him by the collar of his coat, and lower him into the waiting arms of Kane and Brigid.

Sindri strode down Pennsylvania Avenue. Kane noticed that a number of the small buildings bore old bullet pocks in their facades, some of them patched, most of them not.

"Hell of a firefight here at one time," he muttered to no one in particular.

They walked without speaking. Suffused sea-green light filtered down from above, giving them the impression they walked on the bottom of an ocean. What they could make out of the roof seemed to be all pitted and corroded girders and cross beams. Sindri's gait acquired something of a swagger, as if he enjoyed feeling like a giant for one of the few times in his life.

Brigid made motion-detector sweeps, but nothing registered. "Clear."

"That doesn't mean very much," Kane responded quietly. "Blastermen could be hiding behind any of these buildings."

His pointman's sixth sense rang a sudden, insistent alarm, and he came to a halt, latching on to the arms of Lakesh and Brigid. "Sindri," he said urgently.

The little man looked at him over his shoulder but continued walking. "We're almost there."

"Almost where?" Kane demanded. "Where are you taking us?"

The crack of a rifle split the air, cutting off whatever reply Sindri might have made. The round sang past Kane's head, buzzing in his ear like a giant wasp. It struck the cornice of a building to his right and ricocheted away.

"Down!" he shouted, hauling Lakesh and Brigid to the cover provided by an office building. Sindri and his transadapts scrambled out of the street, hunkering down behind structures.

A thundering full-auto salvo stitched holes in the miniature buildings opposite their position, showering Pennsylvania Avenue with rock chips and fragments. One of the transadapts uttered a high-pitched cry of pain and shock, clapping a hand to his hip and staggering.

Sindri stared at the wounded man in disbelief, shouting in outrage, "They got Kenny! You bastards—!"

Brigid took hasty aim with her Iver Johnson at a point behind Kane and squeezed off two door-slamming rounds.

Kane twisted, peered around a corner and glimpsed two business-suited figures brandishing AK-47s duck-walking between buildings. He triggered his Sin Eater in their direction, dousing the walls with a 9 mm barrage that sent them scuttling back. Another volley of autofire blazed from the direction from which they had come, steel-jacketed slugs snapping over their heads like whips. Weapons stuttered from both sides, short pencils of blasterfire lighting up the gloom of the alleys.

He looked toward Sindri, who met his gaze with wild eyes. "We can't stay here," he half shouted to the little man. "These sons of bitches can cut off our retreat any time they want."

Sindri nodded. "Follow me! Stay close and low!" he directed.

Brigid hesitated, but Kane told her tersely, "Get going. I'll cover you."

Sindri began a shambling run, paralleling Pennsylvania Avenue. Brigid, Lakesh and the two transadapts followed suit. The wounded dwarf hopped like a club-footed frog. More shots sounded, chewing up the fake tarmac of the miniature street.

Kane hung back, crouching as he tried to place the positions of the gunners. He glimpsed three figures fanning out two streets over, and dashed to intercept them. He unhooked the incendiary gren from his combat harness, primed it and lobbed it in a looping arc toward the blastermen's position.

Propelling himself into a dive, he hugged the floor as the sharp detonation of the gren banged behind him. He twisted onto his back in time to see two of the men nearest the bloom of the explosion pitch forward amid a scattering of stone, tossed by the force of the blast. Their clothes fluttered wildly with a wreath of blue fire.

Sindri yelled something, but Kane couldn't understand him, due to the rolling echoes of the detonation. The third blasterman lurched drunkenly toward Kane, fumbling to bring his autorifle to bear.

Kane triggered a long burst from the Sin Eater, red-hot Parabellums pulping the rifleman's chest, a greenish-red muck belching out of his back. He slammed into the wing of a building and fell from sight.

Rising to his feet, Kane returned to Pennsylvania Avenue, sprinting as fast as he could after his party. Four men moved from either side of the street to cut him off, two to a side, crouching in tight defensive postures. Their AKs began to stutter, and Kane stumbled from a triple-hammer blow against his lower torso. The rounds didn't penetrate the tough Kevlar weave of his coat, but the impacts nearly knocked him off his feet.

Fighting against the impulse to double over, blinking back the pain haze from his eyes, Kane depressed the Sin Eater's trigger, dousing the four men with a prolonged figure-eight pattern, toppling all four of them under a blazing barrage. One of them spun like a top, a pinkish ichor spurting from a hole in his head.

Kane began running again, gasping in pain and exertion, fumbling for another clip attached to the harness beneath his coat. He heard Brigid shout his name and he swerved in the direction of her voice.

The stink of corrupted flesh suddenly filled his nostrils, and he wheeled around just as a business-suited man lunged from an alley, leading with his AK. Kane swept his unloaded Sin Eater against the autorifle's barrel, jarring it from the man's grip and sending it clattering to the floor.

The man didn't back off. He reached for Kane with talonlike fingers from which dangled shreds of soft, slippery matter. Kane could smell the putrefaction literally oozing out of his pores. The man's face was little more than a blotch of peeling, diseased tissue.

Kane drove his left fist into the man's solar plexus, and as the man doubled over he shot his right hand upward, the barrel of the Sin Eater connecting with the man's chin on the way up. The front blade sight ripped a scrap of flesh away, exposing the metal implant beneath. His head flew back until his stub of a nose pointed at the ceiling, exposing his neck.

Kane drove the extended fingers of his left hand into the man's Adam's apple and felt his windpipe collapse like a hollow reed. Clawing at his throat, the man fell onto his back with a sound like a wet sack of cement dropped from a great height. The man gagged as he writhed and kicked. Kane backed away from him, then turned and began sprinting again.

The miniature city ended abruptly, the demarcation point as precise and as sudden as a knife cut. Kane saw Sindri, Lakesh, Brigid and the pair of transadapts with their backs against two very tall double doors, bound with thick braces of verdegris-discolored brass.

Emblazoned in the center of the right-hand door was a bordered disk-shaped insignia. Within the circular border, depicted in black-and-gold paint, was the representation of a bald eagle with its wings outstretched. Kane recognized the image as the great seal of the United States. A faded empty circle of the same size, with nail holes around the rim, showed where an identical seal had once been affixed on the left door.

Sindri fumbled with the doorknob, shouting, "We'll be safe in here! It's defensible and it's where I was bringing you."

Brigid gazed keenly at the city as Kane joined them, then she raised her blaster in a double-handed grip and fired off three rounds in quick succession. Kane couldn't see whom or what she shot at.

"I want them to keep their distance," she said grimly.

Kane detached the ammo clip from his harness, but before he could eject the spent one from his Sin Eater, Sindri shouldered open the door. It swung noisily on rusted hinges. All of them pelted over the dim threshold, the two transadapts pushing the door into place and putting their backs against it.

Kane, Lakesh and Brigid silently surveyed the gloomy interior of the big, high-ceilinged room. It was at least twenty yards long, lined on three sides with bookshelves that reached to the ceiling. Upholstered armchairs were scattered about. In a far corner, a huge globe of the Earth lay in pieces on the floor. The carpet beneath their feet was a medium shade of blue, and a replica of the seal emblazoned on the door was embroidered into it with thick gold thread.

"This used to be General Kettridge's private office," Lakesh whispered.

The atmosphere of the room held a blended variety of cloying smells, from charred wood, to dusty velvet, to rotting meat, to rancid butter and burned sulfur.

An immense circular desk dominated the fourth wall. The surface seemed bare except for a patina of damp dust. A tall, high-backed chair rose from behind it, the seat turned away from them.

Purposefully, Sindri strode across the office toward the massive desk. "I found the blueprint for the plot behind the desk. I'll fetch it."

Kneading his sore midsection where the bullets had struck, Kane peered through the murk, seeing nothing but the chair. "Where?"

As if his query were a stage cue, the chair swiveled swiftly around. He glimpsed only the shadowy outline of the figure seated in it, but he leveled his Sin Eater just the same.

At the same instant, he heard Brigid and Lakesh

cry out in pain. He started to whirl, but then a sun of pain went nova behind his eyes, accompanied by a sizzle. He felt his muscles convulse and cramp as agony streaked down the back of his head into his hips. He was dimly aware of his finger spasming on the trigger stud of his blaster, but the firing pin struck an empty chamber.

As he slid wetly into the long night, his last conscious thought was that his pointman's instincts had been right all along. He felt no satisfaction. After the first blaze of pain, he felt nothing at all.

Chapter 22

There was not enough light for Lakesh to make out the face that leaned over and looked down into his own. It seemed to swim and pulsate in cadence with his heartbeat. Someone spoke, and at first he thought it was his mother.

"Mohandas..."

It was not his mother's voice, but he didn't recognize it. The voice held a strange, strained quality as if the larnyx that produced it was unaccustomed to making any coherent sound.

"Mohandas," said the hoarse, feminine whisper. "Mohandas Lakesh Singh. Look at me."

Lakesh tried, but he could see nothing but the shifting of shadows.

"Mohandas. See me."

He felt a light touch on his cheek and he recoiled from the chill-fingered caress. Then slowly, at the end of an unimaginably long, black-walled tunnel, a shape acquired form and substance. It rushed toward him or he lunged toward it—he wasn't sure. The darkness fell away and Dian was there, standing over him. He realized he was very cold and he shivered violently, the memory of an arcing thread-thin electrical current drifting to his consciousness.

"Shockstick?" he murmured.

"Yes. It was regrettable but necessary."

Dian's voice was as throaty as he remembered, but it creaked and the words sifted, like the rustle of ashes against violin strings. Her face floated into focus. Lakesh steeled himself, determined not to avert his eyes. The left side of her face was as hauntingly beautiful as always, without a line of age or stress marring it, but still there was something horrible in the beauty, juxtaposed as it was with travesty and ruin.

The left side of her face was more than a cruel parody of loveliness; it was an obscenity, scarred and encrusted tissue studded here and there with steel surgical staples, The gaps between the staples in her flesh leaked a pinkish fluid that was not blood. Lakesh stared at her steadily, ignoring the wave of nausea in his throat. If both sides of her face had been the same, either distorted or lovely, he could have accepted it.

"So you made it back," she said in a low voice. "How you've changed."

Lakesh made no reply, trying to meet her gaze. Her left eye looked like a milky marble with dull blue highlights. Its dead quality only made the bright glint of her right eye seem more ghastly.

He stirred and realized he could scarcely move. His body was strapped to a narrow platform, canvas restraints pinning his arms, chest and legs. Slowly he lifted his head and saw medical equipment and examination tables around him. He recognized the place as the laboratory where Dian had once labored.

"Where are Brigid and Kane?" he croaked. His tongue felt clumsy and thick, his throat parched.

"They live," whispered Dian. "They've been removed so you and I can speak privately."

"A trap," he managed to husk out. "Nothing but a trap."

"Not for you, Mohandas. Never for you." Her tone acquired a silken, almost seductive note with an edge of genuine happiness.

Lakesh squinted, realizing his vision was blurred due to the absence of his glasses. Still he saw she wore a bizarre ensemble of a tailored business suit with a short, pleated skirt, high heels and charcoal stockings that bore splits and runs. He looked her up and down, a carefully calculated neutral expression on his face. "You've changed, too, Dian."

She shifted position restlessly, turning the disfigured side of her face away from him. "You always told me how beautiful I was. The most beautiful woman in the world, you said. Why don't you tell me that now?"

"You're the most beautiful woman in the world," he rasped, despising the quaver in his voice.

Dian turned around, displaying her left profile. In an intense tone, she said, "If only you could've awakened when you were supposed to, in twenty years. I waited three times that for you to tell me I was beautiful again. I waited for you so long my heart aches to think of it."

Her voice caught in her throat. She uttered a strangulated sob, then burst into a screeching, raging invective that was almost incomprehensible. It was not what she said that made Lakesh's heart jerk, because he only understood one word out of ten, but her unrestrained fury, bordering on complete madness.

Dian stomped around the laboratory, sweeping glass beakers and petri dishes from the tables. They shattered with splintering jangles, and with each crash, she shrilled all the louder.

Lakesh silently watched the outburst, fearing she would pick up a shard of razor-edged glass and use it on him or herself.

Her mindless rantings finally wound down, and she panted between clenched teeth. She glared at him with the lust of murder in her eye, but he realized the crazed passion and venom was not directed solely at him. Gutturally she said, "I watched you, Mohandas."

"When?" he asked, striving for a calm, reasonable tone.

"Over the years when you came back here. I allowed you to take government property from the storage vault. You used the mat-trans to remove things from the installation. I lived for the times you visited, just to see you on the security monitors. I kept the others from killing you.

"You were older, but you were still Mohandas. You were my dream walking. Then one day, you didn't come back. I always wondered if you thought about me while you were here."

Very quietly, very sincerely, he said, "I thought

about you all the time whether I was here or not. Why didn't you show yourself to me?"

Dian stared at him as if he had gone insane. She placed her hands on her face. "I do not have the appearance that was once mine, that which you loved."

"It wasn't only your face I loved, Dian. If I'd known you still lived—" He broke off, coughed and said, "I asked about you when I was revived. I was told—"

"I *know* what you were told!" she cried angrily. "They told you what I commanded them to tell you!"

She heeled about and kicked at the litter of broken glass on the floor. In a high, fierce half scream, she keened, "What fucking difference would it have made? You had your duties. I had mine. Duty! Service! Loyalty!"

Lakesh tested the canvas straps, but they held him fast. "Dian—"

"Out of duty, service and loyalty, I remained here. The few of us left behind died or went mad and we were forced to kill them. The keystone of the new world order, the future of humanity, became nothing but a tomb, a crypt for those of us who existed in a twilight state between life and death."

She inhaled a slow, shuddery breath, making a sound like steel sliding along wet leather. Dian shrugged. "Duty, service, loyalty for the future. But you are here now, Mohandas and we can share our own future, make our own plans."

Lakesh stiffened. "And what are your plans for me?"

Dian stepped close to him and put a hand on his upper thigh. Her lips twisted in a rictus, in a grotesque imitation of a coquettish smile. She whispered, "We will fly from this tomb, into the sunlight again. The little man showed me the way. We can be together from here on out."

Breathing hard, she offered an expression of icy calm. Then quite deliberately and horrifyingly, she began touching him.

THE PAIN IN KANE'S HEAD throbbed right next to his mind. It took a long while for him to consciously register it, then he felt cramping pains shooting through his legs and forearms. A hot spasm burned in his side where the three bullets had struck him.

Everything was a blur in his memory, the pain and sight and sounds mixed together. I've been shot in the head, he thought aloofly. No, struck. No, shocked.

He wanted to just slip back into oblivion, away from the pain, away from the knowledge he had ignored his instincts and strolled blithely into a trap.

Opening his eyes was an act of great resolve. He saw nothing but dim shapes at first, and he craned a neck that felt stabbed through and through with hot daggers. He looked around, not understanding why everything appeared unreal and strange. He blinked curiously at the two legs and feet suspended above him before realizing they were his own.

Then Kane understood he hung upside down, ankles bound together by nylon rope and tethered to an aluminum crossbar. His wrists were tied behind him. He tugged at the bindings, but each movement sent needles lancing through his head. His hands and wrists were numb.

He felt very cold and saw he was no longer wearing his coat. It lay wadded up on the floor beneath him. There was a stink in his nostrils, and when he took a deep breath he gagged on air that was thick and clammy and smelled like dead fish left in the sun.

A pleasant voice, bubbling with genuine amusement, said, "The petty little mind rouses."

Sindri's face filled his field of vision. He looked distorted, his head far larger than his body. Kane's sense of perspective returned in piecemeal fashion, and he saw Sindri was leaning forward, hands on his knees. He also saw the black rod of a Shockstick in his right hand.

"My apologies for the discomfort, Mr. Kane, but it was the easiest way to both search you and make sure you wouldn't cause me any trouble."

Adrenaline surged through Kane, and he bucked and twisted, trying to see all of his surroundings. As far as he could tell, he and Sindri were alone in a small, murky room. The only illumination came from a floor lamp in one corner. By the light it shed, he saw that the chamber was a treasure house. There were large open crates filled with jewelry, from pearl necklaces to gold ingots. Magnificent oil paintings leaned against the walls, and even bundles of predark cash and coinage were scattered carelessly on the floor.

"My private hoard," Sindri said, voice purring with mirth. "The treasury of my new government taken from the old. They'll never miss it."

Kane shook his throbbing head to clear it, failed and muttered groggily, "You're overplaying your hand again, Sindri."

"It fooled you, didn't it?"

Kane didn't respond to the question. "Where are Brigid and Lakesh?"

"They're very safe, Mr. Kane. I have no reason to harm either one of them. You, on the other hand, are a different matter entirely."

Forcing a note of disinterest into his voice, Kane stated, "So this trap was about revenge, for what happened on Mars and on the space station."

Sindri pursed his lips and straightened up. "You consistently—and disrespectfully—ascribe the most base motivations to me. I don't waste my time and energy scheming to avenge wrongs. A reckoning always occurs. Years may pass, but it is inevitable. I could afford to be patient."

Kane's temples continued to throb as the blood rushed poundingly to his head. "Then what's this about?"

"What it's always about, Mr. Kane. Exodus, the survival of me and my people. A new world in which to live."

"One in which you make all the rules."

Sindri sighed. "I'm not a big man, as you can see.

But you can even the odds if you have a big enough fulcrum.'' He lowered his voice and quoted, '''In every wound of Caesar that should move the stones of Rome to rise and mutiny.'''

''What the hell does that mean?'' Kane's sinuses felt clogged, and his voice sounded congested even in his own ears.

Patiently, patronizingly, Sindri said, ''I have the weapon to wound the barons, overthrow the villes and inspire the people to rise and mutiny.''

''And rally around you?''

''Of course.''

''Isn't that what you wanted to do the last time? Your philosophy of destroying the majority in order to save the easily ruled minority?''

''That's still my philosophy,'' replied Sindri, ''but now I have the means to visit a less indiscriminate form of destruction on the tyrants.''

Kane tried to snort in derision, but because of his stuffy nasal passages he couldn't quite pull it off. ''Nukes and biological contagions aren't exactly precision weapons.''

Sindri's eyes flashed with irritation. ''You keep going on about that. You're really starting to piss me off. I'm not insane, you know.''

''No,'' Kane said in a calm tone. ''I didn't.''

Raising the Shockstick, Sindri passed the crackling tip back and forth in front of Kane's eyes. Thickly he growled, ''Do you have any idea how difficult it is to fight the temptation to use this on you? To inflict upon you such agony that you'll scream and beg me for death?"

Flatly, Kane said, "That'll never happen."

"Probably not," he agreed in a deadly monotone. "Granted, there are scores to even between you and me. But I can put it on the back burner for a little while to get what I want."

The Shockstick trembled almost imperceptibly within Sindri's grasp. His face contorted in sudden rage. "But I don't like the idea of keeping you alive, Mr. Kane. I don't like it one bit. But I can't take the chance—"

He broke off, turning away, obviously trying to compose himself.

"You can't take the chance," Kane finished for him, a hint of mockery in his voice, "if you're trying to convince Baptiste you're not the maniac I claim you are. You can't afford to indulge your taste for murder."

Sindri thumbed the power switch of the Shockstick to the off position and faced him. He prodded his shoulder gently with the double-pronged tip, setting him swaying like a pendulum. "That's one consideration, I won't deny. But it might be I need you. The creatures here are unpredictable."

"You're in cahoots with them, then?"

"Yes."

"Then why did they try to chill us?"

Sindri shook his head in exasperation. "If you think I'm a maniac, Mr. Kane, you ought to try to hold a rational conversation with one of them. They were ordered to simply fire off a few guns, to make the state of hostility seem legitimate. Instead, they got carried away. Or they forgot their orders. At any rate, none of them will make much of a crew."

"Crew?" Kane echoed. "Crew for what?"

Sindri laughed, a sinister rattlesnake laugh that stood the hairs on the back of Kane's neck at attention. "Of my ship, Mr. Kane. The flagship of freedom sailing the skyways of the world, bringing terror to despots and hope to the despondent."

Kane surreptitiously studied the little man's face, examining it for signs of complete dementia. Then he made a mental connection. "Death from above?"

"Exactly." He tapped Kane's chest with the Shockstick. "See, you're not quite as dense as I think you are."

He made a sudden, expansive wave with the rod, as if it were a scepter. "Let him down."

Instantly the tension suspending Kane's weight disappeared and he plunged straight down. Only the cushion provided by his coat saved him from a fractured skull or a broken neck. As it was, he went rolling clumsily, cursing as his head swam with a sickening vertigo.

He lay on his side, panting for a few moments until the dizziness abated and the blood no longer thumped in his ears. Then he struggled into a sitting position. He found himself face-to-face with a smirking Leland, holding the nylon rope in his hands. Kane kicked out at him with his bound feet, but the effort made him fall over. Leland chuckled snidely and watched him thrash to achieve a sitting position again.

"Calm down," Sindri said. "Be thankful you're right side up."

Glaring at him from beneath lowered brows, Kane demanded, "This whole deal, the tape, sending Leland to us, it was all a ruse."

Sindri sneered. "Well, duh."

"How'd you get these cadavers to go along with you if they're so fused out? What did you offer them?"

"Wrong approach, Mr. Kane," Sindri answered smoothly. "The commander made an offer to me if I figured out a way to bring you here."

Kane stared at him in disbelieving silence for a couple of seconds. "She wanted you to trap us?"

"Essentially."

"How did she even know about us?"

Sindri wagged the Shockstick at him admonishingly. "The commander knew about only one of you."

"Lakesh?"

"Dr. Mohandas Lakesh Singh himself. When I and my party first arrived here, I thought this installation was abandoned many years ago. That initial assessment wasn't too far off the mark, either."

"What do you mean?"

"Apparently the Anthill suffered major damage a century or so ago. It was so severe the people here were never able to completely repair it. They were only able patch things up so as to forestall the inevitable catastrophic shutdown of its life-sustaining systems. It was like a row of dominoes. When one essential system failed, it affected others. Almost all of the personnel perished. Only a handful remain—diseased ragbags of rot, shadows of human beings."

Sindri didn't even try to suppress a shudder of complete revulsion.

"How do you know this?" Kane asked.

"I hacked into their computer system, their personnel records, their maintenance and repair logs. That's when I came across the file on Dr. Singh and I recalled you, Mr. Grant and Miss Brigid mentioning his name when you were on *Parallax Red.*

"I knew it couldn't be a coincidence, two eminent predark physicists with the same name...especially when I learned he had spent nearly 150 years hibernating in this place."

Kane unobtrusively explored his bonds, but his fingertips were so numb he couldn't even be sure of the kind of material trapping his wrists.

"Is that the file you encrypted?" he inquired.

Sindri shook his head. "By no means. I was attempting to access a complete inventory of the items stored here. I came across one word, which then led me to another file and then to a monumental discovery."

Kane grunted. "And what was that one word?"

A slow smile creased Sindri's face, one full of satisfaction and triumph. "I doubt it will mean anything to you, inasmuch as your education regarding predark history is frightfully limited."

"Tell me anyway," Kane suggested sarcastically.

Sindri's smile became smug and superior. "Aurora, Mr. Kane. Aurora."

"DIAN," LAKESH SAID, forcing himself to keep his eyes upon her face, fighting to keep the revulsion from sounding in his voice. There was no point in cringing away even if he surrendered to the impulse. "This isn't the way. Let me up, please."

The woman continued to stroke him. "You'll leave me again."

He shook his head. "You have my word I will not. I've found you again, beloved, after all these years. I won't leave you."

Dian's hands stopped moving, then they slid over to the buckles of the straps. She worked the strap over his chest free of its buckle, but before Lakesh could push himself up, she thrust her face close to his. "Who is that girl with you? A lover? A wife? Who?"

Her whispered question was full of suspicion and jealousy. The stench of necrotic tissue made Lakesh's skin crawl and his belly churn with cold nausea, but he said firmly, "Once you let me up, I'll tell you. And you'll be pleasantly surprised. Happy, even."

"Happy?" Dian repeated, rolling the word around contemptuously. *"Happy?"*

"Happy," Lakesh confirmed.

Dian continued to stare into his face as if searching for any signs of duplicity and then undid the other two restraints. Lakesh sat up, swinging his legs over the side of the table. In as intimate a croon as he could muster, he said, "Dian, beloved, when I thought you were lost to me forever, I searched for any piece of you that might have survived. That girl is it. Her first name is Brigid. Her last name is Baptiste."

Dian did not react in any way.

"She is part of you," Lakesh continued. "Part of *us*. She is much like you—brilliant, curious, compassionate. In many ways, I look at her as the daughter you and I should have had."

Dian remained silent for a tense moment. Then, in a steady, clipped and clinical tone of voice, she declared, "She is a product of my in-vitro genetic samples, on file with Scenario Joshua."

Lakesh's heart gave a great leap of hope as echoes of the Dian Baptiste he remembered rose from the clouds of madness.

"I often wondered if I had any descendants sharing my genotype, if my samples were ever put to use."

"Brigid is living proof of it. I sought her out and looked after her."

Dian sighed, shook her head. "Does she know of her lineage, of her connection to me—to us?"

"She does. I told her after I saw you on the tape."

Dian's face twitched in a macabre caricature of a shy smile. "You saw me?"

"Yes."

"You knew it was me and came anyway?"

Lakesh nodded.

"The little man—Sindri—thought the tale of finding a terrible menace would be sufficient to lure you here."

Earnestly, Lakesh stated, "If it was only that, I would not have come myself. It was the sight of you, beloved. Only that."

Her right eye brimmed with tears, but she blinked them back. When next she spoke, her voice was vacant, distant, as if her clarity of thought had been only a temporary phenomenon, as capricious as her temper tantrum.

"Now we can always be together, Mohandas. A family. You, me and our daughter."

She extended a hand toward him, his eyeglasses held between her fingers. "Come. Let's go tell her the good news."

Chapter 23

The Shockstick attack didn't render Brigid unconscious, but the excruciating touch of voltage incapacitated her.

Writhing on the carpeted floor of the office, she had watched with dazed eyes as transadapts leaped from concealed nooks and crannies, repeatedly stroking Kane and Lakesh with the crackling batons. Although she received only a fragmented impression of the figure seated in the chair, she heard a hoarse but unmistakably feminine voice shout, "Enough! He's not to be harmed!"

Sindri's voice, carrying a surprising note of deference, replied, "I promised you he wouldn't be, Commander."

When she felt tiny hands groping her, inserting themselves into her coat pockets, she struggled to rise and fight back, but her arms were jerked roughly behind her back. She recognized Leland's voice whispering near her ear. "I'm sorry about this, Miss Brigid."

Two transadapts dragged her across the carpet, to an opening between a pair of tall bookcases. Only when she was inside a small elevator did they allow her to get to her feet. The trolls brandished their autoblasters in silent threats.

After the door panel hissed shut, the elevator rose very quietly and only for a few seconds. Then their ascent stopped, the door opened and the transadapts urged her out with nudges from gun barrels. She entered a room that at first glance seemed much like the Cerberus ops center, but at least twice as large.

It was filled with the most sophisticated electronic equipment she had ever seen, some of it so advanced and unfamiliar she could only guess at its function. But all the consoles and panels were dark and soundless. A bank of monitor screens ran the length of one wall, and they were dark, as well.

As she went in the direction the transadapts urged, she saw that each screen bore an identification label: Tango, Zulu, Oscar, Bravo, Alpha and so on. She recognized the code names for the redoubts connected to the Totality Concept's varied divisions and subdivisions. As Lakesh had said, the Anthill had been intended to serve as the coordinating point of all the Concept's installations and projects.

As she walked farther into the room, she saw a shadowy shape bulking on the far side. Blue-green armaglass slabs glinted dully in the feeble light. It was the biggest mat-trans gateway unit she had ever seen, three times or more the size of the one in which they had materialized. It was certainly large enough to accommodate several vehicles like the Sandcat or the Hotspur.

She saw a freestanding control console facing the

jump chamber's massive door. Power-indicator lights glowed on it, so that at least was functional.

Her dwarfish escort pointed her to a chair at a control console, and she sat down. She sat for the better part of thirty minutes, worrying and wondering. The transadapts flanked her like grim and silent watchdogs, refusing to answer any questions she put to them.

Brigid found herself worried less about Lakesh than Kane in the custody of Sindri. She didn't think the little man was the type to torture a helpless captive, but then again he had expertly managed to quell her suspicions about a trap. Once more, Kane's instincts had been sound.

As for Lakesh, she didn't know what to think. If the woman who had spoken in the office was indeed Dian Baptiste, she was obviously concerned about his welfare.

None of the Anthill's personnel appeared in the control center, and she was just as glad. The very thought of them awakened a queasiness within her, a xenophobic shrinking of the like she hadn't experienced since her first sight of Balam. The creatures lurking in the vast catacombs were worse. They bore the superficial aspects of humanity, but it was truly a case of appearances being only skin-deep, and then not real skin at all. Although she didn't want to, she couldn't help but wonder what sustained them.

She managed to sneak a peek at her wrist chron without having a gun barrel shoved in her face. In a little under three hours, Grant and Domi would try to make the jump. She was fairly certain Sindri had closed off the transit lines between the Anthill and the Cerberus gateway.

Brigid heard the elevator door sigh open and she turned her head in that direction. Two figures approached her, crossing the large room. She recognized Lakesh, but the woman was a stranger, despite her having seen before-and-after images of her in Cerberus. She consciously strove to maintain her poker face.

"Dearest Brigid," Lakesh said wearily. "I'm told you weren't harmed."

"You were told right." She fixed a steady gaze on his companion and started to rise from the chair.

One of the transadapts planted a restraining hand on Brigid's shoulder to keep her seated. The woman with Lakesh reacted as if she had been subjected to a jolt from a Shockstick.

Uttering a wild, enraged shriek, she launched a vicious kick at the dwarf with his hand on Brigid. The toe of her shoe caught the transadapt on the underside of the jaw and sent him reeling backward, arms windmilling. His blaster clattered to the floor.

"Take your filthy paws off my daughter!"

Brigid felt her carefully composed mask of neutrality fall away and she stared in speechless surprise as the woman pursued the transadapt around the console. She kicked at him, picking up loose objects from the desktops and pelting him with them.

The unregenerate madness in her voice, bearing and actions shook Brigid to the roots of her soul. Lakesh watched the crazed activity, obviously sickened by it. He raised his reedy voice in a shout. "Dian, stop it! Enough!"

The woman paid him no need, continuing to chase the little man, who scuttled and cowered out of range of her feet. His companion stared with wide eyes.

"Stop!" Lakesh yelled stridently. "You're making a bad impression on Brigid."

The woman stopped her wrathful screams so suddenly it was as if Lakesh's words had thrown a switch. She spun around and strode stiffly back to Brigid. The other transadapt edged away. As Brigid stood up, Lakesh murmured, "Dian, this is Brigid."

Dian smiled, reaching out with cold, clumsy fingers to touch Brigid's hair, then to cup her cheek. Brigid stood stock-still, trying to return the grotesque smile.

"You don't need to introduce me to our daughter," Dian cooed. "She knew who I was right off, didn't you, sweetheart?"

Brigid groped for a response. Before she found an appropriate one, Dian caught her up in a fierce embrace, stroking her hair, patting her back, rocking her to and fro. She hummed a wordless, off-key lullaby into her ear.

Lakesh met her eye and he shook his head helplessly, placing a finger at his lips, warning her not to say or do anything that might trigger another demented outburst.

With great effort, Brigid forced the tension from her posture, emptying her mind of all thoughts. Her heart thudded frantically in her chest, either from compassion or revulsion, she wasn't sure.

She heard and saw the elevator doors open again, discharging Kane, Sindri and Leland. Kane walked gingerly, as if his feet pained him. His black coat lay draped over his shoulders, and when he drew closer, she saw how his arms were pinioned at his back.

Leland carried the holstered Sin Eater, with Kane's web belt slung over a shoulder. Sindri jauntily twirled a Shockstick as if it were a walking stick. Grinning broadly, he announced, "'Journeys end in lovers meeting' and all that sentimental rot."

Dian acted as if she hadn't heard, still hugging Brigid and crooning in her ear.

Sindri eyed both women curiously and cleared his throat loudly. "Forgive my interruption, Commander, but we have matters to discuss."

"Go away," Dian murmured dreamily. "You'll wake the baby."

Sindri visibly blanched, completely taken aback. He glanced up at Kane questioningly. Lakesh shuffled his feet, then focused his vision on some faraway point.

In a gentle, cajoling tone, Sindri ventured, "Commander, I've fulfilled my side of our bargain. I respectfully request you put this reunion—or whatever it is—in abeyance until our business is concluded."

Dian made a spitting, snarling sound. She whirled around with such speed and violence Brigid stumbled back a pace. Kane's eyes widened when he saw her face, but he said nothing, nor did he move.

Looming over Sindri, Dian grated, "How dare you, you deformed little mutant? *I* decide when our business is complete, not you!"

Swallowing his anger, Sindri stood his ground, fearlessly staring up into her disfigured face. "At great risk, I did as you bade. Your own people violated our truce, but I take into account their impaired judgment and mental faculties. I remind you that what I have given you, I have the power to take away."

He paused and added in a colorless, matter-of-fact tone, "I would do so reluctantly, regretfully, but I must insist you provide me with the entrance procedure."

Dian lifted her hands, curving her bony fingers as if she intended to fit them around Sindri's neck. The transadapt she had assaulted began sidling up to her, picking up his XP-900 pistol in the process.

Lakesh barked, "Dian, enough is enough. Friend Sindri is quite right. A bargain is a bargain."

Dian cast him a reproachful look, her one eye seething with resentment. Then she inhaled a calming breath. "As you wish, beloved. I don't want to fight in front of our daughter."

Both Kane and Sindri jerked in reaction to her statement. Kane began, "What the hell are you—?"

Brigid cut off the rest of his words by asking loudly, "Kane, are you all right?"

He nodded once, staring slit eyed at Dian. She felt his stare and demanded, "Who are you?"

"He's a friend of mine," Brigid interjected hastily.

"Just a friend?"

Brigid hesitated a fraction of a second before saying, "Just a friend."

"Good." Dian looked Kane up and down with a judgmental eye. "I don't like the looks of him. He's got the eyes of a moral reprobate, a hoodlum."

Sindri chuckled. "We find ourselves in agreement on that score, Commander."

Dian turned sharply on her heel. "Follow me." She strode off across the room without a backward glance.

Lakesh stepped close to Kane, murmuring, "We must go along with her. She's unstable."

"You think?" Kane snapped sarcastically. "Who is she?"

"The commander of this place. Her real name is Dian Baptiste."

Sindri overheard and shot a surprised searching look toward Brigid. "But she's not really your—"

"No," Brigid said harshly.

"Then what relation is she to you?" Kane asked.

Dian's imperious call prevented either Brigid or Lakesh from offering a response. "Come on!"

They started after her, but Kane distinctly heard Lakesh whisper, his tone thick with agony, "A damned soul."

Kane, Lakesh, Brigid, Leland and the two transadapts joined Dian at the freestanding console. She keyed in a sequence, then strode to the cargo gateway unit. The door, despite its massive proportions, opened easily. All of them climbed in.

"Where are we going?" Kane asked.

"Silence," Dian ordered.

The door shut behind them, and the process began. The hexagonal floor plates took on a shimmering glow, and wisps of cottony vapor drifted down from the ceiling. Kane made a motion to stand beside Brigid—and stumbled facefirst against an armaglass wall.

He blinked in surprise, turning around, seeing he was on the opposite side of the big chamber from everyone else. The transition had been so brief he did not experience any sense of time passing.

Dian popped open the door by its handle and stepped out of the gateway into what appeared to be, at first glance, total darkness. However, the air was fairly warm and held no hint of the dank chill of the Anthill. He gratefully breathed in somewhat stale, but untainted air.

All of them filed out. Kane felt rather than saw the pressure of mighty walls of stone all around them. Glancing to his right, he saw sunlight shafting through a distant, irregular opening and what appeared to be a rock-strewed gorge beyond. To his left, he saw only a congealed mass of blackness.

As his eyes adjusted to the dark, he saw Dian stride to the nearest rock wall and pass her hand over a projecting knob of stone. A tiny needle of red light sprang up from within it, casting her fingertips in a ruddy tint. Circuits clicked and hummed faintly.

For a second, nothing happened. Then above them grew a dim glow of light. It grew steadily brighter until it provided an illumination equal to direct sunlight on a very overcast day.

On the cavern ceiling, more lights flickered and flashed, a series of them. The lamps were so deeply inset into roof fissures that unless someone knew they were there, they would have been completely invisible.

Dian marched purposefully toward the nether end of the cavern, the others trailing behind her.

"Where the hell are we?" Kane asked lowly.

"In a canyon about two miles away from Mount Rushmore," answered Lakesh.

"And where the hell are we going?"

The old man shook his head. "I've never been here. I didn't have the security clearance for it."

"Sindri said—"

Dian swung her head around. "Shut up!" Her knife-edged cry echoed, the cavern walls beating it back.

"You heard her," Sindri commented with a taunting grin.

"You, too, you little mutant!" Dian snapped.

Kane estimated they walked for some three minutes beneath the halogen glow, then the cavern ended against a bulwark of rock. Dian continued walking toward it, as if she didn't see the grim gray stone or she expected it to turn into something else.

She didn't come to a stop until the toes of her shoes pressed against the down-slanting edge. She raised her right hand, and again came the clicking sound of circuits. A wavery funnel of red light sprayed out from a crack and washed over her palm, then slid over her face, haloing her right eye.

In a clear, concise voice, she announced, "Cincom two, Clearance Omega, ID Passcode 0712, Mission Snowbird. Admit."

A grinding rumble slowly built, punctuated, then was overlaid by a series of squeaks, creaks and hisses. Long disused gears, pulleys and hydraulics slowly moved. A huge square of rock laboriously began to shake loose from the cavern wall, dislodging pebbles. Although Kane had no way of knowing, he guessed the massive stone panel hadn't moved in a very long time, perhaps since the days of skydark or before.

Dian stepped away as the slab fell outward, supported by metal cables and chains the thickness of a human arm. Beyond it, down a short foyerlike passageway, stood a disk-shaped portal made of gleaming steel surrounded by a double thickness of riveted metal collars. Affixed to the wall beside it was a keypad with a small LCD window.

Sindri shivered, hugging himself in gleeful anticipation. "Here we go," he chanted. "Here we go."

Dian climbed the ramp formed by the disguised rock wall and punched in a three-digit sequence. Kane experienced a quiver of surprised unease when the glowing numbers, 2-5-3, appeared on the display. The numerical code was the reverse of the one input to open up a Totality Concept redoubt.

With a rumble and a squeal, the massive disk rolled to the left between a pair of baffled slots. The bottom lip of the encircling collars sank into the floor, making a seamless threshold. Light sprang up on the other side, but they couldn't see its source.

Dian crossed over the threshold, and Sindri elbowed between Kane and Lakesh, scrambling up the slanting platform. The two transadapts watched him with nervous eyes, then gestured suggestively with the barrels of their autoblasters. Leland, Brigid, Lakesh and Kane strode up the ramp and through the circular opening.

All of them came to unsteady halts at a metal railing. An array of halogen lights shone down from a domed ceiling into an immense gallery.

Chapter 24

Standing on a platform set high on one wall of the enormous, artificial cavern, they all fell silent, even Sindri.

Sharply cut from the bedrock in the shape of a pentagon, the walls stretched almost out of sight. Above a certain height, they were unfinished stone, but below that they were sheathed in polished alloy. A wide, railed aisle enclosed the center.

"Look at those things," Sindri said almost with a reverence.

Many of the shapes scattered about the vast floor were recognizable. Kane identified treaded digging machines outfitted with huge drill bits and saws, hovertanks and helicopters. But other vehicles defied his ability to categorize them; they might have been designed to crawl, fly or even swim for all he knew.

He saw a double-tiered black box structure thrusting out of the floor, topped by a rotating cube. His eyes followed the snaking power cables. They disappeared beneath a monstrous obsidian form resting on a raised plateau of concrete. It held the outline of a manta ray, but magnified a thousandfold. Its shark-fin, swept-back wings spanned at least a hundred feet. The craft was sleek and black, razor sharp on the leading edge of the wings and the prow. The flat-bodied fuselage put him in mind of a cobra's hood.

In a voice trembling with delighted awe, Sindri said, "Death from above. Aurora."

Although Sindri's earlier mention of the word had prepared Kane somewhat for the sight of the aircraft, he had envisioned the same kind of vessel they had seen and destroyed in New Mexico. That craft was like a child's toy beside this one. A Cobra rocket would have as much effect on it as a snowball.

The Aurora crouching below them looked far broader and longer than any machine intended to fly. He saw weapons emplacements recessed into its ebony sleekness. From the tapering prow bristled a cluster of slender rods, tipped with silver spheres. They looked tiny in comparison to the overall size of the aircraft, but Kane guessed each one was twice the diameter of his head.

Tilting his head back, he saw a spider's maze of catwalks and beams strung from metal cables and wires, surrounding the bowl-shaped roof. Above them, higher yet, glowed the lights.

Dian led them to a small elevator cage running on a steel track. They climbed into it, and she pulled down a lever. As the elevator began slowly moving down, Sindri pressed his face against the grille, standing on tiptoes to gaze at the Aurora.

Kane asked, "So that's what you found in the database and encrypted?"

Sindri bobbed his head. "All the specs and operational instructions for not just the Aurora but all of these other experimental prototypes. Evidently some of the later models were shipped off to other places, primarily to a base in New Mexico. The fully functional and debugged prototypes were stored here."

Lakesh looked toward Dian. "He found the data pertaining to it and rather than open hostilities to take it by force, he negotiated with you?"

"Not at first," she replied faintly. A faint sheen of perspiration glistened on her face, and Kane wondered if it was due to the higher temperature. "He and my people did exchange fire. Two of his were killed."

"Those were the bodies we saw on the tape?" inquired Brigid.

Sindri grinned. "We merely restaged a similar incident from two days before in the same place. Quite the convincing piece of cinema veritié, wasn't it?"

Dian regarded Brigid gravely. "When he hacked into the database and found the references to Aurora, he sent an emissary to me. Sindri offered me anything if I allowed him access to this storage vault. All I wanted was Mohandas, and that was a wish no one could deliver. Or so I thought."

She reached up to chuck Brigid beneath the chin. "You were an unexpected but very welcome bonus."

With an icy irony, Kane said, "That's you all over, Sindri. The great deliverer of unexpected and unrequested bonuses."

Sindri bowed his head, mocking a gracious nod. "Thank you, Mr. Kane. I hope to deliver an unexpected and unwelcome bonus to you in the very near future."

The elevator settled with a clank at the bottom of the track. Sindri rushed out into the immense room, running to the elevated platform holding the Aurora. From the gallery, the aircraft had looked big, but now it appeared absolutely monstrous. He figured it was 150 feet long. Three flat-footed steel pedestals supported its weight, each protruding from one of the vessel's three corners. The support stanchions were taller than Kane and thicker than his body. A hollow transparent cylinder stretched down from amidships to the concrete surface. Kane guessed it was some kind of lift, a way to enter the aircraft.

Sindri scaled the short flight of stairs that led up to the top of the platform. He walked beneath the Aurora, in its shadow, gazing up at its black undercarriage with ebullient eyes. "Stupendous, the pinnacle of avionic achievement! Hidden safe and snug from Armageddon, preserved for posterity."

Brigid called up, "What makes you think you can pilot that thing?"

"I may not have your eidetic gifts," Sindri replied, "but I take pride in being a quick study. Over the past few days, I memorized everything and anything pertaining to its operation."

He pointed toward one of the huge concave disks humping down from its underside. "What drives the Aurora is a pulsating force field generated by three integrated gravity-wave engines. They allow vertical takeoffs, landings and horizontal flight."

He walked to the prow and gestured to the sphere-tipped rods projecting from the nose. "The field cohesion is maintained by these magnetohydrodynamic air spikes. They focus microwaves on a point in the air in front of the craft, which then bends pressure waves backward in a parabola, enclosing the Aurora. Therefore, you have a simple inertialess and frictionless motive power."

Sindri clenched one delicate fist. "Imagine the Aurora as a wet bar of soap and the atmosphere as your hand. The tighter you squeeze, the more pressure you exert, sends the soap squirting out of your grip. The same principle is at work here."

He walked back beneath the aircraft. "Of course, how big a parabolic field and how much mass it affects depends on the generator's power. A big ship like this would emit such a large field, it would envelop other objects, even those on the ground. That's why so many reports of the Aurora's test flights back in the twentieth century were associated with power surges and overloads—not to mention alien spaceships."

Sindri pointed at the hull. "The hull is made of several layers of low-density ceramic-polymer composites. The layers are separated by a chemically bonded foam that provides thermal insulation. And of course, the black color is a means of absorbing sunlight while the Aurora soars into the subzero temperatures of the stratosphere."

Despite himself, Kane was deeply impressed. Not just with the aircraft itself but with Sindri's familiarity with it. Still, he said, "Memorizing the specs and being able to fly the damn thing aren't the same."

Sindri shrugged. "That's what we're here to discover. Now, if you will please join me—"

No one moved. Dian snapped, "The deal was to grant you access to this hangar. That has been done. You're on your own."

"The deal," replied Sindri in a tone sibilant with menace, "was to give me a fully functioning and operable Aurora. That has yet to be proved. Until it has been, the bargain isn't complete."

The two armed transadapts lifted their autopistols, beady eyes glinting. "Do as he says," Leland warned.

"You want all of us to get aboard that ship?" Lakesh demanded.

"I believe that was the general idea I was trying to convey, Dr. Singh."

"That craft hasn't moved in nearly two centuries. Diagnostics need to be run on its systems."

Sindri smiled and said silkily, "A man with your background will be invaluable to me in that area." The smile vanished from his face. "Now get up here. I won't tell you again."

Kane put his foot on the first metal riser of the staircase, but Brigid blocked him with an arm, jaw set at a stubborn, defiant angle. "You want me with you, too, Sindri?"

"Of course, Miss Brigid. Particularly you. There are many things we need to discuss about our future."

"Cut Kane loose first."

Sindri shook his head. "I'm afraid not. I don't trust an unfettered Mr. Kane around delicate instruments."

"Do it," Brigid grated, "or you won't be able to trust me, either."

Sindri's face darkened in frustrated anger. He glared down at her, but she locked eyes with him, not blinking or looking away. After several seconds, he fluttered a dismissive hand through the air. "Oh, all right. But I intend to hold you responsible for his actions. Leland, set him free."

Leland glowered unhappily but he unsheathed Kane's combat knife from the web belt and moved behind him, lifting his coat to one side. Kane felt the pressure of cold steel against his wrists, then his hands fell to his sides.

He repressed a sigh of relief as the ache in his shoulders abated. Bringing his hands up, he massaged his wrists, noting the angry red indentations encircling them. Without much surprise, he saw a set of nylon cuffs lying on the floor. He stoically withstood the burning pain of returning circulation in his hands.

"You don't need Dian for any of this, certainly not a test flight," Lakesh objected loudly. "Leaving her controlled environment might be fatal to her."

"Who could tell?" Sindri shot back scornfully. "Besides, leaving her behind might be fatal to *me.* As long as she's with me, she can't issue orders to her drones or plot a betrayal."

He turned smartly on his heel toward the hollow cylinder extending down from the Aurora. "I'm done arguing. I'm in charge here. If any of you insist on staying behind, you'll do so as corpses."

Kane quirked a quizzical eyebrow at Brigid, then walked up the staircase.

ONCE ALL OF THEM were aboard the Aurora, Sindri led them down a narrow, grille-floored gangway to the flight deck. Considering the size of the ship, it seemed surprisingly small and stripped down. There were no windows or ports, just large squares running the length of the interior bulkheads. Kane saw only four chairs placed before four control boards. Each one came equipped with a crisscrossing harness.

Sindri pointed at them one at a time, saying, "Pilot, copilot, bombardier, communications."

"Bombardier?" Kane repeated. "In your little dissertation, you didn't say anything about weapons."

"A deliberate omission, Mr. Kane. I didn't want to give you any notions."

Sindri sat down in the pilot's chair and waved Lakesh toward the copilot's seat. "Miss Brigid, Mr. Kane, please find seats for yourselves. Commander, there's no need for your presence here. I can't stomach the smell or sight of you any longer. Leland, find a place where she can be confined. Stay with her."

Dian raised her voice in a screechy protest, but when the transadapts pointed their XP-900 pistols, Lakesh said reasonably but sternly, "Dian, do as he says, at least for the time being."

Her lips writhed back from her discolored teeth as

if she were going to spit at him. "I don't like the way that little mutant looks at Brigid!"

Kane almost muttered, *That makes two of us,* but decided to keep silent.

"She'll be safe," Lakesh told her reassuringly. "Now, please go."

Reluctantly, at gunpoint, Dian left the cabin in company of Leland and another of the transadapts. She murmured imprecations under her breath.

Sindri's fingers tapped buttons on a control board. "First thing is to get the air recyclers working to offset that woman's ghastly choice in perfumes."

"Shut your mouth," Lakesh snapped as he sat down in the copilot's chair. "She's as much of a victim of scientific circumstance as you claim you and your people are."

Sindri shot him a narrow-eyed stare. "There's one important difference, Dr. Singh. We didn't volunteer."

Kane and Brigid sat down in the chairs, and the lone transadapt buckled the straps around their torsos. They weren't helpless—their limbs were free—but neither one could make any sudden moves, let alone swift ones.

Sindri continued pushing buttons. He didn't activate the air conditioner. The blank squares on the bulkheads seemed to vanish in segments. They weren't windows but view screens, the images transmitted by external scanners, providing an almost 360-degree perspective of their surroundings.

Sindri experimented with the controls, adjusting

view, focus and range. The images on the screens shifted with each touch of a button. One screen showed the bowl-shaped ceiling of the hangar.

Lakesh flicked a few switches, and all of the consoles emitted a hum like a swarm of bees. Tiny lights flashed and blinked purposefully. An array of monitor screens blurred with pixels, then resolved into sharp focus.

In a voice light with relief and cheer, Sindri crowed, "All the systems are coming on-line—map position scopes, radar-echo altimeters, wave-guide conformals. It all still works!"

Lakesh fastened his attention on a small screen that displayed scrolling machine talk. Sounding enthralled himself, he announced, "An automatic diagnostic program has already kicked in."

Swiveling his chair slightly, Kane tried to catch Brigid's eye. Her face was taut with repressed emotion. He leaned toward her and whispered, "Baptiste, who is that woman?"

"Like Lakesh said, a damned soul." Brigid's voice was barely audible. "She's been living in the Anthill for nearly two hundred years, half alive, half dead."

Kane winced in sympathy. "No wonder she's fused out. What's her connection to you and Lakesh?"

The other dwarf returned to the compartment. As the bore of his blaster jerked in his direction, Kane fell silent and straightened.

Sindri pushed keys and thumbed toggles, blunting the figures appearing on a monitor screen. Cool air from a ventilator suddenly touched all of their faces.

For the next few minutes, Lakesh and Sindri, eyes fastened to the readout screens, asked each other questions in monotones and answered in equally flat voices.

"Guidance system nexus?"

"Enabled."

"Tracking and control radars?"

"Nominal."

"GPS linkup?"

"Dead."

"VTOL cross ties?"

"Green."

The deckplates vibrated beneath their feet, in tandem with a whine that grew in pitch. Dimly came metallic clacking sounds.

"Power umbilici detached," Sindri declared. "Takeoff prep systems engaged."

A siren began hooting, and a light panel flashed Launch System Enabled.

Sindri turned toward the transadapts, pointing to three niches recessed into the far wall. "Strap yourselves in."

On the central view screen, motion flickered. Two great leaves of the domed roof swung outward on gigantic hinges and pivots. The sky above showed dim gray masses of clouds, glowing vaguely with the light of the obscured sun. Kane guessed by the quality of light that the time was late afternoon.

"Withdrawing the landing gear," Lakesh said.

The drone and the vibration sang into harmony, and the Aurora began to rise.

Chapter 25

With a breathless swiftness, the Aurora rose to the open canopy and seemed to hang motionless between the two leaves. Then slowly, the climb resumed.

Sindri's graceful fingers played over the keys of a control board. He murmured to himself about vectors and valences, consulting the instrument displays, then the images on the view screen array.

Kane couldn't help but stare in fascination as the Aurora ascended smoothly, as if drawn by the attraction of a celestial magnet. He felt little sense of motion, only a slight sinking sensation in the pit of his stomach.

The screens offered different vantage points of the ascent and Kane's eyes darted from one to another. The Aurora's vertical climb felt nothing like that of a Deathbird. It was as if the huge aircraft rested on the palm of a hand made of compressed air, which lifted the craft straight up to the heavens.

He watched as the canyon and rocky crags receded so quickly they became mere ripples of contrasting texture and color. High mountain peaks appeared, then shrank into little snowcapped cones. Then the Aurora plunged into cloud cover, and the screens displayed only billowing, misty froth.

Kane glanced over at Brigid, half-expecting to see her eyes screwed up tight, with a white-knuckled grip on the edge of her chair. She had reacted in such a fashion during a flight from Russia to Mongolia some months before. To his pleased surprise, he saw her attention was riveted on the view screens, too. Her posture, though tense, wasn't one of fear.

He doubted she had overcome her fear of flying. Being aboard the Aurora bore no resemblance to the old Soviet Tu-114 cargo plane, with its roaring propellers, unpressurized cabin and shaking superstructure.

Wispy scraps of mist slid past the Aurora's external cameras, and suddenly full sunlight streamed into the cockpit. The sky was a blue canopy without brilliance. In it, far above the cloud ceiling, the sun shone, yet its light was filtered by the scanners so they could peer directly at it without damaging the eye. The bowl of deep azure was edged by blue and white, its rim resting upon the horizon.

Lakesh intoned, "Preset zenith reached. Our altitude is forty thousand feet."

Sindri reached for a control board. "Gravity-wave engines engaged. Let's see what she'll do."

The acceleration of the lateral thrust smashed down on them, slamming Kane's spine so hard against the back of his chair that he fancied he could feel the steel support bar. At the edges of his hearing he heard a ripping roar. The pressure didn't stop; instead it grew stronger, squeezing the air out of his lungs and the sight from his eyes. He heard Sindri yip in pure exultation, then shout, "Mach 1.5!"

The weight suddenly vanished from Kane's body, and he squinted dazedly toward the view screens. They showed nothing but a trackless expanse of blue sky. Without some object as a frame of reference, it appeared the Aurora was still hovering.

But the airspeed gauge proved they weren't. Kane watched the numbers reel up like a panicked clock. Brigid gazed at it, too, breathing hard.

The tearing roar sounded again, and the ship shuddered as if it had struck a rut in the sky. Once more they were slapped back against their seats, but the G-force assault lasted only a second.

"Mach 2!" Sindri crowed.

The Aurora banked, and on the screens the horizon appeared to wheel crazily around them.

"Skin temperature is rising," Lakesh warned.

Sindri tapped a pair of keys, and the craft's velocity dropped with only a distant jar to indicate deceleration. He experimented with the key commands, frequently giggling, occasionally exclaiming "Whoops!"

The Aurora leaped onto a tangential course, and it seemed to Kane he could feel the bones in his face cracking under the stress of acceleration. But always, right on the verge of tolerance, inertia dampers kicked in.

Under Sindri's guidance, the aircraft performed barrel rolls, loops and wide, swinging yaws. The images on the viewers blurred to a chaotic jumble of streaking colors.

The fabric of the ship moaned, quivered, shuddered, swayed. In an instant of terror, Kane thought the craft was breaking up and prepared himself for the whistle of air through ruptured hull plates. But the Aurora held as Sindri put it through its paces, testing all of its flight limitations and capabilities.

The aircraft tilted to starboard, curving back in a wide, flat turn. Sindri swiveled his chair to face Kane and Brigid, his eyes glittering and wild. "Any place you care to visit? Any country, any province, any far corner, just name it. Almost every coordinate for any region on Earth is in the tracking and map computers. All I have to do is feed in some numbers."

Kane said, "You don't intend to use this thing just to play tourist."

"Quite right," replied the little man. "It's my flying fortress, my mobile base of operations, completely safe from attack or invasion."

"Base of operations for what?" Brigid asked.

Sindri fluttered a hand. "For a lot of things. Retribution comes to mind."

"Retribution?" demanded Kane. "Why?"

Sindri made an expansive gesture that encompassed both himself and the two transadapts strapped into bulkhead niches. "For us being born, created as a slave race. Aren't your barons the culmination of the selfsame genetic experiments that birthed us? While we occupy the lowest level of Overproject Excalibur's many labors, the barons sit at the highest point."

"That's true," Brigid admitted. "But do you intend to knock them off the ladder so you can take their place?"

Sindri's eyes blazed with a blue messianic flame. "And why shouldn't I? My destiny as a slave was chosen for me before I was even born. Now that I hold the whip hand, the destinies of the baronies are mine to choose. I've chosen to destroy them."

"And then," Kane ventured, "you think you'll reign supreme over a new empire you'll build out of the ruins of the villes?"

Sindri smiled, a bitter twisting of his mobile mouth. "The fact is the world is about to change, Mr. Kane. Whether a new empire arises or not, I control the most powerful engine of war ever conceived. The Aurora will be the axis around which a new Armageddon revolves."

Lakesh said quietly, "You may be premature. The weapons systems, even if they're fully functional, weren't designed to be offensive. Above all else, the Aurora is a stealth plane, a vehicle of reconnaissance, not of war."

Sindri cast him an incredulous glance and laughed uproariously. "The Aurora carries ten Lance rockets with subkiloton fission warheads. Those are more than sufficient to wage a war against nine baronies."

"And wipe out a goodly portion of their surrounding territories," Brigid bit out grimly.

"True," he conceded. "But I seriously doubt I'll be forced to make more than one or two examples before the others fall into line."

"And then what?" Kane demanded. "Even wiping out the villes won't solve the extinction facing your people."

Sindri opened his mouth to retort, but Brigid declared coldly, flatly, "He doesn't consider that a problem at all. On Mars he told me how he really feels about his poor, abused people."

"Shut up," hissed Sindri.

Affecting not to have heard him, Brigid turned to the transadapts strapped to the bulkhead. "Your great liberator said to me, and I quote, 'I could give the proverbial rat's ass about the transadapts.... Stupid, filthy, childish creatures.'"

"That's a lie!" Sindri bellowed.

Brigid continued calmly, "'The Committee of One Hundred was right. They cannot govern themselves, they should have no decision-making abilities. They are useful only as legs and arms and strong backs.... Unfortunately, they were the only followers I had available.'"

"A lie!" Sindri tried to leap from his chair, but the harness kept him planted within it. He struggled with the catch-release tab. "Lies, *lies!*"

The eyes of the dwarfs flicked uncertainly from Brigid to Sindri.

"I have a photographic memory," she went on. "I don't forget anything I see or hear, and I certainly wouldn't forget a hypocritical admission like that one."

Sindri managed to get to his feet. Kane noticed how

Lakesh surreptitiously reached for the control board as soon as the little man turned his back.

Thrusting out his jaw pugnaciously, Sindri addressed the transadapts. "She's lying, I swear to you, trying to spread dissension. I explained my plan to you—the Anthill has all the advanced medical and bioengineering equipment we need to start a gene-therapy program and cure our sterility."

Kane uttered a sneering laugh. "You're full of shit." He swiveled his chair toward the transadapts. "You saw the condition of that pesthole and the people who live there. If there was any kind of a miracle cure in the place, don't you think those poor bastards would have used it on themselves?"

Sindri's face turned the color of old ashes. He balled his fists, the knuckles straining at the skin like ivory knobs. His small body trembled and his eyes flared with a maddened light. In a soft voice, he said, "Your life and presence aboard the Aurora is no longer an advantage, Mr. Kane. I have Miss Brigid and Dr. Singh, and therefore you are superfluous."

He snapped his fingers and pointed to the transadapts. "Take him below and shoot him four times in the head. When we're at a lower altitude, we'll jettison his carcass like so much trash."

The pair of little men didn't stir for a moment.

Sindri shrieked and stamped his foot. "Do as I say, goddamn you! Do it or I'll dump your malformed asses along with his!"

The transadapts unbuckled the harnesses and stepped out of the niches, moving toward Kane. At that instant, Lakesh slapped a series of keys in tandem. The Aurora surged forward, riding a booming Mach 4 shock wave.

The sudden acceleration pinned Kane and Brigid to their chairs, snapping at the air, and blind. The jump in velocity catapulted Sindri off the deck as if he had been shot from an artillery piece. He bowled into the transadapts, his body turned into a battering ram. He knocked them backward, and all three of them cartwheeled out of the cockpit and into the gangway.

When the crushing pressure of the G-forces lessened, Kane didn't wait until his lungs were full or his vision clear before fumbling for the release catch on his harness. He clicked it open, sprang from his chair and bounded across the cockpit toward the three-body pileup on the deck.

Sindri lay more or less atop the heap, kicking his legs feebly, breathing in wheezes. Snatching him by the collar of his buckskin jacket, Kane wrenched him upright. Beneath him, eyes glazed and blood streaming from a flattened nose, a transadapt peered up over the barrel of his XP-900.

Kane released Sindri, letting him fall into the cockpit, and threw himself to the right, flattening his body against the bulkhead. The gangway filled with the stuttering thunder of full autofire.

The 9 mm rounds thumped the air past Kane's upper body. He felt one pluck at the shoulder of his coat and then crease across his back. He heard a crash and shatter from the cockpit, then a wordless bleat of terror burst from Lakesh's throat.

The big aircraft suddenly slipped to port and Kane staggered, but twisted and fell atop the prone trans-adapt. He managed to grab the spindly barrel of the XP-900 just as the bloody-faced troll triggered it again. The rounds punched through the bulkhead within a finger's width of Kane's face. Sparks flared from the bullet holes stitched in the wall, then a terrible suction began, seeming to snatch at Kane's hair and draw it into the punctures.

Almost immediately oxygen seemed to be sucked from the gangway while freezing air shrieked in, sounding like a hundred teakettles on full boil. Kane's heart fluttered and he felt his throat constrict. The terrific cold struck him like a blow, as if his body had been suddenly submerged in the waters of a polar sea.

Chapter 26

Each breath a struggle, his surroundings fading with every microsecond, Kane fought with the transadapt for the autopistol. He managed to insert a thumb into the trigger guard to keep him from firing another burst, but that one response was the limit of his actions.

The little man was bred to survive in a rarefied atmosphere and low temperatures, and so he didn't suffer from the depressurization as severely as Kane. The troll took vicious advantage of Kane. He bit, he gouged for Kane's eyes, he head-butted and his foot-hands sought out Kane's groin.

Kane barely felt the punishment. Despite the insulation of his coat, he was engulfed in a cold more intense, more penetrating than he had ever known before. His body was so stiff it was almost immovable. His heart trip-hammered; his breath beat in and out of his straining lungs.

At the far edges of his hearing, he heard Brigid and Lakesh shouting, then a piercing, resonant hissing sound. His eardrums registered a brief pressure, then the icy knives thrusting into his body withdrew and he was able to take in a deep breath of air.

He tore himself desperately backward. The transadapt still clung tenaciously to the XP-900, and Kane wrenched him up from the deck. He thrust the crown of his head forward. The dwarf tried to duck and took the blow on his already broken nose. More blood sprayed from his nostrils, and the back of his skull hit the grillwork with a nonmusical chime. His grip loosened and slithered away from the autopistol. He sprawled on the deck and twitched.

Dizzy and still shivering, but now able to breathe more or less normally, Kane quickly examined the other transadapt. He lay on his side, mouth slightly agape, eyes open but lusterless. Kane couldn't determine if the troll was dead or simply unconscious, and at the moment he didn't give much of a damn. He yanked the little man's blaster from his unresisting hand and staggered back into the cockpit.

Both Lakesh and Brigid breathed with labored gasps. Lakesh husked out, "I activated a shutoff valve that compensated for the loss of pressure and restored the oxygen. Temporary measure."

Kane handed Brigid one of the autopistols and gave Sindri a critical appraisal. The little man sat hunched with his back to a chair, cradling his head in his hands and rocking back and forth. Between his fingers, Kane saw the spreading blotch of a purple bruise.

"Why is it temporary?"

Lakesh inhaled deeply, harshly. "We're going down. The automatic stabilizers are keeping us from going into a dive, but we're losing altitude fast."

Looking toward the altimeter, Kane saw numbers

scrolling across it too fast to decipher. "Can't you do anything?"

Lakesh waved in frustration to the control board. Through bullet-smashed holes, circuit boards gleamed and sparks sputtered. "All manual-piloting functions are off-line, overridden by the navigational computers. There's not even a way to reset or reboot. We're dealing with a hardware failure."

"How much time do we have?" Brigid asked, eyeing the view screens. They showed only wispy clouds whipping past the prow of the Aurora.

"At our airspeed, we could hit the ground in less than five minutes...if the turbulence doesn't break us up first."

"Hit where?"

"Sindri had already set the computers to return us to base, so we'll crash somewhere in the vicinity of Mount Rushmore, if not against it. We're still right on course, if that's any comfort."

"It isn't." Kane nudged Sindri with a boot, and he wasn't gentle about it. "Get it together, pissant. There's got to be a way off this damn ship in case of an emergency."

Sindri lowered his hands from his face and looked up, eyes bearing a glassy, dazed sheen. Scarlet oozed from a laceration on his puffy lower lip. Faintly he said, "There is, but I don't remember exactly—"

Kane kicked him hard on the ankle. "You'd better!"

Squatting, Kane jammed the bore of the blaster against Sindri's high forehead, giving it a cruel half twist against the draining bruise. "If you don't remember, I'll shoot you in the head four times."

Sindri blinked repeatedly, grimacing in pain. "Belowdecks," he blurted. "Ejection seats."

Kane straightened up, hauling him erect by the front of his jacket. "Show us."

The deck underfoot suddenly tilted at a sharp angle. All of them staggered, grabbing seat backs to keep from sliding against the forward instrument panel. They felt the ship bump and sway and heard the stressed whine of internal gyroscopic stabilizers. Gradually, the Aurora leveled off.

"We'll stay on course without anyone at the controls," Lakesh said tensely. "But our angle of descent depends on a lot of variables."

The screens still showed clouds, but through gaps torn in them they saw a wide plain far below, marked here and there with rocky crags and vegetation. Even in the few seconds Kane looked at the images, the landscape expanded.

Shoving Sindri ahead of him at blasterpoint, Kane led the way down the passage, past the bodies of the transadapts.

"Dian," Lakesh rasped. "We've got to find her."

"No need," Sindri said over his shoulder. "I told Leland to take her below, and that's where we're going."

At the end of the gangway, Sindri climbed down into a square, metal-walled well, scampering down the aluminum ladder rungs. Kane followed quickly, nearly stepping on Sindri's hands.

The ladder led down to a large, well-lit compartment. Ten-foot-long missiles were stored in racks poised by launch tubes, like gigantic ammo clips. As Lakesh dropped down from the access hatch, Kane asked him, "Won't these things go off when the ship crashes?"

Lakesh spared them a swift, almost feverish stare and said, "Unlikely. The detonators haven't been armed."

Despite his quick, facile answer, the old man sounded doubtful of his own words.

Sindri ran recklessly along a catwalk that seemed to stretch the length of the lower level. Kane, Brigid and Lakesh dashed after him, their feet clanging on the metal grates.

At a branching in the catwalk, Sindri paused, looking frantically to the left and right. One part of it went to a sealed compartment door, and the other stretched down and forward. Lakesh took advantage of Sindri's indecision to cup his hands around his mouth and shout stridently, "Dian!"

A muffled voice responded behind the door, and Lakesh pushed Kane aside. "We've got no time!" Sindri yelled after him. "The ejection pod is this way!"

Brigid laid the barrel of the blaster against the side of the little man's head. "We'll make time."

Kane followed Lakesh closely. The old man reached the door, fumbled with the latch and yanked it open. Leland sprang out in a headfirst lunge. He pistoned his head into Lakesh's midsection, bending him double and sending him stumbling against Kane. The transadapt's swart face was a mask of bewilderment. As Lakesh leaned against him, Kane grabbed a rail with one hand and raised the XP-900 with the other, drawing a bead on Leland.

The transadapt crashed facedown on the surface of the catwalk, making no attempt to check his fall. Kane's combat knife sprouted from the base of his neck, nearly half of its length buried in the thick lumps of muscle.

Dian appeared in the door, her blue eye ablaze with a crazed ferocity, the right side of her mouth upturned in a grin of savage satisfaction. She held Kane's web belt in one hand, and he understood instantly what had happened—when Leland was distracted by Lakesh's call, Dian snatched the belt from him, unsheathed the knife and stabbed him with it.

Bracing himself on the catwalk's handrails, Lakesh straightened, biting at air. "Dian, the Aurora is going down. We've got to get off it!"

Kane stooped and plucked his holstered Sin Eater from Leland's slack fingers, cramming it into a coat pocket. When he reached for the knife in the transadapt's back, Dian thrust a knee hard against his jaw, rocking him back on his heels. Before he recovered his balance, she whipped the dagger free, a streamer of scarlet trailing from the blued blade.

Kane leveled the autopistol. "Drop it."

Dian swished the long knife through the air. She sneered, "Bite me."

A prolonged, racking shudder ran the length of the

Aurora. The catwalk rattled noisily, jumping violently beneath their feet. Dian pitched forward, the knife blade plunging down.

Lakesh twisted, crying out. He staggered back, feet seeking purchase on the trembling metal grille. Kane glimpsed the rent in his shirt and the blood bubbling up through it.

Sindri shouted, his voice a wild keen of fear, "Shoot the bitch and be done with it!"

Grabbing Brigid's wrist, he tried to haul her down the catwalk. She grappled with him, struggling to wrest free of his grasp.

Kane manhandled Lakesh to one side, trying to keep his blaster trained on the disfigured woman. He backed away from her. "Drop it, goddamn it!"

Dian's flaccid lips writhed, and what little spark of reason that gleamed in her good eye vanished in a blaze of madness. She lunged forward, knife slicing the air in a downward stroke.

Kane dodged and the point of the blade struck the handrail, knocking sparks off the metal. Encumbered with Lakesh, he wasn't able to stop her as the woman body-blocked him aside. She bounded down the catwalk where Brigid and Sindri wrestled at the branching-off point.

Not thinking, reacting completely from instinct, Kane reverted to training and to a level of awareness far deeper than training. He tracked the woman swiftly, centered the sights of the XP-900 on an area between her shoulderblades and squeezed the trigger.

The three rounds slammed into Dian with the impact of a triple sledgehammer blow. Her bound became an arch-backed leap, and it ended in Brigid's arms. The combat knife slashed down and sank deep into Sindri's left shoulder, just below the collarbone. His cry of pain was drowned out by Brigid's full-throated scream of angry anguish.

As she sagged beneath the weight of the woman, Lakesh shoved himself away from Kane, muttering thickly, "What have you done?"

They joined Brigid as she cradled Dian's body in her lap, ignoring Sindri's whimpers as he clung to a handrail and made tentative efforts to tug the blade from his body.

Dian looked up into Lakesh's face. Liquid strings of crimson, brought up from bullet-riven lungs, crawled out of her mouth. She croaked, "Mohandas...if only we had met differently...you and I...our daughter...together we..." She stopped and drew in a shuddery breath. "But that's not the way it is. Many happy returns."

Her body trembled, then went stiff. Kane gazed down at her gaping red mouth and staring eyes and felt sick. The ship yawed, listing to port and then to starboard. Kane took Brigid by the arm and pulled her to her feet. She kept her eyes locked on the dead woman's Janus face.

"I thought she was coming after you, not Sindri—" he said, faltingly.

"You didn't think at all," she said bitterly.

When she raised her gaze to him, he recoiled inwardly at the rage glinting in her emerald eyes. Brigid struck him openhanded as hard as she could, across the face. The blow twisted his head sideways on his neck, and he stumbled back half a pace.

Lakesh closed a hand around Brigid's arm. "Dian was dead already—can't you understand that? She was lost to me, lost to you, a long time ago. Kane can't be blamed."

Not looking away from him, eyes seething with fury and more than fury, Brigid snapped, "Can't he?"

The Aurora rocked again, a motion like a stone skipping across the surface of a pond. Gripping the hilt of the knife to keep it from tearing even more flesh and muscle, Sindri staggered drunkenly down the catwalk. Lakesh, Brigid and Kane followed him.

They entered a small enclosed space, not much more than a module with convex walls. From five ovals perforating the far bulkhead, small chairs projected, equipped with parachute packs and harnesses. Hand levers were attached to the bases of the seats.

Sindri started to scramble into one of them, but Brigid grabbed him by his ponytail. He squalled as she yanked him back, clawing for her hand. Eyes glittering with jade sparks of hatred, she grated between clenched teeth, "You're staying here, with her."

In a shocked voice, Lakesh said, "Brigid, that won't solve anything—"

"Shut up," she snapped. She glared into Sindri's bulging eyes. "You're responsible for bringing her out of her tomb. You can keep her company in this one."

Ruthlessly, Brigid closed a hand on the combat knife by the hilt and exerted pressure on it. Sindri shrieked in agony, dropping to his knees, convulsing and flailing, spittle spraying from his lips.

Kane didn't like the merciless, vengeful light in her eyes, but he said nothing as he strapped himself into a harness. Brigid and Lakesh secured themselves to the seats while Sindri thrashed on the deck, sobbing in agony, uttering wordless pleas.

The three people threw the chair levers more or less simultaneously. The ejection ports behind them popped open. Rockets beneath the seats blasted, wind roared and then blue screamed all around them, the horizon tipping up on edge, falling over, tipping up again.

They tumbled like wobbling tops in midair, pierced by a gut-numbing cold. Then came the spine-compressing, teeth-clattering shock of the glider chutes popping open with loud whip cracks. All of them felt the increased pressure of the chairs against their backs and thighs. The chaotic confusion of free fall came to an abrupt end.

Kane grasped the guide cords and gained a stable attitude. He looked for his companions and saw them both, swaying pendulum fashion beneath the belled canopies. Below him he saw stretches of green forest interspersed with gray stone. Twisting his head, he tried to find any trace of the Aurora and at first did not see anything.

Then, far in the distance, at least two miles away, he sighted a black speck, ebony against the charcoal color of a mountain range. A shaved sliver of an instant later, the obsidian speck vanished, replaced by a yellow-orange puffball. Seconds later he heard a dull explosion.

Kane tugged at the shrouds to spill air from the chute and drift him toward a treeless expanse. Brigid and Lakesh followed his example as they floated down.

Kane sprawled on the rocky ground, the chute dragging him, but he fought his way out of the harness and the ejection seat. Lakesh and Brigid came down within yards of him, and he helped them shed their chutes and straps. Only Lakesh offered a murmured word of thanks.

Kane eyed the sun sinking in a welter of crimson behind the pinnacle of mountain peaks and asked, "Do you have any idea where in hell we are?"

Lakesh caught his breath and winced as he touched the shallow cut on his ribs. "By my calculations, we should be within a few miles of Mount Rushmore. A day of hiking will get us back to the canyon and the mat-trans unit there. We can use it to return to Cerberus."

Kane spit in the dust. "It'll mean a night out in the open. A cold camp."

"It's preferable to the Anthill," Lakesh replied in a vague voice.

Both men turned toward Brigid Baptiste. Although her eyes no longer gleamed with a merciless resolve, her mane of hair was a tangle, her features pinched, lips compressed in a grim line.

"Dearest Brigid—" Lakesh began sympathetically.

She cut him off with a sharp, savage gesture. "I don't want to hear it. It's done, it's over. Sindri's punishment may not have fit his crime, but it's all I could improvise."

"I wasn't going to reprimand you," Lakesh replied gently. "I want you to understand about Dian. The woman she was, the woman I loved, died many, many years ago, long before you were born. What you met was just a shell, a warped imitation of the real person. Even if Kane had not done what he did, she was far beyond saving."

He lowered his voice to a rustling whisper. "She died believing she was protecting her child. She died in peace, her existence justified."

Brigid blinked back angry tears. "Died in peace," she echoed contemptuously. "Shot in the back like a slagger."

Kane coughed self-consciously. "Baptiste, I thought she was trying to kill you. Under the circumstances, I did what needed to be done."

Brigid locked her unblinking, glimmering eyes on his. "Just like you always do, no matter what promises you make. You're a cruel man, Kane, and the more I'm in your company, the more your cruelty contaminates me."

She wheeled away from him.

"What the hell does that mean?" Kane demanded angrily.

Brigid didn't respond. She stalked swiftly and

stiffly toward a copse of aspen trees. Kane started to go after her, but Lakesh laid a restraining hand on his shoulder. "Let her go."

Slapping the man's hand away, Kane snarled, "All of this was more your fault than Sindri's."

Lakesh nodded in bleak acceptance of the charge. "I won't presume to debate you. But sometimes drastic measures must be taken to lay the past to rest. That must be done before any kind of future can be conceived, much less lived. In time, Brigid will come to understand that. After she mourns."

"What is there to mourn?" Kane demanded impatiently. "She didn't know the woman."

In a rustling, unsteady voice, Lakesh said, "Brigid doesn't grieve for the woman who died on the Aurora. Like me, she mourns the loss of what might have been."

Epilogue

Abrams quietly traversed a long series of arches. Despite his crippled leg, he could move like a wraith when he saw a reason for it, and he saw a very good reason now.

It was nearly 0300, and the corridors of this wing of A Level were as silent as an Outland cemetery at midnight. They were almost as dark; the overhead neon strips shed a muted glow, as if to simulate moonlight. He crept down the corridor, following the curving wall, walking heel to toe on the green, square floor tiles.

Abrams's body was wrapped in a black Kevlar-weave coat, and his Sin Eater was holstered securely on his right forearm. He carried a war bag over his shoulder. The bag bulged with odds and ends taken not only from the armory on B Level but from the survival stores. He had no idea how long he would be gone, but in his estimation it would require at least five days to adequately explore the Anthill. Depending on what he found there, he might not return to Cobaltville at all—and if he did so, it would not be as the baron's creature.

The intel regarding the vast COG installation was spotty, but it still contained sufficient lures to draw him there for a personal recce. Abrams also had the enabling codes for the Anthill's mat-trans gateways.

No one knew what he was doing, not even pathetic Guende. If all went according to his hopes, Guende would be one of the few spared in his purge.

Abrams passed beneath another arch, which opened up into another stretch of silent hallway. This part of the baron's aerie was designed intentionally like a labyrinth, to confuse an intruder's sense of direction. But Abrams had been here before and knew his way. He did not have fond memories of his last visit to this wing.

At the thought of Baron Cobalt taking a smirking satisfaction in his maze, Abrams smirked himself. If the baron had hoped to cement Abrams's subservience when he exposed the Archon Directorate as a myth, the exact opposite effect had been achieved. Instead of an increase in his loyalty to the united baronies, anger and thirst for rebellion boiled in equal measure in Abrams's heart.

Perhaps if Baron Cobalt hadn't ordered the disastrous and humiliating mission to the Darks, if he had heeded his counsel, Abrams would still have held him in a degree of awe and fear. But when the baron had proved himself to be just as vulnerable to unreasoning, irrational passions as the inferior humans he and his kind ruled, the awe simply died. For if the oligarchy was vulnerable in that area, it stood to reason they had other weaknesses that could be exploited.

If the Anthill installation held medical facilities that would serve as a substitute for the Dulce installation,

Abrams intended to secure and control the Anthill. And barring that, he would destroy it. If he could not stage an open rebellion against the barons, he'd settle for watching them sicken and die.

The wall curved and ended against a door. Abrams thumbed the solenoid stud on the frame, unlocking the panel, which slid noiselessly open. He stepped into the rooms that contained Baron Cobalt's private mat-trans gateway, its existence known only to the Trust and its use forbidden to all but the baron.

He walked across the small control room, paying no attention to chittering consoles and flickering light panels. He went through another door and entered an anteroom, just large enough for a marble, round-topped table, two chairs and the jump chamber itself. A green-tinted neon strip ran the length of the ceiling. The armaglass walls of the gateway unit were pewter-colored, the hue of distant rain clouds.

He punched in the memorized code on the keypad mounted beside the jump chamber's door and stepped in, swinging the heavy armaglass door closed. He stood and waited for the automatic jump initiator to engage and begin the cycle.

A lilting voice reached him, penetrating the armaglass walls. "I've interrupted the connection between the initiator and the autosequencer. You're not going anywhere, Abrams. At least, not out of Cobaltville."

The sudden shock of fear was almost like a physical blow. For a second, the air seized in Abrams's lungs and he was unable to breathe or even to move.

"Come on out of there," Baron Cobalt called, his tone oily and passionless.

Slowly, Abrams heaved up on the door handle and shouldered the translucent slab aside. The baron leaned casually against the console in the control room and regarded him with mild eyes, no particular expression on his high-planed face. Beside him stood Guende, his balding head bowed, eyes disconsolate, lower lip trembling.

Abrams felt his shoulders slumping at the realization of betrayal, but with a great effort of will, he straightened his spine and strode across the antechamber to the control room. He gazed levelly at Baron Cobalt.

"My lord," he said politely.

Baron Cobalt patted Guende comfortingly on the shoulder. "Don't blame him, Abrams. I learned nothing from him. I didn't need to."

A lazy smile stretched the baron's thin lips. "Did you really think you could continue to deceive me with that childish bit of tampering with the spy-eye in your office? I've known about it for years, Abrams. *Years.* A new surveillance system was installed there a long time ago. One of your own Intel section officers did little more than watch you and report on what you said and did."

Abrams nodded. "I shouldn't have underestimated you. My error."

"More than one, actually. I pardoned you and gave you the Mount Rushmore installation assignment as something of a test, to gauge your resentment toward me, to find out if you could still be trusted after your incarceration. I calculated that if you did harbor ill will toward me, the temptation to take covert action would be too much for you to pass up.''

Baron Cobalt paused and shook his head, his eyelids drooping sadly. ''It grieves me to the soul that my calculations proved to be correct.''

Abrams surprised the baron—and to an extent, himself—by laughing. ''Spare me the martyrdom. These pious psychological games you love so much prove nothing.''

Sudden golden fury flared in Baron Cobalt's eyes. ''They prove that humanity is inherently self-destructive, instinctively savage and will at the first opportunity turn on their benefactors.''

Abrams peeled his lips back from his teeth in a snarling grin. ''Fuck you, my lord. You and your kind aren't our benefactors—you're not even our conquerors. You're parasites and we're your hosts. We can live without you, but you can't live without us.''

He stiffened his wrist tendons, and the Sin Eater slapped solidly into Abrams's waiting hand. The roar of the single shot sounded obscenely loud in the quiet control room, like a thunderclap bursting without warning from a clear, cloudless sky.

Abrams's head jerked violently back on his neck. A piece of scalp exploded from the rear of his skull, riding a slurry of blood and brain matter. They splattered the armaglass walls of the gateway unit with an abstract, artless pattern of gore.

Abrams's body collapsed, half in and half out of

the control room and the antechamber. His legs shook in a brief postmortem spasm.

Baron Cobalt gusted out a weary sigh and turned to face Kearney as he stepped from a wedge of shadow. A faint curl of smoke twisted up from the bore of his Sin Eater.

"Well-done," said the baron.

Kearney nodded in reverence. "I thank you, my lord. I live only to serve you."

Baron Cobalt smiled and knuckled Guende's double chins. "Hear that, Guende? He lives only to serve me. Isn't that a nice sentiment? Why don't you tell me things like that?"

Guende's mouth opened and closed like a fish stranded on dry land. Finally, he husked out, "I live only to serve you, my lord. Ever and always."

The baron pushed his fist against Guende's jaw, forcing his head up and back so the small man had no choice but to look directly at the looming Kearney. In a musical whisper, he said, "Tell him that, too."

"I live only to serve you," he half gasped.

"And for how long?" Baron Cobalt persisted.

"Ever and always."

The baron stepped back from Guende and pushed him away. "I don't think so. What do you think, Kearney?"

The huge man pondered the query for a silent second, then said, "I don't think so either, my lord baron."

Kearney raised his Sin Eater and placed Guende's head before the bore. "Even a wounded lion is still a lion," he murmured, and squeezed the trigger.